Scholastic LIBRARY Editions

Mark Twain's Best

Eight Short Stories by
America's Master Humorist

Illustrated by Wayne Blickenstaff

SCHOLASTIC BOOK SERVICES
50 West 44th Street, New York, N. Y. 10036

Published by Scholastic Book Services,
a division of Scholastic Magazines, Inc.,
"Creative Publishers for America's Classrooms."

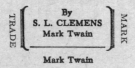

TRADE { By
S. L. CLEMENS
Mark Twain } MARK

Mark Twain

3rd printing...November 1964

Printed in the U.S.A.

Price: 50¢. Quantity prices available on request.

Introduction

This introduction will be brief. It will be brief because there isn't much that should be said between the title page of this book and the massive talent represented by these eight stories.

To most readers, *The Adventures of Tom Sawyer* and *The Adventures of Huckleberry Finn* are the beginning and the end of Mark Twain. The fact that he came into the public's view via a short story[1] is usually forgotten.

The stories in this book, you must remember, are not advertised as Mark Twain's best-*known* stories, but they will give any serious student of nonsense, worth his "wabe in mimsey,"[2] a long afternoon of pleasurable reading.[3] Now for some helpful words about these stories:

"How I Edited an Agricultural Paper" is *not* a true story. Although Twain spent several years as a reporter, most scholars agree that he did not have sufficient farming experience to speak with authority on the subject of farming.

---

[1] "The Notorious Jumping Frog of Calaveras County," which deserves a long, nonanthologized rest: it must be tired after making 371 dutiful appearances—372, if you count its short-lived inclusion in one edition of the *Fine Foods Storybook*, an Eater's Digest Book Club selection. An overearnest assistant editor, instructed to include a story about frogs' *legs*, thought he was to find a story about frogs' *leaps*—or so went his testimony in the pretrial hearing of his suit to recover his job. He maintained that a drop of celery batter from a cinnamon steak smudged the word—he was testing a new recipe in the line of duty—and therefore he could not be held responsible. He lost the case on a technicality.

[2] The reference here, of course, is to Lewis Jabberwocky's famous "Carroll"—a kind of musical lyric without music and, according to some deep critics, without words.

[3] Slow readers are urged to put pressure on their state legislatures for more Daylight Saving Time.

"The Story of the Good Little Boy" is a warning to all who think that Dame Success is monogamous.

"Some Learned Fables for Good Old Boys and Girls"—don't be misled by the title; you too can read it.

"The McWilliamses and the Burglar Alarm" can stand on its own feet as an amusing tale of incredible gullibility, but evidence is slowly accumulating that there is more to this story than comic bungling.[4]

"The Diary of Adam and Eve"—in which Twain proves that he can be both amusing and tender.

"The £1,000,000 Bank-Note" is probably the best example of a master's storyteller's handling of the "What-would-happen-if . . ." question. Could this story really have happened? Twain makes us think so.

"Extract from Captain Stormfield's Visit to Heaven" — at first a thinly disguised plea for humility in the light of this planet's minor role in the universe; then a barrage of wit brings down scores of muddy thinkers[5] who had little regard for logic in their concept of the hereafter.

"The Mysterious Stranger" — read it carefully; you'll find you're somewhat ashamed of the human race, but less confused about how to improve it. And what will help you is this sentence: "For your race, in its poverty, has unquestionably one really effective weapon: laughter."

MORRIS GOLDBERGER

---

[4] Note Twain's subtle indication of his debt to Thoreau's *Walden*. He too includes an itemized list of expenses. But credit Twain for "economy of material"—his total was only $19.77, as compared with Thoreau's $28.12½.

[5] Readers may be reminded of other famous muddy thinkers. There was Louisa May Muffet, who frequented the roulette tables of Las Vegas and Monte Carlo, chanting, "Where there's a wheel, there's a way." And let's not forget James Fenimore Nero, who wore strips cut from a street map in his hair, singing (*a capella*, of course), "A man's Rome is his tassel." Also Henry Wadsworth Woolworth, who refused to open a department store in Alaska and constantly muttered, "Keep the Nome buyers yearning."

Contents

How I Edited
an Agricultural Paper

I did not take temporary editorship of an agricultural paper without misgivings. Neither would a landsman take command of a ship without misgivings. But I was in circumstances that made the salary an object. The regular editor of the paper was going off for a holiday and I accepted the terms he offered, and took his place.

The sensation of being at work again was luxurious, and I wrought all the week with unflagging pleasure. We went to press, and I waited a day with some solicitude to see whether my effort was going to attract any notice. As I left the office, toward sundown, a group of men and boys at the foot of the stairs dispersed with one impulse, and gave me passageway, and I heard one or two of them say: "That's him!" I was naturally pleased by this incident. The next morning I found a similar group at the foot of the stairs,

and scattering couples and individuals standing here and
there in the street and over the way, watching me with
interest. The group separated and fell back as I approached,
and I heard a man say, "Look at his eye!" I pretended not
to observe the notice I was attracting, but secretly I was
pleased with it, and was purposing to write an account of it
to my aunt. I went up the short flight of stairs, and heard
cheery voices and a ringing laugh as I drew near the door,
which I opened, and caught a glimpse of two young rural-
looking men, whose faces blanched and lengthened when
they saw me, and then they both plunged through the
window with a great crash. I was surprised.

In about half an hour an old gentleman, with a flowing
beard and a fine but rather austere face, entered, and sat
down at my invitation. He seemed to have something on his
mind. He took off his hat and set it on the floor, and got out
of it a red silk handkerchief and a copy of our paper.

He put the paper on his lap, and while he polished his
spectacles with his handkerchief he said, "Are you the new
editor?"

I said I was.

"Have you ever edited an agricultural paper before?"

"No," I said; "this is my first attempt."

"Very likely. Have you had any experience in agriculture
practically?"

"No; I believe I have not."

"Some instinct told me so," said the old gentleman, putting
on his spectacles, and looking over them at me with asperity,
while he folded his paper into convenient shape. "I wish to
read you what must have made me have that instinct. It was
this editorial. Listen, and see if it was you that wrote it:

> Turnips should never be pulled; it injures them.
> It is much better to send a boy up and let him
> shake the tree.

"Now, what do you thing of that?—for I really suppose you wrote it?"

"Think of it? Why, I think it is good. I think it is sense. I have no doubt that every year millions and millions of bushels of turnips are spoiled in this township alone by being pulled in a half-ripe condition, when, if they had sent a boy up to shake the tree—"

"Shake your grandmother! Turnips don't grow on trees!"

"Oh, they don't, don't they? Well, who said they did? The language was intended to be figurative, wholly figurative. Anybody that knows anything will know that I meant that the boy should shake the vine."

Then this old person got up and tore his paper all into small shreds, and stamped on them, and broke several things with his cane, and said I did not know as much as a cow; and then went out and banged the door after him, and, in short, acted in such a way that I fancied he was displeased about something. But not knowing what the trouble was, I could not be any help to him.

Pretty soon after this a long, cadaverous creature, with lanky locks hanging down to his shoulders, and a week's stubble bristling from the hills and valleys of his face, darted within the door, and halted, motionless, with finger on lip, and head and body bent in listening attitude. No sound was heard. Still he listened. No sound. Then he turned the key in the door, and came elaborately tiptoeing toward me till he was within long reaching distance of me, when he stopped and, after scanning my face with intense interest for a while, drew a folded copy of our paper from his bosom, and said:

"There, you wrote that. Read it to me—quick! Relieve me. I suffer."

I read as follows; and as the sentences fell from my lips I could see the relief come, I could see the drawn muscles relax, and the anxiety go out of the face, and rest and peace

steal over the features like the merciful moonlight over a
desolate landscape:

> The guano is a fine bird, but great care is neces-
> sary in rearing it. It should not be imported earlier
> than June or later than September. In the winter
> it should be kept in a warm place, where it can
> hatch out its young.
>
> It is evident that we are to have a backward
> season for grain. Therefore it will be well for the
> farmer to begin setting out his corn-stalks and
> planting his buckwheat cakes in July instead of
> August.
>
> Concerning the pumpkin. This berry is a favorite
> with the natives of the interior of New England,
> who prefer it to the gooseberry for the making of
> fruit-cake, and who likewise give it the preference
> over the raspberry for feeding cows, as being more
> filling and fully as satisfying. The pumpkin is the
> only esculent of the orange family that will thrive
> in the North, except the gourd and one or two va-
> rieties of the squash. But the custom of planting it
> in the front yard with the shrubbery is fast going
> out of vogue, for it is now generally conceded that
> the pumpkin as a shade tree is a failure.
>
> Now, as the warm weather approaches, and the
> ganders begin to spawn—

The excited listener sprang toward me to shake hands, and
said:

"There, there—that will do. I know I am all right now,
because you have read it just as I did, word for word. But,
stranger, when I first read it this morning, I said to myself,
I never, never believed it before, notwithstanding my friends
kept me under watch so strict, but now I believe I *am* crazy;
and with that I fetched a howl that you might have heard
two miles, and started out to kill somebody—because, you

know, I knew it would come to that sooner or later, and so I might as well begin. I read one of them paragraphs over again, so as to be certain, and then I burned my house down and started. I have crippled several people, and have got one fellow up a tree, where I can get him if I want him. But I thought I would call in here as I passed along and make the thing perfectly certain; and now it *is* certain, and I tell you it is lucky for the chap that is in the tree. I should have killed him sure, as I went back. Good-by, sir, good-by; you have taken a great load off my mind. My reason has stood the strain of one of your agricultural articles, and I know that nothing can ever unseat it now. *Good*-by, sir."

I felt a little uncomfortable about the cripplings and arsons this person had been entertaining himself with, for I could not help feeling remotely accessory to them. But these thoughts were quickly banished, for the regular editor walked in! [I thought to myself, Now if you had gone to Egypt as I recommended you to, I might have had a chance to get my hand in; but you wouldn't do it, and here you are. I sort of expected you.]

The editor was looking sad and perplexed and dejected.

He surveyed the wreck which that old rioter and those two young farmers had made, and then said: "This is a sad business—a very sad business. There is the mucilage-bottle broken, and six panes of glass, and a spittoon, and two candlesticks. But that is not the worst. The reputation of the paper is injured—and permanently, I fear. True, there never was such a call for the paper before, and it never sold such a large edition or soared to such celebrity;—but does one want to be famous for lunacy, and prosper upon the infirmities of his mind? My friend, as I am an honest man, the street out here is full of people, and others are roosting on the fences, waiting to get a glimpse of you, because they think you are crazy. And well they might after reading your editorials. They are a disgrace to journalism. Why, what put it into your head that you could edit a paper of this nature? You do not seem to know the first rudiments of agriculture. You speak of a furrow and a harrow as being the same thing; you talk of the moulting season for cows; and you recommend the domestication of the pole-cat on account of its playfulness and its excellence as a ratter! Your remark that clams will lie quiet if music be played to them was superfluous—entirely superfluous. Nothing disturbs clams. Clams *always* lie quiet. Clams care nothing whatever about music. Ah, heavens and earth, friend! if you had made the acquiring of ignorance the study of your life, you could not have graduated with higher honor than you could to-day. I never saw anything like it. Your observation that the horse-chestnut as an article of commerce is steadily gaining in favor is simply calculated to destroy this journal. I want you to throw up your situation and go. I want no more holiday—I could not enjoy it if I had it. Certainly not with you in my chair. I would always stand in dread of what you might be going to recommend next. It makes me lose all patience every time I think of your discussing oyster-beds under the head of 'Landscape Gardening.' I want you to go. Nothing on earth could persuade me to take another holiday. Oh! why didn't you *tell* me you didn't know anything about agriculture?"

"*Tell* you, you corn-stalk, you cabbage, you son of a cauliflower? It's the first time I ever heard such an unfeeling remark. I tell you I have been in the editorial business going on fourteen years, and it is the first time I ever heard of a man's having to know anything in order to edit a newspaper. You turnip! Who write the dramatic critiques for the second-rate papers? Why, a parcel of promoted shoemakers and apprentice apothecaries, who know just as much about good acting as I do about good farming and no more. Who review the books? People who never wrote one. Who do up the heavy leaders on finance? Parties who have had the largest opportunities for knowing nothing about it. Who criticize the Indian campaigns? Gentlemen who do not know a war-whoop from a wigwam, and who never have had to run a foot-race with a tomahawk, or pluck arrows out of the several members of their families to build the evening camp-fire with. Who write the temperance appeals, and clamor about the flowing bowl? Folks who will never draw another sober breath till they do it in the grave. Who edit the agricultural papers, you—yam? Men, as a general thing, who fail in the poetry line, yellow-colored novel line, sensation-drama line, city-editor line, and finally fall back on agriculture as a temporary reprieve from the poor-house. *You* try to tell *me* anything about the newspaper business! Sir, I have been through it from Alpha to Omaha, and I tell you that the less a man knows, the bigger the noise he makes and the higher the salary he commands. Heaven knows if I had but been ignorant instead of cultivated, and impudent instead of diffident, I could have made a name for myself in this cold, selfish world. I take my leave, sir. Since I have been treated as you have treated me, I am perfectly willing to go. But I have done my duty. I have fulfilled my contract as far as I was permitted to do it. I said I could make your paper of interest to all classes—and I have. I said I could run your circulation up to twenty thousand copies, and if I had had two more weeks I'd have done it. And I'd have given you the best class of readers that ever an agricultural paper had—not a farmer in it, nor a solitary individual who could tell a watermelon-tree from a peach-vine to save his life. *You* are the loser by this rupture, not me, Pie-plant. *Adios.*"

I then left.

The Story of
the Good Little Boy

Once there was a good little boy by the name of Jacob
Blivens. He always obeyed his parents, no matter how absurd
and unreasonable their demands were; and he always learned
his book, and never was late at Sabbath-school. He would
not play hookey, even when his sober judgment told him it
was the most profitable thing he could do. None of the other
boys could ever make that boy out, he acted so strangely.
He couldn't lie, no matter how convenient it was. He just
said it was wrong to lie, and that was sufficient for him. And
he was so honest that he was simply ridiculous. The curious
ways that Jacob had, surpassed everything. He wouldn't play
marbles on Sunday, he wouldn't rob birds' nests, he wouldn't
give hot pennies to organ-grinders' monkeys; he didn't seem
to take any interest in any kind of rational amusement. So
the other boys used to try to reason it out and come to an

understanding of him, but they couldn't arrive at any
satisfactory conclusion. As I said before, they could only
figure out a sort of vague idea that he was "afflicted," and
so they took him under their protection, and never allowed
any harm to come to him.

This good little boy read all the Sunday-school books;
they were his greatest delight. This was the whole secret of
it. He believed in the good little boys they put in the Sunday-
school books; he had every confidence in them. He longed to
come across one of them alive once; but he never did. They
all died before his time, maybe. Whenever he read about a
particularly good one he turned over quickly to the end to
see what became of him, because he wanted to travel
thousands of miles and gaze on him; but it wasn't any use;
that good little boy always died in the last chapter, and there
was a picture of the funeral, with all his relations and the
Sunday-school children standing around the grave in panta-
loons that were too short, and bonnets that were too large,
and everybody crying into handkerchiefs that had as much
as a yard and a half of stuff in them. He was always headed
off in this way. He never could see one of those good little
boys on account of his always dying in the last chapter.

Jacob had a noble ambition to be put in a Sunday-school
book. He wanted to be put in, with pictures representing him
gloriously declining to lie to his mother, and her weeping
for joy about it; and pictures representing him standing on
the doorstep giving a penny to a poor beggar-woman with
six children, and telling her to spend it freely, but not to be
extravagant, because extravagance is a sin; and pictures of
him magnanimously refusing to tell on the bad boy who
always lay in wait for him around the corner as he came from
school, and welted him over the head with a lath, and then
chased him home, saying, "Hi! hi!" as he proceeded. That
was the ambition of young Jacob Blivens. He wished to be
put in a Sunday-school book. It made him feel a little

uncomfortable sometimes when he reflected that the good little boys always died. He loved to live, you know, and this was the most unpleasant feature about being a Sunday-school-book boy. He knew it was not healthy to be good. He knew it was more fatal than consumption to be so supernaturally good as the boys in the books were; he knew that none of them had ever been able to stand it long, and it pained him to think that if they put him in a book he wouldn't ever see it, or even if they did get the book out before he died it wouldn't be popular without any picture of his funeral in the back part of it. It couldn't be much of a Sunday-school book that couldn't tell about the advice he gave to the community when he was dying. So at last, of course, he had to make up his mind to do the best he could under the circumstances—to live right, and hang on as long as he could, and have his dying speech all ready when his time came.

But somehow nothing ever went right with this good little boy; nothing ever turned out with him the way it turned out with the good little boys in the books. They always had a good time, and the bad boys had the broken legs; but in his case there was a screw loose somewhere, and it all happened just the other way. When he found Jim Blake stealing apples, and went under the tree to read to him about the bad little boy who fell out of a neighbor's apple tree and broke his arm, Jim fell out of the tree, too, but he fell on *him* and broke *his* arm, and Jim wasn't hurt at all. Jacob couldn't understand that. There wasn't anything in the books like it.

And once, when some bad boys pushed a blind man over in the mud, and Jacob ran to help him up and receive his blessing, the blind man did not give him any blessing at all, but whacked him over the head with his stick and said he would like to catch him shoving *him* again, and then pretending to help him up. This was not in accordance with any of the books. Jacob looked them all over to see.

One thing that Jacob wanted to do was to find a lame dog that hadn't any place to stay, and was hungry and persecuted, and bring him home and pet him and have that dog's imperishable gratitude. And at last he found one and was happy; and he brought him home and fed him, but when he was going to pet him the dog flew at him and tore all the clothes off him except those that were in front, and made a spectacle of him that was astonishing. He examined authorities, but he could not understand the matter. It was of the same breed of dogs that was in the books, but it acted very differently. Whatever this boy did he got into trouble. The very things the boys in the books got rewarded for turned out to be about the most unprofitable things he could invest in.

Once, when he was on his way to Sunday-school, he saw some bad boys starting off pleasuring in a sailboat. He was filled with consternation, because he knew from his reading that boys who went sailing on Sunday invariably got drowned. So he ran out on a raft to warn them, but a log turned with him and slid him into the river. A man got him out pretty soon, and the doctor pumped the water out of him, and gave him a fresh start with his bellows, but he caught cold and lay sick abed nine weeks. But the most unaccountable thing about it was that the bad boys in the boat had a good time all day, and then reached home alive and well in the most surprising manner. Jacob Blivens said there was nothing like these things in the books. He was perfectly dumfounded.

When he got well he was a little discouraged, but he resolved to keep on trying anyhow. He knew that so far his experiences wouldn't do to go in a book, but he hadn't yet reached the allotted term of life for good little boys, and he hoped to be able to make a record yet if he could hold on till his time was fully up. If everything else failed he had his dying speech to fall back on.

He examined his authorities, and found that it was now time for him to go to sea as a cabin-boy. He called on a ship-captain and made his application, and when the captain asked for his recommendations he proudly drew out a tract and pointed to the word, "To Jacob Blivens, from his affectionate teacher." But the captain was a coarse, vulgar man, and he said, "Oh, that be blowed! *that* wasn't any proof that he knew how to wash dishes or handle a slush-bucket, and he guessed he didn't want him." This was altogether the most extraordinary thing that ever happened to Jacob in all his life. A compliment from a teacher, on a tract, had never failed to move the tenderest emotions of ship-captains, and open the way to all offices of honor and profit in their gift—it never had in any book that ever *he* had read. He could hardly believe his senses.

This boy always had a hard time of it. Nothing ever came out according to the authorities with him. At last, one day, when he was around hunting up bad little boys to admonish, he found a lot of them in the old iron-foundry fixing up a little joke on fourteen or fifteen dogs, which they had tied together in long procession, and were going to ornament with empty nitroglycerin cans made fast to their tails. Jacob's heart was touched. He sat down on one of those cans (for he never minded grease when duty was before him), and he took hold of the foremost dog by the collar, and turned his reproving eye upon wicked Tom Jones. But just at that moment Alderman McWelter, full of wrath, stepped in. All the bad boys ran away, but Jacob Blivens rose in conscious innocence and began one of those stately little Sunday-school-book speeches which always commence with "Oh, sir!" in dead opposition to the fact that no boy, good or bad, ever starts a remark with "Oh, sir." But the alderman never waited to hear the rest. He took Jacob Blivens by the ear and turned him around, and hit him a whack in the rear with the flat of his hand; and in an instant that good little boy shot out through the roof and soared away toward the sun, with the fragments of those fifteen dogs stringing after him like the tail of a kite. And there wasn't a sign of that alderman or that old iron-foundry left on the face of the earth; and, as for young Jacob Blivens, he never got a chance to make his last dying speech after all his trouble fixing it up, unless he made it to the birds; because, although the bulk of him came down all right in a tree-top in an adjoining county, the rest of him was apportioned around among four townships, and so they had to hold five inquests on him to find out whether he was dead or not, and how it occurred. You never saw a boy scattered so.*

Thus perished the good little boy who did the best he could, but didn't come out according to the books. Every boy who ever did as he did prospered except him. His case is truly remarkable. It will probably never be accounted for.

---

* This glycerin catastrophe is borrowed from a floating newspaper item, whose author's name I would give if I knew it.   M.T.

Some Learned Fables
for Good Old Boys and Girls

PART I

How the Animals of the Wood
Sent Out a Scientific Expedition

Once the creatures of the forest held a great convention and appointed a commission consisting of the most illustrious scientists among them to go forth, clear beyond the forest and out into the unknown and unexplored world, to verify the truth of the matters already taught in their schools and colleges and also to make discoveries. It was the most imposing enterprise of the kind the nation had ever embarked in. True, the government had once sent Dr. Bull Frog, with a picked crew, to hunt for a northwesterly passage through the swamp to the right-hand corner of the wood, and had since sent out many expeditions to hunt for Dr. Bull

Frog; but they never could find him, and so government finally gave him up and ennobled his mother to show its gratitude for the services her son had rendered to science. And once government sent Sir Grass Hopper to hunt for the sources of the rill that emptied into the swamp; and afterward sent out many expeditions to hunt for Sir Grass, and at last they were successful—they found his body, but if he had discovered the sources meanwhile, he did not let on. So government acted handsomely by deceased, and many envied his funeral.

But these expeditions were trifles compared with the present one; for this one comprised among its servants the very greatest among the learned; and besides it was to go to the utterly unvisited regions believed to lie beyond the mighty forest—as we have remarked before. How the members were banqueted, and glorified, and talked about! Everywhere that one of them showed himself, straightway there was a crowd to gape and stare at him.

Finally they set off, and it was a sight to see the long procession of dry-land Tortoises heavily laden with savants, scientific instruments, Glow-Worms and Fire-Flies for signal service, provisions, Ants and Tumble-Bugs to fetch and carry and delve, Spiders to carry the surveying chain and do other engineering duty, and so forth and so on; and after the Tortoises came another long train of ironclads—stately and spacious Mud Turtles for marine transportation service; and from every Tortoise and every Turtle flaunted a flaming gladiolus or other splendid banner; at the head of the column a great band of Bumble-Bees, Mosquitoes, Katy-Dids, and Crickets discoursed martial music; and the entire train was under the escort and protection of twelve picked regiments of the Army Worm.

At the end of three weeks the expedition emerged from the forest and looked upon the great Unknown World. Their eyes were greeted by an impressive spectacle. A vast level plain stretched before them, watered by a sinuous stream;

and beyond there towered up against the sky a long and lofty barrier of some kind, they did not know what. The Tumble-Bug said he believed it was simply land tilted up on its edge, because he knew he could see trees on it. But Professor Snail and the others said:

"You are hired to dig, sir—that is all. We need your muscle, not your brains. When we want your opinion on scientific matters, we will hasten to let you know. Your coolness is intolerable, too—loafing about here meddling with august matters of learning, when the other laborers are pitching camp. Go along and help handle the baggage."

The Tumble-Bug turned on his heel uncrushed, unabashed, observing to himself, "If it isn't land tilted up, let me die the death of the unrighteous."

Professor Bull Frog (nephew of the late explorer) said he believed the ridge was the wall that inclosed the earth. He continued:

"Our fathers have left us much learning, but they had not traveled far, and so we may count this a noble new discovery. We are safe for renown now, even though our labors began and ended with this single achievement. I wonder what this wall is built of? Can it be fungus? Fungus is an honorable good thing to build a wall of."

Professor Snail adjusted his field-glass and examined the rampart critically. Finally he said:

"The fact that it is not diaphanous convinces me that it is a dense vapor formed by the calorification of ascending moisture dephlogisticated by refraction. A few endiometrical experiments would confirm this, but it is not necessary. The thing is obvious."

So he shut up his glass and went into his shell to make a note of the discovery of the world's end, and the nature of it.

"Profound mind!" said Professor Angle-Worm to Professor Field-Mouse; "profound mind! nothing can long remain a mystery to that august brain."

Night drew on apace, the sentinel crickets were posted, the Glow-Worm and Fire-Fly lamps were lighted, and the camp sank to silence and sleep. After breakfast in the morning, the expedition moved on. About noon a great avenue was reached, which had in it two endless parallel bars of some kind of hard black substance, which raised the height of the tallest Bull Frog above the general level. The scientists climbed up on these and examined and tested them in various ways. They walked along them for a great distance, but found no end and no break in them. They could arrive at no decision. There was nothing in the records of science that mentioned anything of this kind. But at last the bald and venerable geographer, Professor Mud Turtle, a person who, born poor, and of a drudging low family, had, by his own native force raised himself to the headship of the geographers of his generation, said:

"My friends, we have indeed made a discovery here. We have found in a palpable, compact, and imperishable state what the wisest of our fathers always regarded as a mere thing of the imagination. Humble yourselves, my friends, for we stand in a majestic presence. These are parallels of latitude!"

Every heart and every head was bowed, so awful, so sublime was the magnitude of the discovery. Many shed tears.

The camp was pitched and the rest of the day given up to writing voluminous accounts of the marvel, and correcting astronomical tables to fit it. Toward midnight a demonical shriek was heard, then a clattering and rumbling noise, and the next instant a vast terrific eye shot by, with a long tail attached, and disappeared in the gloom, still uttering triumphant shrieks.

The poor camp laborers were stricken to the heart with fright, and stampeded for the high grass in a body. But not the scientists. They had no superstitions. They calmly proceeded to exchange theories. The ancient geographer's opinion was asked. He went into his shell and deliberated long and profoundly. When he came out at last, they all knew by his worshiping countenance that he brought light. Said he:

"Give thanks for this stupendous thing which we have been permitted to witness. It is the Vernal Equinox!"

There were shoutings and great rejoicings.

"But," said the Angle-Worm, uncoiling after reflection, "this is dead summer-time."

"Very well," said the Turtle, "we are far from our region; the season differs with the difference of time between the two points."

"Ah, true. True enough. But it is night. How should the sun pass in the night?"

"In these distant regions he doubtless passes always in the night at this hour."

"Yes, doubtless that is true. But it being night, how is it that we could see him?"

"It is a great mystery. I grant that. But I am persuaded that the humidity of the atmosphere in these remote regions is such that particles of daylight adhere to the disk, and it was by aid of these that we were enabled to see the sun in the dark."

This was deemed satisfactory, and due entry was made of the decision.

But about this moment those dreadful shriekings were heard again; again the rumbling and thundering came speeding up out of the night; and once more a flaming great eye flashed by and lost itself in gloom and distance.

The camp laborers gave themselves up for lost. The savants were sorely perplexed. Here was a marvel hard to account for. They thought and they talked, they talked and they thought. Finally the learned and aged Lord Grand-Daddy-Longlegs, who had been sitting in deep study, with his slender limbs crossed and his stemmy arms folded, said:

"Deliver your opinions, brethren, and then I will tell my thought—for I think I have solved this problem."

"So be it, good your lordship," piped the weak treble of the wrinkled and withered Professor Woodlouse, "for we shall hear from your lordship's lips naught but wisdom." [Here the speaker threw in a mess of trite, threadbare, exasperating quotations from the ancient poets and philosophers, delivering them with unction in the sounding grandeurs of the original tongues, they being from the Mastodon, the Dodo, and other dead languages.] "Perhaps I ought not to presume to meddle with matters pertaining to astronomy at all, in such a pretense as this, I who have made it the business of my life to delve only among the riches of the extinct languages and unearth the opulence of their ancient lore; but still, as unacquainted as I am with the noble science of astronomy, I beg with deference and humility to suggest that inasmuch as the last of these wonderful apparitions proceeded in exactly the opposite direction from that pursued by the first, which you decide to be the Vernal Equinox, and greatly resembled it in all particulars, is it not possible, nay certain, that this last is the *Autumnal* Equi—"

"O-o-o!" O-o-o! go to bed! go to bed!" with annoyed derision from everybody. So the poor old Woodlouse retreated out of sight, consumed with shame.

Further discussion followed, and then the united voice of the commission begged Lord Longlegs to speak. He said:

"Fellow-scientists, it is my belief that we have witnessed a thing which has occurred in perfection but once before in the knowledge of created beings. It is a phenomenon of inconceivable importance and interest, view it as one may, but its interest to us is vastly heightened by an added knowledge of its nature which no scholar has heretofore possessed or even suspected. This great marvel which we have just witnessed, fellow-savants (it almost takes my breath away), is nothing less than the transit of Venus!"

Every scholar sprang to his feet pale with astonishment. Then ensued tears, hand shakings, frenzied embraces, and the most extravagant jubilations of every sort. But by and by, as emotion began to retire within bounds, and reflection to return to the front, the accomplished Chief Inspector Lizard observed:

"But how is this? Venus should traverse the sun's surface, not the earth's."

The arrow went home. It carried sorrow to the breast of every apostle of learning there, for none could deny that this was a formidable criticism. But tranquilly the venerable Duke crossed his limbs behind his ears and said:

"My friend has touched the marrow of our mighty discovery. Yes—all that have lived before us thought a transit of Venus consisted of a flight across the sun's face; they thought it, they maintained it, they honestly believed it, simple hearts, and were justified in it by the limitations of their knowledge; but to us has been granted the inestimable boon of proving that the transit occurs across the earth's face, for we have *seen* it!"

The assembled wisdom sat in speechless adoration of this imperial intellect. All doubts had instantly departed, like night before the lightning.

The Tumble-Bug had just intruded, unnoticed. He now came reeling forward among the scholars, familiarly slapping first one and then another on the shoulder, saying "Nice ('ic!) nice old boy!" and smiling a smile of elaborate content. Arrived at a good position for speaking, he put his left arm akimbo with his knuckles planted in his hip just under the edge of his cut-away coat, bent his right leg, placing his toe on the ground and resting his heel with easy grace against his left shin, puffed out his aldermanic stomach, opened his lips, leaned his right elbow on Inspector Lizard's shoulder, and—

But the shoulder was indignantly withdrawn and the hardhanded son of toil went to earth. He floundered a bit, but came up smiling, arranged his attitude with the same careful detail as before, only choosing Professor Dogtick's shoulder for a support, opened his lips and—

Went to earth again. He presently scrambled up once more, still smiling, made a loose effort to brush the dust off his coat and legs, but a smart pass of his hand missed entirely, and the force of the unchecked impulse slewed him suddenly around, twisted his legs together, and projected him, limber and sprawling, into the lap of the Lord Longlegs. Two or three scholars sprang forward, flung the low creature head over heels into a corner, and reinstated the patrician, smoothing his ruffled dignity with many soothing and regretful speeches. Professor Bull Frog roared out:

"No more of this, sirrah Tumble-Bug! Say your say and then get you about your business with speed! Quick—what is your errand? Come—move off a trifle; you smell like a stable; what have you been at?"

"Please ('ic!) please your worship I chanced to light upon a find. But no m (*e-uck!*) matter 'bout that. There's b ('ic!) been another find which—beg pardon, your honors, what was that th ('ic!) thing that ripped by here first?"

"It was the Vernal Equinox."

"Inf ('ic!) fernal equinox. 'At's all right. D ('ic!) Dunno *him*. What's other one?"

"The transit of Venus."

"G ('ic!) Got me again. No matter. Las' one dropped something."

"Ah, indeed! Good luck! Good news! Quick—what is it?"

"M ('ic!) Mosey out 'n' see. It'll pay."

No more votes were taken for four-and-twenty hours. Then the following entry was made:

"The commission went in a body to view the find. It was found to consist of a hard, smooth, huge object with a rounded summit surmounted by a short upright projection resembling a section of a cabbage stalk divided transversely. This projection was not solid, but was a hollow cylinder plugged with a soft woody substance unknown to our region —that is, it had been so plugged, but unfortunately this obstruction had been heedlessly removed by Norway Rat, Chief of the Sappers and Miners, before our arrival. The vast object before us, so mysteriously conveyed from the glittering domains of space, was found to be hollow and nearly filled with a pungent liquid of a brownish hue, like rain water that has stood for some time. And such a spectacle as met our view! Norway Rat was perched upon the summit engaged in thrusting his tail into the cylindrical projection, drawing it out dripping, permitting the struggling multitude of laborers to suck the end of it, then straightway reinserting it and de-livering the fluid to the mob as before. Evidently this liquor had strangely potent qualities; for all that partook of it were immediately exalted with great and pleasurable emotions, and went staggering about singing ribald songs, embracing, fighting, dancing, discharging irruptions of profanity, and de-fying all authority. Around us struggled a massed and un-controlled mob—uncontrolled and likewise uncontrollable, for the whole army, down to the very sentinels, were mad like the rest, by reason of the drink. We were seized upon by these reckless creatures, and within the hour we, even we, were undistinguishable from the rest—the demoralization was complete and universal. In time the camp wore itself out with its orgies and sank into a stolid and pitiable stupor, in whose mysterious bonds rank was forgotten and strange bedfellows made, our eyes, at the resurrection, being blasted and our souls petrified with the incredible spectacle of that intol-erable stinking scavenger, the Tumble-Bug, and the il-lustrious patrician my Lord Grand Daddy, Duke of Longlegs, lying soundly steeped in sleep, and clasped lovingly in each other's arms, the like whereof hath not been seen in all the ages that tradition compasseth, and doubtless none shall ever in this world find faith to master the belief of it save only we that have beheld the damnable and unholy vision. Thus inscrutable be the ways of God, whose will be done!

"This day, by order, did the engineer-in-chief, Herr Spider, rig the necessary tackle for the overturning of the vast reservoir, and so its calamitous contents were discharged in a torrent upon the thirsty earth, which drank it up, and now there is no more danger, we reserving but a few drops for experiment and scrutiny, and to exhibit to the king and subsequently preserve among the wonders of the museum. What this liquid is has been determined. It is without question that fierce and most destructive fluid called lightning. It was wrested, in its container, from its storehouse in the clouds, by the resistless might of the flying planet, and hurled at our feet as she sped by. An interesting discovery here results. Which is, that lightning, kept to itself, is quiescent; it is the assaulting contact of the thunderbolt that releases it from captivity, ignites its awful fires, and so produces an instantaneous combustion and explosion which spread disaster and desolation far and wide in the earth."

After another day devoted to rest and recovery, the expedition proceeded upon its way. Some days later it went into camp in a pleasant part of the plain, and the savants sallied forth to see what they might find. Their reward was at hand. Professor Bull Frog discovered a strange tree, and called his comrades. They inspected it with profound interest. It was very tall and straight, and wholly devoid of bark, limbs, or foliage. By triangulation Lord Longlegs determined its altitude; Herr Spider measured its circumference at the base and computed the circumference at its top by a mathematical demonstration based upon the warrant furnished by the uniform degree of its taper upward. It was considered a very extraordinary find; and since it was a tree of hitherto unknown species, Professor Woodlouse gave it a name of a learned sound, being none other than that of Professor Bull Frog translated into the ancient Mastodon language, for it had always been the custom with discoverers to perpetuate their names and honor themselves by this sort of connection with their discoveries.

Now Professor Field-Mouse, having placed his sensitive ear to the tree, detected a rich, harmonious sound issuing from it. This surprising thing was tested and enjoyed by each scholar in turn, and great was the gladness and the astonishment of all. Professor Woodlouse was requested to add to and extend the tree's name so as to make it suggest the musical quality it possessed—which he did, furnishing the addition *Anthem Singer*, done into the Mastodon tongue.

By this time Professor Snail was making some telescopic inspections. He discovered a great number of these trees, extending in a single rank, with wide intervals between, as far as his instrument would carry, both southward and northward. He also presently discovered that all these trees were bound together, near their tops, by fourteen great ropes, one above another, which ropes were continuous, from tree to tree, as far as his vision could reach. This was surprising. Chief Engineer Spider ran aloft and soon reported that these ropes were simply a web hung there by some colossal member of his own species, for he could see its prey dangling here and there from the strands, in the shape of mighty shreds and rags that had a woven look about their texture and were no doubt the discarded skins of prodigious insects which had been caught and eaten. And then he ran along one of the ropes to make a closer inspection, but felt a smart sudden burn on the soles of his feet, accompanied by a paralyzing shock, wherefore he let go and swung himself to the earth by a thread of his own spinning, and advised all to hurry at once to camp, lest the monster should appear and get as much interested in the savants as they were in him and his works. So they departed with speed, making notes about the gigantic web as they went. And that evening the naturalist of the expedition built a beautiful model of the colossal spider, having no need to see it in order to do this, because he had picked up a fragment of its vertebræ by the tree, and so knew exactly what the creature looked like and what its habits and its preferences were by this simple evidence alone. He built it with a tail, teeth, fourteen legs, and a snout, and said it ate grass, cattle, pebbles, and dirt with equal enthusiasm. This animal was regarded as a very precious addition to science. It was hoped a dead one might be found to stuff. Professor Woodlouse thought that he and his brother scholars, by lying hid and being quiet, might maybe catch a live one. He was advised to try it. Which was all the attention that was paid to his suggestion. The conference ended with the naming of the monster after the naturalist, since he, after God, had created it.

"And improved it, mayhap," muttered the Tumble-Bug, who was intruding again, according to his idle custom and his unappeasable curiosity.

PART II

How the Animals of the Wood Completed Their Scientific Labors

A week later the expedition camped in the midst of a collection of wonderful curiosities. These were a sort of vast caverns of stone that rose singly and in bunches out of the plain by the side of the river which they had first seen when they emerged from the forest. These caverns stood in long, straight rows on opposite sides of broad aisles that were bordered with single ranks of trees. The summit of each cavern sloped sharply both ways. Several horizontal rows of great square holes, obstructed by a thin, shiny, transparent substance, pierced the frontage of each cavern. Inside were caverns within caverns; and one might ascend and visit these minor compartments by means of curious winding ways consisting of continuous regular terraces raised one above another. There were many huge, shapeless objects in each compartment which were considered to have been living creatures at one time, though now the thin brown skin was shrunken and loose, and rattled when disturbed. Spiders were here in great number, and their cobwebs, stretched in all directions and wreathing the great skinny dead together, were a pleasant spectacle, since they inspired with life and wholesome cheer a scene which would otherwise have brought to the mind only a sense of forsakenness and desolation. Information was sought of these spiders, but in vain. They were of a different nationality from those with the expedition, and their language seemed but a musical, meaningless jargon. They were a timid, gentle race, but ignorant, and heathenish worshipers of unknown gods. The expedition detailed a great detachment of missionaries to teach them the true religion, and in a week's time a precious work had been wrought among those darkened creatures, not three families being by that time at peace with each other or having a settled belief in any system of religion whatever. This encouraged the expedition to establish a colony of missionaries there permanently, that the work of grace might go on.

But let us not outrun our narrative. After close examination of the fronts of the caverns, and much thinking and exchanging of theories, the scientists determined the nature of these singular formations. They said that each belonged mainly to the Old Red Sandstone period; that the cavern fronts rose in innumerable and wonderfully regular strata high in the air, each stratum about five frog-spans thick, and that in the present discovery lay an overpowering refutation

of all received geology; for between every two layers of Old
Red Sandstone reposed a thin layer of decomposed limestone; so instead of their having been but one Old Red Sandstone period there had certainly been not less than a hundred and seventy-five! And by the same token it was plain
that there had also been a hundred and seventy-five flood-
ings of the earth and depositings of limestone strata! The
unavoidable deduction from which pair of facts was the over-
whelming truth that the world, instead of being only two
hundred thousand years old, was older by millions upon
millions of years! And there was another curious thing: every
stratum of Old Red Sandstone was pierced and divided at
mathematically regular intervals by vertical strata of limestone. Up-shootings of igneous rock through fractures in water
formations were common; but here was the first instance
where water-formed rock had been so projected. It was a
great and noble discovery, and its value to science was
considered to be inestimable.

A critical examination of some of the lower strata demonstrated the presence of fossil ants and tumble-bugs (the latter accompanied by their peculiar goods), and with high gratification the fact was enrolled upon the scientific record; for
this was proof that these vulgar laborers belonged to the first
and lowest orders of created beings, though at the same
time there was something repulsive in the reflection that the
perfect and exquisite creature of the modern uppermost order
owed its origin to such ignominious beings through the mysterious law of Development of Species.

The Tumble-Bug, overhearing this discussion, said he was
willing that the parvenus of these new times should find what
comfort they might in their wise-drawn theories, since as far
as he was concerned he was content to be of the old first families and proud to point back to his place among the old
original aristocracy of the land.

"Enjoy your mushroom dignity, stinking of the varnish of

yesterday's veneering, since you like it," said he; "suffice it
for the Tumble-Bugs that they come of a race that rolled their
fragrant spheres down the solemn aisles of antiquity, and
left their imperishable words embalmed in the Old Red Sandstone to proclaim it to the wasting centuries as they file
along the highway of Time!"

"Oh, take a walk!" said the chief of the expedition, with
derision.

The summer passed, and winter approached. In and about
many of the caverns were what seemed to be inscriptions.
Most of the scientists said they were inscriptions, a few said
they were not. The chief philologist, Professor Woodlouse,
maintained that they were writings, done in a character utterly unknown to scholars, and in a language equally unknown. He had early ordered his artists and draftsmen to
make facsimiles of all that were discovered; and had set himself about finding the key to the hidden tongue. In this work
he had followed the method which had always been used by
decipherers previously. That is to say, he placed a number of
copies of inscriptions before him and studied them both col-
lectively and in detail. To begin with, he placed the following
copies together:

The American Hotel
The Shades
Boats for Hire Cheap
Billiards
The A1 Barber Shop
Keep Off the Grass
Cottages for Rent During the Watering Season
For Sale Cheap
For Sale Cheap
Meals at All Hours
No Smoking
Union Prayer Meeting, 4 P.M.
The Waterside Journal

Telegraph Office
Try Brandreth's Pills
For Sale Cheap
For Sale Cheap

At first it seemed to the professor that this was a sign-language, and that each word was represented by a distinct sign: further examination convinced him that it was a written language, and that every letter of its alphabet was represented by a character of its own; and finally he decided that it was a language which conveyed itself partly by letters, and partly by signs or hieroglyphics. This conclusion was forced upon him by the discovery of several specimens of the following nature:

He observed that certain inscriptions were met with in greater frequency than others. Such as "For Sale Cheap"; "Billiards"; "S. T.—1860—X"; "Keno"; "Ale on Draught." Naturally, then, these must be religious maxims. But this idea was cast aside by and by, as the mystery of the strange alphabet began to clear itself. In time, the professor was enabled to translate several of the inscriptions with considerable plausibility, though not to the perfect satisfaction of all the scholars. Still, he made constant and encouraging progress.

Finally a cavern was discovered with these inscriptions upon it:

WATERSIDE MUSEUM

Open at all Hours—Admission 50 Cents

WONDERFUL COLLECTIONS OF
WAX-WORKS, ANCIENT FOSSILS, ETC.

Professor Woodlouse affirmed that the word "Museum" was equivalent to the phrase "*lumgath molo*," or "Burial

Place." Upon entering, the scientists were well astonished. But what they saw may be best conveyed in the language of their own official report:

"Erect, in a row, were a sort of rigid great figures which struck us instantly as belonging to the long extinct species of reptile called MAN, described in our ancient records. This was a peculiarly gratifying discovery, because of late times it has become fashionable to regard this creature as a myth and a superstition, a work of the inventive imaginations of our remote ancestors. But here, indeed, was Man, perfectly preserved, in a fossil state. And this was his burial place, as already ascertained by the inscription. And now it began to be suspected that the caverns we had been inspecting had been his ancient haunts in that old time that he roamed the earth—for upon the breast of each of these tall fossils was an inscription in the character heretofore noticed. One read, 'Captain Kidd, the Pirate'; another, 'Queen Victoria'; another, 'Abe Lincoln'; another, 'George Washington,' etc.

"With feverish interest we called for our ancient scientific records to discover if perchance the description of Man there set down would tally with the fossils before us. Professor Woodlouse read it aloud in its quaint and musty phraseology, to wit:

> In ye time of our fathers Man still walked ye earth, as by tradition we know. It was a creature of exceeding great size, being compassed about with a loose skin, sometimes of one color, sometimes of many, the which it was able to cast at will; which being done, the hind legs were discovered to be armed with short claws like to a mole's but broader, and ye forelegs with fingers of a curious slimness and a length much more prodigious than a frog's, armed also with broad talons for scratching in ye earth for its food. It had a sort

of feathers upon its head such as hath a rat, but longer, and a beak suitable for seeking its food by yᵉ smell thereof. When it was stirred with happiness, it leaked water from its eyes; and when it suffered or was sad, it manifested it with a horrible hellish cackling clamor that was exceeding dreadful to hear and made one long that it might rend itself and perish, and so end its troubles. Two Mans being together, they uttered noises at each other like this: "Haw-haw-haw—dam good, dam good," together with other sounds of more or less likeness to these, wherefore yᵉ poets conceived that they talked, but poets be always ready to catch at any frantic folly, God he knows. Sometimes this creature goeth about with a long stick yᵉ which it putteth to its face and bloweth fire and smoke through yᵉ same with a sudden and most damnable bruit and noise that doth fright its prey to death, and so seizeth it in its talons and walked away to its habitat, consumed with a most fierce and devlish joy.

"Now was the description set forth by our ancestors wonderfully indorsed and confirmed by the fossils before us, as shall be seen. The specimen marked 'Captain Kidd' was examined in detail. Upon its head and part of its face was a sort of furr like that upon the tail of a horse. With great labor its loose skin was removed, whereupon its body was discovered to be of a polished white texture, thoroughly petrified. The straw it had eaten, so many ages gone by, was still in its body, undigested—and even in its legs.

"Surrounding these fossils were objects that would mean nothing to the ignorant, but to the eye of science they were a revelation. They laid bare the secrets of dead ages. These musty Memorials told us when Man lived, and what were his habits. For here, side by side with Man, were the evidences that he had lived in the earliest ages of creation, the compan-

ion of the other low orders of life that belonged to that forgotten time. Here was the fossil nautilus that sailed the pri-
meval seas; here was the skeleton of the mastodon, the ich-
thyosaurus, the cave-bear, the prodigious elk. Here, also,
were the charred bones of some of these extinct animals and
of the young of Man's own species, split lengthwise, showing
that to his taste the marrow was a toothsome luxury. It was
plain that Man had robbed those bones of their contents,
since no toothmark of any beast was upon them—albeit the
Tumble-Bug intruded the remark that 'no beast could mark a
bone with its teeth, anyway.' Here were proofs that Man had
vague, groveling notions of art; for this fact was conveyed by
certain things marked with the untranslatable words, 'Flint
Hatchets, Knives, Arrow-Heads, and Bone Ornaments of Pri-
meval Man.' Some of these seemed to be rude weapons
chipped out of flint, and in a secret place was found some
more in process of construction, with this untranslatable leg-
end, on a thin, flimsy material, lying by:

> Jones, if you don't want to be discharged from
> the Museum, make the next primeaveal weppons
> more careful—you couldn't even fool one of these
> sleapy old syentiffic grannys from the Coledge
> with the last ones. And mind you the animles you
> carved on some of the Bone Ornaments is a blame
> sight too good for any primeaveal man that was
> ever fooled.—Varnum, Manager.

"Back of the burial place was a mass of ashes, showing
that Man always had a feast at a funeral—else why the ashes
in such a place; and showing, also, that he believed in God
and the immortality of the soul—else why these solemn ceremonies?

"To sum up. We believe that Man had a written language.
We *know* that he indeed existed at one time, and is not a

myth; also, that he was the companion of the cave-bear, the mastodon, and other extinct species; that he cooked and ate them and likewise the young of his own kind; also, that he bore rude weapons, and knew nothing of art; that he imagined he had a soul, and pleased himself with the fancy that it was immortal. But let us not laugh; there may be creatures in existence to whom we and our vanities and profundities may seem as ludicrous."

PART III

Near the margin of the great river the scientists presently found a huge, shapely stone, with this inscription:

> In 1847, in the spring, the river overflowed its banks and covered the whole township. The depth was from two to six feet. More than 900 head of cattle were lost, and many homes destroyed. The Mayor ordered this memorial to be erected to perpetuate the event. God spare us the repetition of it!

With infinite trouble, Professor Woodlouse succeeded in making a translation of this inscription, which was sent home, and straightway an enormous excitement was created about it. It confirmed, in a remarkable way, certain treasured traditions of the ancients. The translation was slightly marred by one or two untranslatable words, but these did not impair the general clearness of the meaning. It is here presented:

> One thousand eight hundred and forty-seven years ago, the (fires?) descended and consumed the whole city. Only some nine hundred souls were saved, all others destroyed. The (king?)

commanded this stone to be set up to . . . (untranslatable) . . . repetition of it.

This was the first successful and satisfactory translation
that had been made of the mysterious character left behind
him by extinct man, and it gave Professor Woodlouse such
reputation that at once every seat of learning in his native
land conferred a degree of the most illustrious grade upon
him, and it was believed that if he had been a soldier and
had turned his splendid talents to the extermination of a remote tribe of reptiles, the king would have ennobled him
and made him rich. And this, too, was the origin of that
school of scientists called Manologists, whose specialty is the
deciphering of the ancient records of the extinct bird termed
Man. [For it is now decided that Man was a bird and not a
reptile.] But Professor Woodlouse began and remained chief
of these, for it was granted that no translations were ever
so free from error as his. Others made mistakes—he seemed
incapable of it. Many a memorial of the lost race was afterward found, but none ever attained to the renown and
veneration achieved by the "Mayoritish Stone"—it being so
called from the word "Mayor" in it, which, being translated
"King," "Mayoritish Stone" was but another way of saying
"King Stone."

Another time the expedition made a great "find." It
was a vast round flattish mass, ten frog-spans in diameter and
five or six high. Professor Snail put on his spectacles and examined it all around, and then climbed up and inspected the
top. He said:

"The result of my perlustration and perscontation of this
isoperimetrical proturberance is a belief that it is one of those
rare and wonderful creations left by the Mound Builders. The
fact that this one is lamel-libranchiate in its formation
simply adds to its interest as being possibly of a different

kind from any we read of in the records of science, but yet in no manner marring its authenticity. Let the megalophonous grasshopper sound a blast and summon hither the perfunctory and circumforaneous Tumble-Bug, to the end that excavations may be made and learning gather new treasures."

Not a Tumble-Bug could be found on duty, so the Mound was excavated by a working party of Ants. Nothing was discovered. This would have been a great disappointment, had not the venerable Longlegs explained the matter. He said:

"It is now plain to me that the mysterious and forgotten race of Mound Builders did not always erect these edifices as mausoleums, else in this case, as in all previous cases, their skeletons would be found here, along with the rude implements which the creatures used in life. Is not this manifest?"

"True! true!" from everybody.

"Then we have made a discovery of peculiar value here; a discovery which greatly extends our knowledge of this creature in place of diminishing it; a discovery which will add luster to the achievements of this expedition and win for us the commendations of scholars everywhere. For the absence of the customary relics here means nothing less than this: The Mound Builder, instead of being the ignorant, savage reptile we have been taught to consider him, was a creature of cultivation and high intelligence, capable of not only appreciating worthy achievements of the great and noble of his species, but of commemorating them! Fellow-scholars, this stately Mound is not a sepulcher, it is a monument!"

A profound impression was produced by this.

But it was interrupted by rude and derisive laughter—and the Tumble-Bug appeared.

"A monument!" quoth he. "A monument set up by a Mound Builder! Aye, so it is! So it is, indeed, to the shrewd

keen eye of science; but to an ignorant poor devil who has
never seen a college, it is not a Monument, strictly speaking,
but is yet a most rich and noble property; and with your
worship's good permission I will proceed to manufacture it
into spheres of exceedings grace and—"

The Tumble-Bug was driven away with stripes, and the
draftsmen of the expedition were set to making views of the
Monument from different standpoints, while Professor
Woodlouse, in a frenzy of scientific zeal, traveled all over it
and all around it hoping to find an inscription. But if there
had ever been one, it had decayed or been removed by some
vandal as a relic.

The views having been completed, it was now considered
safe to load the precious Monument itself upon the backs
of four of the largest Tortoises and send it home to the
king's museum, which was done; and when it arrived it was
received with enormous *éclat* and escorted to its future
abiding-place by thousands of enthusiastic citizens, King Bull-
frog XVI himself attending and condescending to sit en-
throned upon it throughout the progress.

The growing rigor of the weather was now admonishing
the scientists to close their labors for the present, so they
made preparations to journey homeward. But even their last
day among the Caverns bore fruit; for one of the scholars
found in an out-of-the-way corner of the Museum or "Burial
Place" a most strange and extraordinary thing. It was nothing
less than a double Man-Bird lashed together breast to breast
by a natural ligament, and labeled with the untranslatable
words, "Siamese Twins." The official report concerning this
thing closed thus:

"Wherefore it appears that there were in old times two distinct species of this majestic fowl, the one being single and
the other double. Nature has a reason for all things. It is plain
to the eye of science that the Double-Man originally inhabited a region where dangers abounded; hence he was paired

together to the end that while one part slept the other might watch; and likewise that, danger being discovered, there might always be a double instead of a single power to oppose it. All honor to the mystery-dispelling eye of godlike Science!"

And near the Double Man-Bird was found what was plainly an ancient record of his, marked upon numberless sheets of a thin white substance and bound together. Almost the first glance that Professor Woodlouse threw into it revealed this following sentence, which he instantly translated and laid before the scientists, in a tremble, and it uplifted every soul there with exultation and astonishment: "In truth it is believed by many that the lower animals reason and talk together."

When the great official report of the expedition appeared, the above sentence bore this comment:

> Then there are lower animals than Man! This remarkable passage can mean nothing else. Man himself is extinct, but *they* may still exist. What can they be? Where do they inhabit? One's enthusiasm bursts all bounds in the contemplation of the brilliant field of discovery and investigation here thrown open to science. We close our labors with the humble prayer that your Majesty will immediately appoint a commission and command it to rest not nor spare expense until the search for this hitherto unsuspected race of the creatures of God shall be crowned with success.

The expedition then journeyed homeward after its long absence and its faithful endeavors, and was received with a mighty ovation by the whole grateful country. There were vulgar, ignorant carpers, of course, as there always are and always will be; and naturally one of these was the obscene Tumble-Bug. He said that all he had learned by his travels was that science only needed a spoonful of supposition to build a mountain of demonstrated fact out of; and that for the future he meant to be content with the knowledge that nature had made free to all creatures and not go prying into the august secrets of the Deity.

The McWilliamses
and the Burglar Alarm

The conversation drifted smoothly and pleasantly along from weather to crops, from crops to literature, from literature to scandal, from scandal to religion; then took a random jump, and landed on the subject of burglar alarms. And now for the first time Mr. McWilliams showed feeling. Whenever I perceive this sign on this man's dial, I comprehend it, and lapse into silence, and give him opportunity to unload his heart. Said he, with but ill-controlled emotion:

I do not go one single cent on burglar alarms, Mr. Twain —not a single cent—and I will tell you why. When we were finishing our house, we found we had a little cash left over, on account of the plumber not knowing it. I was for enlightening the heathen with it, for I was always unaccountably down on the heathen somehow; but Mrs. McWilliams said no, let's have a burglar alarm. I agreed to this compromise. I will explain that whenever I want a thing, and Mrs. McWilliams wants another thing, and we decide upon the thing that Mrs. McWilliams wants—as we always do—she calls that a compromise. Very well: the man came up from New York and put in the alarm, and charged three hundred and twenty-five dollars for it, and said we could sleep without uneasiness now. So we did for awhile—say a month. Then one night we smelled smoke, and I was advised to get up and see what the matter was. I lit a candle, and started toward the stairs, and met a burglar coming out of a room with a basket of tinware, which he had mistaken for solid silver in the dark. He was smoking a pipe. I said, "My friend, we do not allow smoking in this room." He said he was a stranger, and could not be expected to know the rules of the house: said he had been in many houses just as good as this one, and it had never been objected to before. He added that as far as his experience went, such rules had never been considered to apply to burglars, anyway.

I said: "Smoke along, then, if it is the custom, though I think that the conceding of a privilege to a burglar which is denied to a bishop is a conspicuous sign of the looseness of the times. But waving all that, what business have you to be entering this house in this furtive and clandestine way, without ringing the burglar alarm?"

He looked confused and ashamed, and said, with embarrassment: "I beg a thousand pardons. I did not know you had a burglar alarm, else I would have rung it. I beg you will not mention it where my parents may hear of it, for they are old and feeble, and such a seemingly wanton breach of the hallowed conventionalities of our Christian civilization might all too rudely sunder the frail bridge which hangs darkling between the pale and evanescent present and the solemn great deeps of the eternities. May I trouble you for a match?"

I said: "Your sentiments do you honor, but if you will

allow me to say it, metaphor is not your best hold. Spare
your thigh; this kind light only on the box, and seldom there,
in fact, if my experience may be trusted. But to return to
business: how did you get in here?"

"Through a second-story window."

It was even so. I redeemed the tinware at pawnbroker's
rates, less cost of advertising, bade the burglar good-night,
closed the window after him, and retired to headquarters to
report. Next morning we sent for the burglar-alarm man, and
he came up and explained that the reason the alarm did not
"go off" was that no part of the house but the first floor was
attached to the alarm. This was simply idiotic; one might as
well have no armor on at all in battle as to have it only on
his legs. The expert now put the whole second story on the
alarm, charged three hundred dollars for it, and went his
way. By and by, one night, I found a burglar in the third
story, about to start down a ladder with a lot of miscella-
neous property. My first impulse was to crack his head with
a billiard cue; but my second was to refrain from this attention, because he was between me and the cue rack. The
second impulse was plainly the soundest, so I refrained, and
proceeded to compromise. I redeemed the property at former
rates, after deducting ten per cent, for use of ladder, it being
my ladder, and next day we sent down for the expert once
more, and had the third story attached to the alarm, for
three hundred dollars.

By this time the "annunciator" had grown to formidable
dimensions. It had forty-seven tags on it, marked with the
names of the various rooms and chimneys, and it occupied
the space of an ordinary wardrobe. The gong was the size of
a wash-bowl, and was placed above the head of our bed.
There was a wire from the house to the coachman's quarters
in the stable, and a noble gong alongside his pillow.

We should have been comfortable now but for one defect.
Every morning at five the cook opened the kitchen door, in

the way of business, and rip went that gong! The first time
this happened I thought the last day was come sure. I didn't
think it *in* bed—no, but out of it—for the first effect of that
frightful gong is to hurl you across the house, and slam you
against the wall, and then curl you up, and squirm you like
a spider on a stove lid, till somebody shuts the kitchen door.
In solid fact, there is no clamor that is even remotely comparable to the dire clamor which that gong makes. Well,
this catastrope happened every morning regularly at five
o'clock, and lost us three hours sleep; for, mind you, when
that thing wakes you, it doesn't merely wake you in spots;
it wakes you all over, conscience and all, and you are good
for eighteen hours of wide-awakeness subsequently—eighteen hours of the very most inconceivable wide-awakeness
that you ever experienced in your life. A stranger died on
our hands one time, and we vacated and left him in our
room overnight. Did that stranger wait for the general judgment? *No*, sir; he got up at five the next morning in the most
prompt and unostentatious way. I knew he would; I knew it
mighty well. He collected his life-insurance, and lived happy
ever after, for there was plenty of proof as to the perfect
squareness of his death.

Well, we were gradually fading toward a better land, on
account of the daily loss of sleep; so we finally had the expert up again, and he ran a wire to the outside of the door,
and placed a switch there, whereby Thomas, the butler, always made one little mistake—he switched the alarm off at
night when he went to bed, and switched it on again at day-
break in the morning, just in time for the cook to open the
kitchen door, and enable that gong to slam us across the
house, sometimes breaking a window with one or the other
of us. At the end of a week we recognized that this switch
business was a delusion and a snare. We also discovered that
a band of burglars had been lodging in the house the whole
time—not exactly to steal, for there wasn't much left now,
but to hide from the police, for they were hot pressed, and

they shrewdly judged that the detectives would never think of a tribe of burglars taking sanctuary in a house notoriously protected by the most imposing and elaborate burglar alarm in America.

Sent down for the expert again, and this time he struck a most dazzling idea—he fixed the thing so that opening the kitchen door would take off the alarm. It was a noble idea, and he charged accordingly. But you already foresee the result. I switched on the alarm every night at bed-time, no longer trusting on Thomas's frail memory; and as soon as the lights were out the burglars walked in at the kitchen door, thus taking the alarm off without waiting for the cook to do it in the morning. You see how aggravatingly we were situated. For months we couldn't have any company. Not a spare bed in the house; all occupied by burglars.

Finally, I got up a cure of my own. The expert answered the call, and ran another ground wire to the stable, and established a switch there, so that the coachman could put on and take off the alarm. That worked first rate, and a season of peace ensued, during which we got to inviting company once more and enjoying life.

But by and by the irrepressible alarm invented a new kink. One winter's night we were flung out of bed by the sudden music of that awful gong, and when we hobbled to the annunciator, turned up the gas, and saw the word "Nursery" exposed, Mrs. McWilliams fainted dead away, and I came precious near doing the same thing myself. I seized my shotgun, and stood timing the coachman whilst that appalling buzzing went on. I knew that his gong had flung him out, too, and that he would be along with his gun as soon as he could jump into his clothes. When I judged that the time was ripe, I crept to the room next the nursery, glanced through the window, and saw the dim outline of the coachman in the yard below, standing at present-arms and waiting for a chance. Then I hopped into the nursery and fired, and in the same instant the coachman fired at the red flash of my gun. Both

of us were successful; I crippled a nurse, and he shot off all
my back hair. We turned up the gas, and telephoned for a
surgeon. There was not a sign of a burglar, and no window
had been raised. One glass was absent, but that was where
the coachman's charge had come through. Here was a fine
mystery—a burglar alarm "going off" at midnight of its own
accord, and not a burglar in the neighborhood!

The expert answered the usual call, and explained that it
was a "False alarm." Said it was easily fixed. So he overhauled the nursery window, charged a remunerative figure
for it, and departed.

What we suffered from false alarms for the next three
years no stylographic pen can describe. During the next three
months I always flew with my gun to the room indicated, and
the coachman always sallied forth with his battery to support
me. But there was never anything to shoot at—windows all
tight and secure. We always sent down for the expert next
day, and he fixed those particular windows so they would
keep quiet a week or so, and always remembered to send us
a bill about like this:

Wire	$2.15
Nipple	.75
Two hours' labor	1.50
Wax	.47
Tape	.34
Screws	.15
Recharging battery	.98
Three hours' labor	2.25
String	.02
Lard	.66
Pond's Extract	1.25
Springs at 50	2.00
Railroad fares	7.25
	$19.77

At length a perfectly natural thing came about—after we had answered three or four hundred false alarms—to wit, we stopped answering them. Yes, I simply rose up calmly, when slammed across the house by the alarm, calmly inspected the annunciator, took note of the room indicated, and then calmly disconnected that room from the alarm, and went back to bed as if nothing had happened. Moreover, I left that room off permanently, and did not send for the expert. Well, it goes without saying that in the course of time *all* the rooms were taken off, and the entire machine was out of service.

It was at this unprotected time that the heaviest calamity of all happened. The burglars walked in one night and carried off the burglar alarm! yes, sir, every hide and hair of it: ripped it out, tooth and nail; springs, bells, gongs, battery, and all; they took a hundred and fifty miles of copper wire; they just cleaned her out, bag and baggage, and never left us a vestige of her to swear at—swear by, I mean.

We had a time of it to get her back; but we accomplished it finally, for money. The alarm firm said that what we needed now was to have her put in right—with their new patent springs in the windows to make false alarms impossible, and their new patent clock attached to take off and put on the alarm morning and night without human assistance. That seemed a good scheme. They promised to have the whole thing finished in ten days. They began work, and we left for the summer. They worked a couple of days; then *they* left for the summer. After which the burglars moved in, and began *their* summer vacation. When we returned in the fall, the house was as empty as a beer closet in premises where painters have been at work. We refurnished, and then sent down to hurry up the expert. He came up and finished the job, and said: "Now this clock is set to put on the alarm every night at 10, and take it off every morning at 5:45. All you've got to do is to wind her up every week, and then leave her alone —she will take care of the alarm herself."

After that we had a most tranquil season during three months. The bill was prodigious, of course, and I had said I would not pay it until the new machinery had proved itself to be flawless. The time stipulated was three months. So I paid the bill, and the very next day the alarm went to buzzing like ten thousand bee swarms at ten o'clock in the morning. I turned the hands around twelve hours, according to instructions, and this took off the alarm; but there was another hitch at night, and I had to set her ahead twelve hours once more to get her to put the alarm on again. That sort of nonsense went on a week or two, then the expert came up and put in a new clock. He came up every three months during the next three years, and put in a new clock. But it was always a failure. His clocks all had the same perverse defect: they would put the alarm on in the daytime, and they would *not* put it on at night; and if you forced it on yourself, they *would* take it off again the minute your back was turned.

Now there is the history of that burglar alarm—everything just as it happened; nothing extenuated, and naught set down in malice. Yes, sir,—and when I had slept nine years with burglars, and maintained an expensive burglar alarm the whole time, for their protection, not mine, and at my sole cost—for not a d——d cent could I ever get *them* to contribute—I just said to Mrs. McWilliams that I had had enough of that kind of pie; so with her full consent I took the whole thing out and traded it off for a dog, and shot the dog. I don't know what *you* think about it, Mr. Twain; but *I* think those things are made solely in the interest of the burglars. Yes, sir, a burglar alarm combines in its person all that is objectionable about a fire, a riot, and a harem, and at the same time has none of the compensating advantages, of one sort or another, that customarily belong with that combination. Goodby: I get off here.

The Diary of Adam and Eve

PART I

Extracts from Adam's Diary

Monday: This new creature with the long hair is a good deal in the way. It is always hanging around and following me about. I don't like this; I am not used to company. I wish it would stay with the other animals. . . . Cloudy today, wind in the east; think we shall have rain. . . . *We?* Where did I get that word?—I remember now—the new creature uses it.

Tuesday: Been examining the great waterfall. It is the finest thing on the estate, I think. The new creature calls it Niagara Falls—why, I am sure I do not know. Says it *looks* like Niagara Falls. That is not a reason, it is mere waywardness and imbecility. I get no chance to name anything myself. The new creature names everything that comes along, before I can get in a protest. And always that same pretext is offered—it *looks* like the thing. There is the dodo, for instance. Says the moment one looks at it one sees at a glance that it "looks like a dodo." It will have to keep that name, no doubt. It wearies me to fret about it, and it does no good, anyway. Dodo! It looks no more like a dodo than I do.

Wednesday: Built me a shelter against the rain, but could not have it to myself in peace. The new creature intruded. When I tried to put it out it shed water out of the holes it looks with, and wiped it away with the back of its paws, and made a noise such as some of the other animals make when they are in distress. I wish it would not talk; it is always talking. That sounds like a cheap fling at the poor creature, a slur; but I do not mean it so. I have never heard the human voice before, and any new and strange sound intruding itself here upon the solemn hush of these dreaming solitudes offends my ear and seems a false note. And this new sound is so close to me; it is right at my shoulder, right at my ear, first on one side and then on the other, and I am used only to sounds that are more or less distant from me.

Friday: The naming goes recklessly on, in spite of anything I can do. I had a very good name for the estate, and it was musical and pretty: Garden of Eden. Privately, I continue to call it that, but not any longer publicly. The new creature says it is all woods and rocks and scenery, and therefore has no resemblance to a garden. Says it *looks* like a park, and does not look like anything *but* a park. Consequently, without consulting me, it has been new-named Niagara Falls Park. This is sufficiently high-handed, it seems to me. And already there is a sign up:

KEEP OFF THE GRASS

My life is not as happy as it was.

Saturday: The new creature eats too much fruit. We are going to run short, most likely. "We" again—that is *its* word; mine, too, now, from hearing it so much. Good deal of fog this morning. I do not go out in the fog myself. The new creature does. It goes out in all weathers, and stumps right in with its muddy feet. And talks. It used to be so pleasant and quiet here.

Sunday: Pulled through. This day is getting to be more and more trying. It was selected and set apart last November as a day of rest. I had already six of them per week before. This morning found the new creature trying to clod apples out of that forbidden tree.

Monday: The new creature says its name is Eve. That is all right, I have no objections. Says it is to call it by, when I want it to come. I said it was superfluous, then. The word evidently raised me in its respect; and indeed it is a large, good word and will bear repetition. It says it is not an It, it is She. This is probably doubtful; yet it is all one to me; what she is were nothing to me if she would but go by herself and not talk.

Tuesday: She has littered the whole estate with execrable names and offensive signs:

THIS WAY TO THE WHIRLPOOL
THIS WAY TO GOAT ISLAND
CAVE OF THE WINDS THIS WAY

She says this park would make a tidy summer resort if there was any custom for it. Summer resort—another invention of hers—just words, without any meaning. What is a

summer resort? But it is best not to ask her, she has such a
rage for explaining.

Friday: She has taken to beseeching me to stop going
over the Falls. What harm does it do? Says it makes her
shudder. I wonder why; I have always done it—always liked
the plunge, and coolness. I supposed it was what the Falls
were for. They have no other use that I can see, and they must
have been made for something. She says they were only
made for scenery—like the rhinoceros and the mastodon.

I went over the Falls in a barrel—not satisfactory to her.
Went over in a tub—still not satisfactory. Swam the Whirlpool and the Rapids in a fig-leaf suit. It got much damaged.
Hence, tedious complaints about my extravagance. I am too
much hampered here. What I need is change of scene.

Saturday: I escaped last Tuesday night, and traveled two
days, and built me another shelter in a secluded place, and
obliterated my tracks as well as I could, but she hunted me
out by means of a beast which she has tamed and calls a
wolf, and came making that pitiful noise again, and shedding
that water out of the places she looks with. I was obliged to
return with her, but will presently emigrate again when occasion offers. She engages herself in many foolish things;
among others, to study out why the animals called lions and
tigers live on grass and flowers, when, as she says, the sort of
teeth they wear would indicate that they were intended
to eat each other. This is foolish, because to do that would be
to kill each other, and that would introduce what, as I understand it, is called "death"; and death, as I have been told,
has not yet entered the Park. Which is a pity, on some accounts.

Sunday: Pulled through.

Monday: I believe I see what the week is for: it is to give time to rest up from the weariness of Sunday. It seems a good idea. . . . She has been climbing that tree again. Clodded her out of it. She said nobody was looking. Seems to consider that a sufficient justification for chancing any dangerous thing. Told her that. The word justification moved her admiration—and envy, too, I thought. It is a good word.

Tuesday: She told me she was made out of a rib taken from my body. This is at least doubtful, if not more than that. I have not missed any rib. . . . She is in much trouble about the buzzard; says grass does not agree with it; is afraid she can't raise it; thinks it was intended to live on decayed flesh. The buzzard must get along the best it can with what is is provided. We cannot overturn the whole scheme to accommodate the buzzard.

Saturday: She fell in the pond yesterday when she was looking at herself in it, which she is always doing. She nearly strangled, and said it was most uncomfortable. This made her sorry for the creatures which live in there, which she calls fish, for she continues to fasten names on to things that don't need them and don't come when they are called by them, which is a matter of no consequence to her, she is such a numskull, anyway; so she got a lot of them out and brought them in last night and put them in my bed to keep warm, but I have noticed them now and then all day and I don't see that they are any happier there than they were before, only quieter. When night comes I shall throw them outdoors. I will not sleep with them again, for I find them clammy and unpleasant to lie among when a person hasn't anything on.

Sunday: Pulled through.

Tuesday: She has taken up with a snake now. The other animals are glad, for she was always experimenting with them and bothering them; and I am glad because the snake talks, and this enables me to get a rest.

Friday: She says the snake advises her to try the fruit of that tree, and says the result will be a great and fine and noble education. I told her there would be another result, too—it would introduce death into the world. That was a mistake—it had been better to keep the remark to myself; it only gave her an idea—she could save the sick buzzard, and furnish fresh meat to the despondent lions and tigers. I advised her to keep away from the tree. She said she wouldn't. I foresee trouble. Will emigrate.

Wednesday: I have had a variegated time. I escaped last night, and rode a horse all night as fast as he could go, hoping to get clear out of the Park and hide in some other country before the trouble should begin; but it was not to be. About an hour after sun-up, as I was riding through a flowery plain where thousands of animals were grazing, slumbering, or playing with each other, according to their wont, all of a sudden they broke into a tempest of frightful noises, and in one moment the plain was a frantic commotion and every beast was destroying its neighbor. I knew what it meant—Eve had eaten that fruit, and death was come into the world. . . . The tigers ate my horse, paying no attention when I ordered them to desist, and they would have eaten me if I had stayed—which I didn't, but went away in much haste. . . . I found this place, outside the Park, and was farily comfortable for a few days, but she has found me out. Found me out, and has named the place Tonawanda—says it *looks* like that. In fact I was not sorry she came, for there are but meager pickings here, and she brought some of those apples. I was obliged to eat them, I was so hungry. It

was against my principles, but I find that principles have no
real force except when one is well fed. . . . She came cur-
tained in boughs and bunches of leaves, and when I asked
her what she meant by such nonsense, and snatched them
away and threw them down, she tittered and blushed. I had
never seen a person titter and blush before, and to me it
seemed unbecoming and idiotic. She said I would soon know
how it was myself. This was correct. Hungry as I was, I
laid down the apple half-eaten—certainly the best one I ever
saw, considering the lateness of the season—and arrayed myself in the discarded boughs and branches, and then spoke
to her with some severity and ordered her to go and get some
more and not make such a spectacle of herself. She did it,
and after this we crept down to where the wild-beast battle
had been, and collected some skins, and I made her patch together a couple of suits proper for public occasions. They are
uncomfortable, it is true, but stylish, and that is the main
point about clothes. . . . I find she is a good deal of a companion. I see I should be lonesome and depressed without
her, now that I have lost my property. Another thing, she
says it is ordered that we work for our living hereafter. She
will be useful. I will superintend.

Ten Days Later: She accuses *me* of being the cause of our
disaster! She says, with apparent sincerity and truth, that the
Serpent assured her that the forbidden fruit was not apples,
it was chestnuts. I said I was innocent, then, for I had not
eaten any chestnuts. She said the Serpent informed her that
"chestnut" was a figurative term meaning an aged and moldy
joke. I turned pale at that, for I have made many jokes to pass
the weary time, and some of them could have been of that
sort, though I had honestly supposed that they were new
when I made them. She asked me if I had made one just at
the time of the catastrophe. I was obliged to admit that I
had made one to myself, though not aloud. It was this. I was

thinking about the Falls, and I said to myself, "How wonderful it is to see that vast body of water tumble down there!" Then in an instant a bright thought flashed into my head, and I let it fly, saying, "It would be a deal more wonderful to see it tumble *up* there!"—and I was just about to kill myself with laughing at it when all nature broke loose in war and death and I had to flee for my life. "There," she said, with triumph, "that is just it; the Serpent mentioned that very jest, and called it the First Chestnut, and said it was coeval with the creation." Alas, I am indeed to blame. Would that I were not witty; oh, that I had never had that radiant thought!

Next Year: We have named it Cain. She caught it while I was up country trapping on the North Shore of the Erie; caught it in the timber a couple of miles from our dug-out— or it might have been four, she isn't certain which. It resembles us in some ways, and may be a relation. That is what she thinks, but this is an error, in my judgment. The difference in size warrants the conclusion that it is a different and new kind of animal—a fish, perhaps, though when I put it in the water to see, it sank, and she plunged in and snatched it out before there was opportunity for the experiment to determine the matter. I still think it is a fish, but she is indifferent about what it is, and will not let me have it to try. I do not understand this. The coming of the creature seems to have changed her whole nature and made her unreasonable about experiments. She thinks more of it than she does of any of the other animals, but is not able to explain why. Her mind is disordered—everything shows it. Sometimes she carries the fish in her arms half the night when it complains and wants to get to the water. At such times the water comes out of the places in her face that she looks out of, and she pats the fish on the back and makes soft sounds with her mouth to soothe it, and betrays sorrow and solicitude in a hundred ways. I have never seen her do like this with any other fish, and it troubles me greatly. She used to carry the young tigers around so, and play with them, before we lost our property, but it was only play; she never took on about them like this when their dinner disagreed with them.

Sunday: She doesn't work, Sundays, but lies around all tired out, and likes to have the fish wallow over her; and she makes fool noises to amuse it, and pretends to chew its paws, and that makes it laugh. I have not seen a fish before that could laugh. This makes me doubt. . . . I have come to like Sunday myself. Superintending all the week tires a body so. There ought to be more Sundays. In the old days they were tough, but now they come handy.

Wednesday: It isn't a fish. I cannot quite make out what it is. It makes curious devilish noises when not satisfied, and says "goo-goo" when it is. It is not one of us, for it doesn't walk; it is not a bird, for it doesn't fly; it is not a frog, for it doesn't hop; it is not a snake, for it doesn't crawl, I feel sure it is not a fish, though I cannot get a chance to find out whether it can swim or not. It merely lies around, and mostly on its back, with its feet up. I have not seen any other animal do that before. I said I believed it was an enigma; but she only admired the word without understanding it. In my judgment it is either an enigma or some kind of a bug. If it dies, I will take it apart and see what its arrangements are. I never had a thing perplex me so.

Three Months Later: The perplexity augments instead of diminishing. I sleep but little. It has ceased from lying around, and goes about on its four legs now. Yet it differs from the other four-legged animals, in that its front legs are unusually short, consequently this causes the main part of its person to stick up uncomfortably high in the air, and this is not attractive. It is built much as we are, but its method of traveling shows that it is not of our breed. The short front legs and long hind ones indicate that it is of the kangaroo family, but it is a marked variation of the species, since the true kangaroo hops, whereas this one never does. Still it is a curious and interesting variety, and has not been catalogued before. As I discovered it, I have felt justified in securing the credit of the discovery by attaching my name to it, and hence have called it *"Kangaroorum Adamiensis."* . . . It must have been a young one when it came, for it has grown exceedingly since. It must be five times as big, now, as it was then, and when discontented it is able to make from twenty-two to thirty-eight times the noise it made at first. Coercion does not modify this, but has the contrary effect. For this reason I discontinued the system. She reconciles it by persuasion, and by giving it things which she had previously told me she wouldn't give it. As already observed, I was not at home when it first came, and she told me she found it in the woods. It seems odd that it should be the only one, yet it must be so, for I have worn myself out these many weeks trying to find another one to add to my collection, and for this one to play with; for surely then it would be quieter and we could tame it more easily. But I find none, nor any vestige of any; and strangest of all, no tracks. It has to live on the ground, it cannot help itself; therefore, how does it get about without leaving a track? I have set a dozen traps, but they do no good. I catch all small animals except that one; animals that merely go into the trap out of curiosity, I think, to see what the milk is there for. They never drink it.

Three Months Later: The Kangaroo still continues to grow, which is very strange and perplexing. I never knew one to be so long getting its growth. It has fur on its head now; not like kangaroo fur, but exactly like our hair except that it is much finer and softer, and instead of being black it is red. I am like to lose my mind over the capricious and harassing developments of this unclassifiable zoological freak. If I could catch another one—but that is hopeless; it is a new variety, and the only sample; this is plain. But I caught a true kangaroo and brought it in, thinking that this one, being lonesome, would rather have that for company than have no kin at all, or any animal it could feel a nearness to or get sympathy from in its forlorn condition here among strangers who do not know its ways or habits, or what to do to make it feel that it is among friends; but it was a mistake—it went into such fits at the sight of the kangaroo that I was convinced it had never seen one before. I pity the poor noisy little animal, but there is nothing I can do to make it happy. If I could tame it—but that is out of the question; the more I try the worse I seem to make it. It grieves me to the heart to see it in its little storms of sorrow and passion. I wanted to let it go, but she wouldn't hear of it. That seemed cruel and not like her; and yet she may be right. It might be lonelier than ever; for since I cannot find another one, how could *it*?

Five Months Later: It is not a kangaroo. No, for it supports itself by holding to her finger, and thus goes a few steps on its hind legs, and then falls down. It is probably some kind of a bear; and yet it has no tail—as yet—and no fur, except on its head. It still keeps on growing—that is a curious circumstance, for bears get their growth earlier than this. Bears are dangerous—since our catastrophe—and I shall not be satisfied to have this one prowling about the place much longer without a muzzle on. I have offered to get her a kangaroo if she would let this one go, but it did no good—she is determined to run us into all sorts of foolish risks, I think. She was not like this before she lost her mind.

A Fortnight Later: I examined its mouth. There is no danger yet: it has only one tooth. It has no tail yet. It makes more noise now than it ever did before—and mainly at night.

I have moved out. But I shall go over, mornings, to breakfast, and see if it has more teeth. If it gets a mouthful of teeth it will be time for it to go, tail or no tail, for a bear does not need a tail in order to be dangerous.

Four Months Later: I have been off hunting and fishing a month, up in the region that she calls Buffalo; I don't know why, unless it is because there are not any buffaloes there. Meantime the bear has learned to paddle around all by itself on its hind legs, and says "poppa" and "momma." It is certainly a new species. This resemblance to words may be purely accidental, of course, and may have no purpose or meaning; but even in that case it is still extraordinary, and is a thing which no other bear can do. This imitation of speech, taken together with general absence of fur and entire absence of tail, sufficiently indicates that this is a new kind of bear. The further study of it will be exceedingly interesting. Meantime I will go off on a far expedition among the forests of the north and make an exhaustive search. There must certainly be another one somewhere, and this one will be less dangerous when it has company of its own species. I will go straightway; but I will muzzle this one first.

Three Months Later: It has been a weary, weary hunt, yet I have had no success. In the meantime, without stirring from the home estate, she has caught another one! I never saw such luck. I might have hunted these woods a hundred years, I never would have run across that thing.

Next Day: I have been comparing the new one with the old one, and it is perfectly plain that they are the same breed. I was going to stuff one of them for my collection, but she is prejudiced against it for some reason or other; so I have relinquished the idea, though I think it is a mistake. It would be an irreparable loss to science if they should get

away. The old one is tamer than it was and can laugh and
talk like the parrot, having learned this, no doubt, from being
with the parrot so much, and having the imitative faculty in
a highly developed degree. I shall be astonished if it turns
out to be a new kind of parrot; and yet I ought not to be astonished, for it has already been everything else it could
think of since those first days when it was a fish. The new one
is as ugly now as the old one was at first; has the same sul-
phur-and-raw-meat complexion and the same singular head
without any fur on it. She calls it Abel.

Ten Years Later: They are *boys;* we found it out long ago.
It was their coming in that small, immature shape that puzzled us; we were not used to it. There are some girls now.
Abel is a good boy, but if Cain had stayed a bear it would
have improved him. After all these years, I see that I was
mistaken about Eve in the beginning; it is better to live
outside the Garden with her than inside it without her. At
first I thought she talked too much; but now I should be sorry
to have that voice fall silent and pass out of my life. Blessed
be the chestnut that brought us near together and taught me
to know the goodness of her heart and the sweetness of her
spirit!

PART II

Eve's Diary
(Translated from the Original)

Saturday: I am almost a whole day old, now. I arrived
yesterday. That is as it seems to me. And it must be so, for
if there was a day-before-yesterday I was not there when it
happened, or I should remember it. It could be, of course,
that it did happen, and that I was not noticing. Very well;
I will be very watchful now, and if any day-before-yesterdays

happen I will make a note of it. It will be best to start right
and not let the record get confused, for some instinct tells
me that these details are going to be important to the histo-
rian some day. For I feel like an experiment, I feel exactly
like an experiment; it would be impossible for a person to
feel more like an experiment than I do, and so I am coming
to feel convinced that that is what I *am*—an experiment; just
an experiment, and nothing more.

Then if I am an experiment, am I the whole of it? No, I
think not; I think the rest of it is part of it. I am the main
part of it, but I think the rest of it has its share in the matter. Is my position assured, or do I have to watch it and take
care of it? The latter, perhaps. Some instinct tells me that
eternal vigilance is the price of supremacy. (That is a good
phrase, I think, for one so young.)

Everything looks better to-day than it did yesterday. In the
rush of finishing up yesterday, the mountains were left in a
ragged condition, and some of the plains were so cluttered
with rubbish and remnants that the aspects were quite distressing. Noble and beautiful works of art should not be
subjected to haste; and this majestic new world is indeed a
most noble and beautiful work. And certainly marvelously
near to being perfect, notwithstanding the shortness of the
time. There are too many stars in some places and not enough
in others, but that can be remedied presently, no doubt. The
moon got loose last night, and slid down and fell out of the
scheme—a very great loss; it breaks my heart to think of it.
There isn't another thing among the ornaments and decora-
tions that is comparable to it for beauty and finish. It should
have been fastened better. If we can only get it back again—

But of course there is no telling where it went to. And besides, whoever gets it will hide it; I know it because I
would do it myself. I believe I can be honest in all other
matters, but I already begin to realize that the core and center of my nature is love of the beautiful, a passion for the

beautiful, and that it would not be safe to trust me with a moon that belonged to another person and that person didn't know I had it. I could give up a moon that I found in the daytime, because I should be afraid some one was looking; but if I found it in the dark, I am sure I should find some kind of an excuse for not saying anything about it. For I do love moons, they are so pretty and so romantic. I wish we had five or six; I would never go to bed; I should never get tired lying on the moss-bank and looking up at them.

Stars are good, too. I wish I could get some to put in my hair. But I suppose I never can. You would be surprised to find how far off they are, for they do not look it. When they first showed, last night, I tried to knock some down with a pole, but it didn't reach, which astonished me; then I tried clods till I was all tired out, but I never got one. It was because I am left-handed and cannot throw good. Even when I aimed at the one I wasn't after I couldn't hit the other one, though I did make some close shots, for I saw the black blot of the clod sail right into the midst of the golden clusters forty or fifty times, just barely missing them, and if I could have held out a little longer maybe I could have got one.

So I cried a little, which was natural, I suppose, for one of my age, and after I was rested I got a basket and started for a place on the extreme rim of the circle, where the stars were close to the ground and I could get them with my hands, which would be better, anyway, because I could gather them tenderly then, and not break them. But it was farther than I thought, and at last I had to give it up; I was so tired I couldn't drag my feet another step; and besides, they were sore and hurt me very much.

I couldn't get back home; it was too far and turning cold; but I found some tigers and nestled in among them and was most adorably comfortable, and their breath was sweet and pleasant, because they live on strawberries. I had never seen a tiger before, but I knew them in a minute by the stripes. If I could have one of those skins, it would make a lovely gown.

To-day I am getting better ideas about distances. I was so eager to get hold of every pretty thing that I giddily grabbed for it, sometimes when it was too far off, and sometimes when it was but six inches away but seemed a foot—alas, with thorns between! I learned a lesson; also I made an axiom, all out of my own head—my very first one: *The scratched Experiment shuns the thorn.* I think it is a very good one for one so young.

I followed the other Experiment around, yesterday afternoon, at a distance, to see what it might be for, if I could. But I was not able to make out. I think it is a man. I had never seen a man, but it looked like one, and I feel sure that that is what it is. I realize that I feel more curiosity about it than about any of the other reptiles. If it is a reptile, and I suppose it is; for it has frowsy hair and blue eyes, and looks like a reptile. It has no hips; it tapers like a carrot; when it stands, it spreads itself apart like a derrick; so I think it is a reptile, though it may be architecture.

I was afraid of it at first, and started to run every time it turned around, for I thought it was going to chase me; but by and by I found it was only trying to get away, so after that I was not timid any more, but tracked it along, several hours, about twenty yards behind, which made it nervous and unhappy. At last it was a good deal worried, and climbed a tree. I waited a good while, then gave it up and went home.

To-day the same thing over. I've got it up the tree again.

Sunday: It is up there yet. Resting, apparently. But that is a subterfuge: Sunday isn't the day of rest; Saturday is appointed for that. It looks to me like a creature that is more interested in resting than in anything else. It would tire me to rest so much. It tires me just to sit around and watch the tree. I do wonder what it is for; I never see it do anything.

They returned the moon last night, and I was *so* happy! I think it is very honest of them. It slid down and fell off again, but I was not distressed; there is no need to worry when one has that kind of neighbors; they will fetch it back. I wish I could do something to show my appreciation. I would like to send them some stars, for we have more than we can use. I mean I, not we, for I can see that the reptile cares nothing for such things.

It has low tastes, and is not kind. When I went there yesterday evening in the gloaming it had crept down and was trying to catch the little speckled fishes that play in the pool, and I had to clod it to make it go up the tree again and let them alone. I wonder if *that* is what it is for? Hasn't it any heart? Hasn't it any compassion for those little creatures? Can it be that it was designed and manufactured for such ungentle work? It has the look of it. One of the clods took it back of the ear, and it used language. It gave me a thrill, for it was the first time I had ever heard speech, except my own. I did not understand the words, but they seemed expressive.

When I found it could talk I felt a new interest in it, for I love to talk; I talk, all day, and in my sleep, too, and I am very interesting, but if I had another to talk to I could be twice as interesting, and would never stop if desired.

If this reptile is a man, it isn't an *it*, is it? That wouldn't be grammatical, would it? I think it would be *he*. I think so. In that case one would parse it thus: nominative, *he;* dative, *him;* possessive, *his'n*. Well, I will consider it a man and call it *he* until it turns out to be something else. This will be handier than having so many uncertainties.

Next Week Sunday: All the week It tagged around after him and tried to get acquainted. I had to do the talking, because he was shy, but I didn't mind it. He seemed pleased to have me around, and I used the sociable "we" a good deal, because it seemed to flatter him to be included.

Wednesday: We are getting along very well indeed, now, and getting better and better acquainted. He does not try to avoid me any more, which is a good sign, and shows that he likes to have me with him. That pleases me, and I study to be useful to him in every way I can, so as to increase his regard. During the last day or two I have taken all the work of naming things off his hands, and this has been a great relief to him, for he has not gift in that line, and is evidently very grateful. He can't think of a rational name to save him, but I do not let him see that I am aware of his defect. Whenever a new creature comes along I name it before he has time to expose himself by an awkward silence. In this way I have saved him many embarrassments. I have no defect like his. The minute I set eyes on an animal I know what it is. I don't have to reflect a moment; the right name comes out instantly, just as if it were an inspiration, as no doubt it is, for I am sure it wasn't in me half a minute before. I seem to know just by the shape of the creature and the way it acts what animal it is.

When the dodo came along he thought it was a wildcat—I saw it in his eyes. But I saved him. And I was careful not to do it in a way that could hurt his pride. I just spoke up in a quite natural way of pleased surprise, and not as if I was dreaming of conveying information, and said, "Well, I do declare, if there isn't the dodo!" I explained—without seeming to be explaining—how I knew it for a dodo, and although I thought maybe he was a little piqued that I knew the creature when he didn't, it was quite evident that he admired me. That was very agreeable, and I thought of it more than once with gratification before I slept. How little a thing can make us happy when we feel that we have earned it!

Thursday: My first sorrow. Yesterday he avoided me and seemed to wish I would not talk to him. I could not believe it, and thought there was some mistake, for I loved to be with him, and loved to hear him talk, and so how could it be that he could feel unkind toward me when I had not done anything? But at last it seemed true, so I went away and sat lonely in the place where I first saw him the morning that we were made and I did not know what he was and was indifferent about him; but now it was a mournful place, and every little thing spoke of him, and my heart was very sore. I did not know why very clearly, for it was a new feeling; I had not experienced it before, and it was all a mystery, and I could not make it out.

But when night came I could not bear the lonesomeness, and went to the new shelter which he has built, to ask him what I had done that was wrong and how I could mend it and get back his kindness again; but he put me out in the rain, and it was my first sorrow.

Sunday: It is pleasant again, now, and I am happy; but those were heavy days; I do not think of them when I can help it.

I tried to get him some of those apples, but I cannot learn to throw straight. I failed, but I think the good intention pleased him. They are forbidden, and he says I shall come to harm; but so I come to harm through pleasing him, why shall I care for that harm?

Monday: This morning I told him my name, hoping it would interest him. But he did not care for it. It is strange. If he should tell me his name, I would care. I think it would be pleasanter in my ears than any other sound.

He talks very little. Perhaps it is because he is not bright, and is sensitive about it and wishes to conceal it. It is such a pity that he should feel so, for brightness is nothing; it is in the heart that the values lie. I wish I could make him understand that a loving good heart is riches, and riches enough, and that without it intellect is poverty.

Although he talks so little, he has quite a considerable vocabulary. This morning he used a surprisingly good word. He evidently recognized, himself, that it was a good one, for he worked it in twice afterward, casually. It was not good casual art, still it showed that he possesses a certain quality of perception. Without a doubt that seed can be made to grow, if cultivated.

Where did he get that word? I do not think I have ever used it.

No, he took no interest in my name. I tried to hide my disappointment, but I suppose I did not succeed. I went away and sat on the moss-bank with my feet in the water. It is where I go when I hunger for companionship, some one to look at, some one to talk to. It is not enough—that lovely white body painted there in the pool—but it is something, and something is better than utter loneliness. It talks when I talk; it is sad when I am sad; it comforts me with its sympathy; it says, "Do not be downhearted, you poor friendless girl; I will be your friend." It *is* a good friend to me, and my only one; it is my sister.

That first time that she forsook me! ah, I shall never forget that—never, never. My heart was lead in my body! I said, "She was all I had, and now she is gone!" In my despair I said, "Break, my heart; I cannot bear my life any more!" and hid my face in my hands, and there was no solace for me. And when I took them away, after a little, there she was again, white and shining and beautiful, and I sprang into her arms!

That was perfect happiness; I had known happiness before, but it was not like this, which was ecstasy. I never doubted her afterward. Sometimes she stayed away—maybe an hour, maybe almost the whole day, but I waited and did not doubt; I said, "She is busy, or she is gone on a journey, but she will come." And it was so: she always did. At night she would not come if it was dark, for she was a timid little thing; but if there was a moon she would come. I am not afraid of the dark, but she is younger than I am; she was born after I was. Many and many are the visits I have paid her; she is my comfort and my refuge when my life is hard—and it is mainly that.

Tuesday: All the morning I was at work improving the estate; and I purposely kept away from him in the hope that he would get lonely and come. But he did not.

At noon I stopped for the day and took my recreation by flitting all about with the bees and the butterflies and reveling in the flowers, those beautiful creatures that catch the smile of God out of the sky and preserve it! I gathered them, and made them into wreaths and garlands and clothed myself in them while I ate my luncheon—apples, of course; then I sat in the shade and wished and waited. But he did not come.

But no matter. Nothing would have come of it, for he does not care for flowers. He calls them rubbish, and cannot tell one from another, and thinks it is superior to feel like that. He does not care for me, he does not care for flowers, he does not care for the painted sky at eventide—is there anything he does care for, except building shacks to coop himself up in from the good clean rain, and thumping the melons, and sampling the grapes, and fingering the fruit on the trees, to see how those properties are coming along?

I laid a dry stick on the ground and tried to bore a hole in it with another one, in order to carry out a scheme that I had, and soon I got an awful fright. A thin, transparent bluish film rose out of the hole, and I dropped everything and ran! I thought it was a spirit, and I *was* so frightened! But I looked back, and it was not coming; so I leaned against a rock and rested and panted, and let my limbs go on trembling until they got steady again; then I crept warily back, alert, watching, and ready to fly if there was occasion; and when I was come near, I parted the branches of a rose-bush and peeped through—wishing the man was about, I was looking so cunning and pretty—but the spirit was gone. I went there, and there was a pinch of delicate pink dust in the hole. I put my finger in, to feel it, and said *ouch!* and took it out again. It was a cruel pain. I put my finger in my mouth; and by standing first on one foot and then the other, and grunting, I presently eased my misery; then I was full of interest, and began to examine.

I was curious to know what the pink dust was. Suddenly the name of it occurred to me, though I had never heard of it before. It was *fire!* I was as certain of it as a person could be of anything in the world. So without hesitation I named it that—fire.

I had created something that didn't exist before; I had added a new thing to the world's uncountable properties; I realized this, and was proud of my achievement, and was going to run and find him and tell him about it, thinking to raise myself in his esteem—but I reflected, and did not do it. No—he would not care for it. He would ask what it was good for, and what could I answer? for if it was not *good* for something, but only beautiful, merely beautiful—

So I sighed, and did not go. For it wasn't good for any-thing; it could not build a shack, it could not improve mel-ons, it could not hurry a fruit crop; it was useless, it was a foolishness and a vanity; he would despise it and say cutting words. But to me it was not despicable; I said, "Oh, you fire, I love you, you dainty pink creature, for you are *beautiful*—and that is enough!" and was going to gather it to my breast. But refrained. Then I made another maxim out of my own head, though it was so nearly like the first one that I was afraid it was only a plagiarism: "The burnt Ex-periment shuns the fire."

I wrought again; and when I had made a good deal of

fire-dust I emptied it into a handful of dry brown grass, intending to carry it home and keep it always and play with it; but the wind struck it and it sprayed up and spat out at me fiercely, and I dropped it and ran. When I looked back the blue spirit was towering up and stretching and rolling away like a cloud, and instantly I thought of the name of it—*smoke!*—though, upon my word, I had never heard of smoke before.

Soon, brilliant yellow and red flares shot up through the smoke, and I named them in an insant—*flames*—and I was right, too, though these were the very first flames that had ever been in the world. They climbed the trees, they flashed splendidly in and out of the vast and increasing volume of tumbling smoke, and I had to clap my hands and laugh and dance in my rapture, it was so new and strange and so wonderful and so beautiful!

He came running, and stopped and gazed, and said not a word for many minutes. Then he asked what it was. Ah, it was too bad that he should ask such a direct question. I had to answer it, of course, and I did. I said it was fire. If it annoyed him that I should know and he must ask, that was not my fault; I had no desire to annoy him. After a pause he asked:

"How did it come?"

Another direct question, and it also had to have a direct answer.

"I made it."

The fire was traveling farther and farther off. He went to the edge of the burned place and stood looking down, and said:

"What are these?"

"Fire-coals."

He picked up one to examine it, but changed his mind and put it down again. Then he went away. *Nothing* interests him.

But I was interested. There were ashes, gray and soft and delicate and pretty—I knew what they were at once. And the embers; I knew the embers, too. I found my apples, and raked them out, and was glad; for I am very young and my appetite is active. But I was disappointed; they were all burst open and spoiled. Spoiled apparently; but it was not so; they were better than raw ones. Fire is beautiful; some day it will be useful, I think.

Friday: I saw him again, for a moment, last Monday at nightfall, but only for a moment. I was hoping he would praise me for trying to improve the estate, for I had meant well and had worked hard. But he was not pleased, and turned away and left me. He was also displeased on another account: I tried once more to persuade him to stop going over the Falls. That was because the fire had revealed to me a new passion—quite new, and distinctly different from love, grief, and those others which I had already discovered—*fear*. And it is horrible!—I wish I had never discovered it; it gives me dark moments, it spoils my happiness, it makes me shiver and tremble and shudder. But I could not persuade him, for he has not discovered fear yet, and so he could not understand me.

Extract from Adam's Diary

Perhaps I ought to remember that she is very young, a mere girl, and make allowances. She is all interest, eagerness, vivacity, the world is to her a charm, a wonder, a mystery, a joy; she can't speak for delight when she finds a new flower, she must pet it and caress it and smell it and talk to it, and pour out endearing names upon it. And she is color-mad: brown rocks, yellow sand, gray moss, green foliage, blue sky; the pearl of the dawn, the purple shadows on the mountains, the golden

islands floating in crimson seas at sunset, the pallid
moon sailing through the shredded cloud-rack, the
star-jewels glittering in the wastes of space—none
of them is of any practical value, so far as I can
see, but because they have color and majesty, that
is enough for her, and she loses her mind over
them. If she could quiet down and keep still a
couple of minutes at a time, it would be a reposeful
spectacle. In that case I think I could enjoy looking
at her; indeed I am sure I could, for I am coming
to realize that she is a quite remarkably comely
creature—lithe, slender, trim, rounded, shapely,
nimble, graceful; and once when she was standing
marble-white and sun-drenched on a boulder, with
her young head tilted back and her hand shading
her eyes, watching the flight of a bird in the sky,
I recognized that she was beautiful.

Monday noon: If there is anything on the planet
that she is not interested in it is not in my list.
There are animals that I am indifferent to, but it is
not so with her. She has no discrimination, she
takes to all of them, she thinks they are all
treasures, every new one is welcome.

When the mighty brontosaurus came striding
into camp, she regarded it as an acquisition, I
considered it a calamity; that is a good sample of
the lack of harmony that prevails in our views of
things. She wanted to domesticate it, I wanted to
make it a present of the homestead and move out.
She believed it could be tamed by kind treatment
and would be a good pet; I said a pet twenty-one
feet high and eighty-four feet long would be no
proper thing to have about the place, because,
even with the best intentions and without meaning
any harm, it could sit down on the house and mash
it, for any one could see by the look of its eye that
it was absent-minded.

Still, her heart was set upon having that monster, and she couldn't give it up. She thought we could start a dairy with it, and wanted me to help her milk it; but I wouldn't; it was too risky. The sex wasn't right, and we hadn't any ladder anyway. Then she wanted to ride it, and look at the scenery. Thirty or forty feet of its tail was lying on the ground, like a fallen tree, and she thought she could climb it, but she was mistaken; when she got to the steep place it was too slick and down she came, and would have hurt herself but for me.

Was she satisfied now? No. Nothing ever satisfies her but demonstration; untested theories are not in her line, and she won't have them. It is the right spirit, I concede it; it attracts me; I feel the influence of it; if I were with her more I think I should take it up myself. Well, she had one theory remaining about this colossus: she thought that if we could tame him and make him friendly we could stand him in the river and use him for a bridge. It turned out that he was already plenty tame enough—at least as far as she was concerned— so she tried her theory, but it failed: every time she got him properly placed in the river and went ashore to cross over on him, he came out and followed her around like a pet mountain. Like the other animals. They all do that.

Friday: Tuesday—Wednesday—Thursday—and to-day: all without seeing him. It is a long time to be alone; still, it is better to be alone than unwelcome.

I *had* to have company—I was made for it, I think—so I made friends with the animals. They are just charming, and they have the kindest disposition and the politest ways; they never look sour, they never let you feel that you are intruding, they smile at you and wag their tail, if they've got one, and they are always ready for a romp or an excursion or anything you want to propose. I think they are perfect gentlemen. All these days we have had such good times, and it hasn't been lonesome for me, ever. Lonesome! No, I should say not. Why, there's always a swarm of them around—sometimes as much as four or five acres—you can't count them; and when you stand on a rock in the midst and look out over the furry expanse it is so mottled and splashed and gay with color and frisking sheen and sun-flash, and so rippled with stripes, that you might think it was a lake, only you know it isn't; and there's storms of sociable birds, and hurricanes of whirring wings; and when the sun strikes all that feathery commotion, you have a blazing up of all the colors you can think of, enough to put your eyes out.

We have made long excursions, and I have seen a great deal of the world; almost all of it, I think; and so I am the first traveler, and the only one. When we are on the march, it is an imposing sight—there's nothing like it anywhere. For comfort I ride a tiger or a leopard, because it is soft and has a round back that fits me, and because they are such pretty animals; but for long distance or for scenery I ride the elephant. He hoists me up with his trunk, but I can get off myself; when we are ready to camp, he sits and I slide down the back way.

The birds and animals are all friendly to each other, and there are no disputes about anything. They all talk, and they all talk to me, but it must be a foreign language, for I cannot make out a word they say; yet they often understand me when I talk back, particularly the dog and the elephant. It makes me ashamed. It shows that they are brighter than I am, and are therefore my superiors. It annoys me, for I want to be the principal Experiment myself —and I intend to be, too.

I have learned a number of things, and am educated, now, but I wasn't at first. I was ignorant at first. At first it used to vex me because, with all my watching, I was never smart enough to be around when the water was running uphill; but now I do not mind it. I have experiemented and experimented until now I know it never does run uphill, except in the dark. I know it does in the dark, because the pool never goes dry, which it would, of course, if the water didn't come back in the night. It is best to prove things by actual experiment; then you *know;* whereas if you depend on guessing and supposing and conjecturing, you will never get educated.

Some things you *can't* find out; but you will never know you can't by guessing and supposing: no, you have to be patient and go on experimenting until you find out that you can't find out. And it is delightful to have it that way, it makes the world so interesting. If there wasn't anything to find out, it would be dull. Even trying to find out and not finding out is just as interesting as trying to find out and finding out, and I don't know but more so. The secret of the water was a treasure until I *got* it; then the excitement all went away, and I recognized a sense of loss.

By experiment I know that wood swims, and dry leaves, and feathers, and plenty of other things; therefore by all that cumulative evidence you know that a rock will swim; but you have to put up with simply knowing it, for there isn't any way to prove it—up to now. But I shall find a way —then *that* excitement will go. Such things make me sad; be-cause by and by when I have found out everything there won't be any more excitements, and I do love excitements so! The other night I couldn't sleep for thinking about it.

At first I couldn't make out what I was made for, but now I think it was to search out the secrets of this wonder-ful world and be happy and thank the Giver of it all for devising it. I think there are many things to learn yet—I hope so; and by economizing and not hurrying too fast I think they will last weeks and weeks. I hope so. When you cast up a feather it sails away on the air and goes out of sight; then you throw up a clod and it doesn't. It comes down, every time. I have tried it and tried it, and it is always so. I wonder why it is? Of course it *doesn't* come down, but why should it *seem* to? I suppose it is an optical illusion. I mean, one of them is. I don't know which one. It may be the feather, it may be the clod; I can't prove which it is, I can only demonstrate that one or the other is a fake, and let a person take his choice.

By watching, I know that the stars are not going to last. I have seen some of the best ones melt and run down the sky. Since one can melt, they can all melt; since they can all melt, they can all melt the same night. That sorrow will come—I know it. I mean to sit up every night and look at them as long as I can keep awake; and I will impress those sparkling fields on my memory, so that by and by when they are taken away I can by my fancy restore those lovely myriads to the black sky and make them sparkle again, and double them by the blur of my tears.

After the Fall

When I look back, the Garden is a dream to me. It was beautiful, surpassingly beautiful, enchantingly beautiful; and now it is lost, and I shall not see it any more.

The Garden is lost, but I have found *him*, and am content. He loves me as well as he can; I love him with all the strength of my passionate nature, and this, I think, is proper to my youth and sex. If I ask myself why I love him, I find I do not know, and do not really much care to know; so I suppose that this kind of love is not a product of reasoning and statistics, like one's love for other reptiles and animals. I think that this must be so. I love certain birds because of their song; but I do not love Adam on account of his singing—no, it is not that; the more he sings, the more I do not get reconciled to it. Yet I ask him to sing, because I wish to learn to like everything he is interested

in. I am sure I can learn, because at first I could not
stand it, but now I can. It sours the milk, but it doesn't
matter; I can get used to that kind of milk.

It is not on account of his brightness that I love him—
no, it is not that. He is not to blame for his brightness, such
as it is, for he did not make it himself; he is as God made
him, and that is sufficient. There was a wise purpose in it,
that I know. In time it will develop, though I think it will
not be sudden; and besides, there is no hurry; he is well
enough just as he is.

It is not on account of his gracious and considerate ways
and his delicacy that I love him. No, he has lacks in these
regards, but he is well enough just so, and is improving.

It is not on account of his industry that I love him—no,
it is not that. I think he has it in him, and I do not know
why he conceals it from me. It is my only pain. Otherwise he is frank and open with me, now. I am sure he keeps
nothing from me but this. It grieves me that he should
have a secret from me, and sometimes it spoils my sleep,
thinking of it, but I will put it out of my mind; it shall
not trouble my happiness, which is otherwise full to over-
flowing.

It is not on account of his education that I love him—no,
it is not that. He is self-educated, and does really know a
multitude of things, but they are not so.

It is not on account of his chivalry that I love him—no,
it is not that. He told on me, but I do not blame him;
it is a peculiarity of sex, I think, and he did not make his
sex. Of course I would not have told on him, I would
have perished first; but that is a peculiarity of sex, too, and
I do not take credit for it, for I did not make my sex.

Then why is it that I love him? *Merely because he is
masculine,* I think.

At bottom he is good, and I love him for that, but I
could love him without it. If he should beat me and

abuse me, I should go on loving him. I know it. It is a matter of sex, I think.

He is strong and handsome, and I love him for that, and I admire him and am proud of him, but I could love him without those qualities. If he were plain, I should love him; if he were a wreck, I should love him; and I would work for him, and slave over him, and pray for him, and watch by his bedside until I died.

Yes, I think I love him merely because he is *mine* and is *masculine*. There is no other reason, I suppose. And so I think it is as I first said: that this kind of love is not a product of reasonings and statistics. It just *comes*—none knows whence—and cannot explain itself. And doesn't need to.

It is what I think. But I am only a girl, and the first that has examined this matter, and it may turn out that in my ignorance and inexperience I have not got it right.

Forty Years Later

It is my prayer, it is my longing, that we may pass from this life together—a longing which shall never perish from the earth, but shall have place in the heart of every wife that loves, until the end of time; and it shall be called by my name.

But if one of us must go first, it is my prayer that it shall be I; for he is strong, I am weak, I am not so necessary to him as he is to me—life without him would not be life; how could I endure it? This prayer is also immortal, and will not cease from being offered up while my race continues. I am the first wife; and in the last wife I shall be repeated.

At Eve's Grave

ADAM: Wheresoever she was, *there* was Eden.

The £1,000,000 Bank-Note

When I was twenty-seven years old, I was a mining-broker's clerk in San Francisco, and an expert in all the details of stock traffic. I was alone in the world, and had nothing to depend upon but my wits and a clean reputation; but these were setting my feet in the road to eventual fortune, and I was content with the prospect.

My time was my own after the afternoon board, Saturdays, and I was accustomed to put it in on a little sailboat on the bay. One day I ventured too far, and was carried out to sea. Just at nightfall, when hope was about gone, I was picked up by a small brig which was bound for London. It was a long and stormy voyage, and they made me work my passage without pay, as a common sailor. When I stepped ashore in London my clothes were ragged and shabby, and I had only a dollar in my pocket. This money fed and sheltered me twenty-four hours. During the next twenty-four I went without food and shelter.

About ten o'clock on the following morning, seedy and hungry, I was dragging myself along Portland Place, when a child that was passing, towed by a nurse-maid, tossed a luscious big pear—minus one bite—into the gutter. I stopped, of course, and fastened my desiring eye on that muddy treasure. My mouth watered for it, my stomach craved it, my whole being begged for it. But every time I made a move to get it some passing eye detected my purpose, and of course I straightened up then, and looked indifferent, and pretended that I hadn't been thinking about the pear at all. This same thing kept happening and happening, and I couldn't get the pear. I was just getting desperate enough to brave all the shame, and to seize it, when a window behind me was raised, and a gentleman spoke out of it, saying:

"Step in here, please."

I was admitted by a gorgeous flunkey, and shown into a sumptuous room where a couple of elderly gentlemen were sitting. They sent away the servant, and made me sit down. They had just finished their breakfast, and the sight of the remains of it almost overpowered me. I could hardly keep my wits together in the presence of that food, but as I was not asked to sample it, I had to bear my trouble as best I could.

Now, something had been happening there a little before, which I did not know anything about until a good many days afterward, but I will tell you about it now. Those two old brothers had been having a pretty hot argument a couple of days before, and had ended by agreeing to decide it by a bet, which is the English way of settling everything.

You will remember that the Bank of England once issued two notes of a million pounds each, to be used for a special purpose connected with some public transaction with a foreign country. For some reason or other only one of these had been used and canceled; the other still lay in the vaults of the Bank. Well, the brothers, chatting along, happened to get to wondering what might be the fate of a perfectly honest and intelligent stranger who should be turned adrift in London without a friend, and with no money but that million-pound bank-note, and no way to account for his being in possession of it. Brother A said he would starve to death; Brother B said he wouldn't. Brother A said he couldn't offer it at a bank or anywhere else, because he would be arrested on the spot. So they went on disputing till Brother B said he would bet twenty thousand pounds that the man would live thirty days, *anyway*, on that million, and keep out of jail, too. Brother A took him up. Brother B went down to the Bank and bought that note. Just like an Englishman, you see; pluck to the backbone. Then he dictated a letter, which one of his clerks wrote out in a beautiful round hand, and then the two brothers sat at the window a whole day watching for the right man to give it to.

They saw many honest faces go by that were not intelligent enough; many that were intelligent, but not honest enough; many that were both, but the possessors were not poor enough, or, if poor enough, were not strangers. There was always a defect, until I came along; but they agreed that I filled the bill all around; so they elected me unanimously, and there I was now waiting to know why I was called in. They began to ask me questions about myself, and pretty soon they had my story. Finally they told me I would answer their purpose. I said I was sincerely glad, and asked what it was. Then one of them handed me an envelope, and said I would find the explanation inside. I was going to open it, but he said no; take it to my lodgings, and look it over carefully, and not be hasty or rash. I was puzzled, and wanted to discuss the matter a little further, but they didn't; so I took my leave, feeling hurt and insulted to be made the butt of what was apparently some kind of a practical joke and yet obliged to put up with it, not being in circumstances to resent affronts from rich and strong folk.

I would have picked up the pear now and eaten it before
all the world, but it was gone; so I had lost that by this
unlucky business, and the thought of it did not soften
my feeling toward those men. As soon as I was out of sight
of that house I opened my envelope, and saw that it con-
tained money! My opinion of those people changed, I can tell
you! I lost not a moment, but shoved note and money into
my vest pocket, and broke for the nearest cheap eating-
house. Well, how I did eat! When at last I couldn't hold any
more, I took out my money and unfolded it, took one glimpse
and nearly fainted. Five millions of dollars! Why, it made
my head swim.

I must have sat there stunned and blinking at the note as
much as a minute before I came rightly to myself again. The
first thing I noticed, then, was the landlord. His eye was on
the note, and he was petrified. He was worshiping, with all
his body and soul, but he looked as if he couldn't stir hand
or foot. I took my cue in a moment, and did the only rational
thing there was to do. I reached the note toward him, and
said, carelessly:

"Give me the change, please."

Then he was restored to his normal condition, and made
a thousand apologies for not being able to break the bill,
and I couldn't get him to touch it. He wanted to look at it,
and keep on looking at it; he couldn't seem to get enough of
it to quench the thirst of his eye, but he shrank from
touching it as if it had been something too sacred for poor
common clay to handle. I said:

"I am sorry if it is an inconvenience, but I must insist.
Please change it; I haven't anything else."

But he said that wasn't any matter; he was quite willing
to let the trifle stand over till another time. I said I might not
be in his neighborhood again for a good while; but he said it
was of no consequence, he could wait, and, moreover, I could
have anything I wanted, any time I chose, and let the ac-

count run as long as I pleased. He said he hoped he wasn't
afraid to trust as rich a gentleman as I was, merely because
I was of a merry disposition, and chose to play larks on the
public in the matter of dress. By this time another customer
was entering, and the landlord hinted to me to put the monster out of sight; then he bowed me all the way to the door,
and I started straight for that house and those brothers, to
correct the mistake which had been made before the police
should hunt me up, and help me do it. I was pretty nervous;
in fact, pretty badly frightened, though, of course, I was no
way in fault; but I knew men well enough to know that when
they find they've given a tramp a million-pound bill when
they thought it was a one-pounder, they are in a frantic rage
against *him* instead of quarreling with their own near-sight-
edness, as they ought. As I approached the house my excitement began to abate, for all was quiet there, which made
me feel pretty sure the blunder was not discovered yet. I
rang. The same servant appeared. I asked for those gentlemen.

"They are gone." This in the lofty, cold way of that
fellow's tribe.

"Gone? Gone where?"

"On a journey."

"But whereabouts?"

"To the Continent, I think."

"The Continent?"

"Yes, sir."

"Which way—by what route?"

"I can't say, sir."

"When will they be back?"

"In a month, they said."

"A month! Oh, this is awful! Give me *some* sort of idea of
how to get a word to them. It's of the last importance."

"I can't, indeed. I've no idea where they've gone, sir."

"Then I must see some member of the family."

"Family's away, too; been abroad months—in Egypt and India, I think."

"Man, there's been an immense mistake made. They'll be back before night. Will you tell them I've been here, and that I will keep coming till it's all made right, and they needn't be afraid?"

"I'll tell them, if they come back, but I am not expecting them. They said you would be here in an hour to make inquiries, but I must tell you it's all right, they'll be here on time and expect you."

So I had to give it up and go away. What a riddle it all was! I was like to lose my mind. They would, be here "on time." What could that mean? Oh the letter would explain, maybe. I had forgotten the letter; I got it out and read it. This is what it said:

> You are an intelligent and honest man, as one may see by your face. We conceive you to be poor and a stranger. Enclosed you will find a sum of money. It is lent to you for thirty days, without interest. Report at this house at the end of that time. I have a bet on you. If I win it you shall have any situation that is in my gift—any, that is, that you shall be able to prove yourself familiar with and competent to fill.

No signature, no address, no date.

Well, here was a coil to be in! You are posted on what had preceded all this, but I was not. It was just a deep, dark puzzle to me. I hadn't the least idea what the game was, nor whether harm was meant me or a kindness. I went into a park, and sat down to try to think it out, and to consider what I had best do.

At the end of an hour my reasonings had crystallized into this verdict.

Maybe those men mean me well, maybe they mean me ill; no way to decide that—let it go. They've got a game, or a scheme, or an experiment, of some kind on hand; no way to determine what it is—let it go. There's a bet on me; no way to find out what it is—let it go. That disposes of the indeterminable quantities; the remainder of the matter is tangible, solid, and may be classed and labeled with certainty. If I ask the Bank of England to place this bill to the credit of the man it belongs to, they'll do it, for they know him, although I don't; but they will ask me how I came in possession of it, and if I tell the truth they'll put me in the asylum, naturally, and a lie will land me in jail. The same result would follow if I tried to bank the bill anywhere or to borrow money on it. I have got to carry this immense burden around until those men come back, whether I want to or not. It is useless to me, as useless as a handful of ashes, and yet I must take care of it, and watch over it, while I beg my living. I couldn't *give* it away if I should try, for neither honest citizen nor highwayman would accept it or meddle with it for anything. Those brothers are safe. Even if I lose their bill, or burn it, they are still safe, because they can stop payment, and the bank will make them whole; but meantime I've got to do a month's suffering without wages or profit—unless I help win that bet, whatever it may be, and get that situation that I am promised. I *should* like to get that; men of their sort have situations in their gift that are worth having.

I got to thinking a good deal about that situation. My hopes began to rise high. Without doubt the salary would be large. It would begin in a month; after that I should be all right. Pretty soon I was feeling first rate. By this time I was tramping the streets again. The sight of a tailorshop gave me a sharp longing to shed my rags, and to clothe myself decently once more. Could I afford it? No; I had nothing in the world but a million pounds. So I forced myself to go on by. But soon I was drifting back again. The temptation persecuted me cruelly. I must have passed that shop back and forth six times during that manful struggle. At last I gave in; I had to. I asked if they had a misfit suit that had been thrown on their hands. The fellow I spoke to nodded his head toward another fellow, and gave me no answer. I went to the indicated fellow, and he indicated another fellow with *his* head, and no words. I went to him, and he said:

" 'Tend to you presently."

I waited tell he was done with what he was at, then he took me into a back room, and overhauled a pile of rejected suits, and selected the rattiest one for me. I put it on. It didn't fit, and wasn't in any way attractive, but it was new, and I was anxious to have it; so I didn't find any fault, but said, with some diffidence:

"It would be an accommodation to me if you could wait some days for the money. I haven't any small change about me."

The fellow worked up a most sarcastic expression of countenance, and said:

"Oh, you haven't? Well, of course, I didn't expect it. I'd only expect gentlemen like you to carry large change."

I was nettled, and said:

"My friend, you shouldn't judge a stranger always by the clothes he wears. I am quite able to pay for this suit; I simply didn't wish to put you to the trouble of changing a large note."

He modified his style a little at that, and said, though still with something of an air:

"I didn't mean any particular harm, but as long as rebukes are going, I might say it wasn't quite your affair to jump to the conclusion that we couldn't change any note that you might happen to be carrying around. On the contrary, we *can*."

I handed the note to him, and said:

"Oh, very well; I apologize."

He received it with a smile, one of those large smiles which go all around over, and have folds in them, and wrinkles, and spirals, and look like the place where you have thrown a brick in a pond; and then in the act of his taking a glimpse of the bill this smile froze solid, and turned yellow, and looked like those wavy, wormy spreads of lava which you find hardened on little levels on the side of Vesuvius. I never before saw a smile caught like that, and perpetuated. The man stood there holding the bill, and looking like that, and the proprietor hustled up to see what was the matter, and said, briskly:

"Well, what's up? what's the trouble? what's wanting?"

I said: "There isn't any trouble. I'm waiting for my change."

"Come, come; get him his change, Tod; get him his change."

Tod retorted: "Get him his change! It's easy to say, sir; but look at the bill yourself."

The proprietor took a look, gave a low, eloquent whistle, then made a dive for the pile of rejected clothing, and began to snatch it this way and that, talking all the time excitedly, and as if to himself:

"Sell an eccentric millionaire such an unspeakable suit as that! Tod's a fool—a born fool. Always doing something like this. Drives every millionaire away from this place, because he can't tell a millionaire from a tramp, and never could. Ah, here's the thing I am after. Please get those things off, sir, and throw them in the fire. Do me the favor to put on this shirt and this suit; it's just the thing, the very thing—plain, rich, modest, and just ducally nobby; made to order for a foreign prince—you may know him, sir, his Serene Highness the Hospodar of Halifax; had to leave it with us and take a mourning-suit because his mother was going to die —which she didn't. But that's all right; we can't always have

things the way we—that is, the way they—there! trousers all
right, they fit you to a charm, sir; now the waistcoat; aha,
right again! now the coat—lord! look at that, now! Perfect—
the whole thing! I never saw such a triumph in all my
experience."

I expressed my satisfaction.

"Quite right, sir, quite right; it'll do for a makeshift, I'm
bound to say. But wait till you see what we'll get up for
you on your own measure. Come, Tod, book and pen; get
at it. Length of leg, 32″ "—and so on. Before I could get in a
word he had measured me, and was giving orders for dress-
suits, morning suits, shirts, and all sorts of things. When I got
a chance I said:

"But, my dear sir, I *can't* give these orders, unless you
can wait indefinitely, or change the bill."

"Indefinitely! It's a weak word, sir, a weak word. Eternal-
ly—*that's* the word, sir. Tod, rush these things through, and
send them to the gentleman's address without any waste of
time. Let the minor customers wait. Set down the gentleman's address and—"

"I'm changing my quarters. I will drop in and leave the
new address."

"Quite right, sir, quite right. One moment—let me show
you out, sir. There—good day, sir, good day."

Well, don't you see what was bound to happen? I drifted
naturally into buying whatever I wanted, and asking for
change. Within a week I was sumptuously equipped with all
needful comforts and luxuries, and was housed in an expensive private hotel in Hanover Square. I took my dinners there,
but for breakfast I stuck by Harris's humble feeding-house,
where I had got my first meal on my million-pound bill. I
was the making of Harris. The fact had gone all abroad that
the foreign crank who carried million-pound bills in his vest
pocket was the patron saint of the place. That was enough.
From being a poor, struggling, little hand-to-mouth enter-

prise, it had become celebrated, and overcrowded with customers. Harris was so grateful that he forced loans upon me,
and would not be denied; and so, pauper as I was, I had
money to spend, and was living like the rich and the great.
I judged that there was going to be a crash by and by, but I
was in now and must swim across or drown. You see there
was just that element of impending disaster to give a serious
side, a sober side, yes, a tragic side, to a state of things which
would otherwise have been purely ridiculous. In the night, in
the dark, the tragedy part was always to the front, and always warning, always threatening; and so I moaned and
tossed, and sleep was hard to find. But in the cheerful daylight the tragedy element faded out and disappeared, and I
walked on air, and was happy to giddiness, to intoxication,
you may say.

And it was natural; for I had become one of the notorieties
of the metropolis of the world, and it turned my head, not
just a little, but a good deal. You could not take up a
newspaper, English, Scotch, or Irish, without finding in it one
or more references to the "vest-pocket million-pounder" and
his latest doings and sayings. At first, in these mentions, I
was at the bottom of the personal-gossip column; next, I was
listed above the knights, next above the baronets, next above
the barons, and so on, and so on, climbing steadily, as my
notoriety augmented, until I reached the highest altitude possible, and there I remained, taking precedence of all dukes
not royal, and of all ecclesiastics except the primate of all
England. But mind, this was not fame; as yet I had achieved
only notoriety. Then came the climaxing stroke—the acco-
lade, so to speak—which in a single instant transmuted the
perishable dross of notoriety into the enduring gold of fame:
Punch caricatured me! Yes, I was a made man now; my
place was established. I might be joked about still, but reverently, not hilariously, not rudely; I could be smiled at, but
not laughed at. The time for that had gone by. *Punch* pic-

tured me all a-flutter with rags, dickering with a beef-eater for the Tower of London. Well, you can imagine how it was with a young fellow who had never been taken notice of before, and now all of a sudden couldn't say a thing that wasn't taken up and repeated everywhere; couldn't stir abroad without constantly overhearing the remark flying from lip to lip, "There he goes; that's him!"—couldn't take his breakfast without a crowd to look on; couldn't appear in an opera-box without concentrating there the fire of a thousand lorgnettes. Why, I just swam in glory all day long—that is the amount of it.

You know, I even kept my old suit of rags, and every now and then appeared in them, so as to have the old pleasure of buying trifles, and being insulted, and then shooting the scoffer dead with the million-pound bill. But I couldn't keep that up. The illustrated papers made the outfit so familiar that when I went out in it I was at once recognized and followed by a crowd, and if I attempted a purchase the man would offer me his whole shop on credit before I could pull my note on him.

About the tenth day of my fame I went to fulfill my duty to my flag by paying my respects to the American minister. He received me with the enthusiasm proper in my case, upbraided me for being so tardy in my duty, and said that there was only one way to get his forgiveness, and that was to take the seat at his dinner-party that night made vacant by the illness of one of his guests. I said I would, and we got to talking. It turned out that he and my father had been schoolmates in boyhood, Yale students together later, and always warm friends up to my father's death. So then he required me to put in at his house all the odd time I might have to spare, and I was very willing, of course.

In fact, I was more than willing; I was glad. When the crash should come, he might somehow be able to save me from total destruction; I didn't know how, but he might think

of a way, maybe. I couldn't venture to unbosom myself to
him at this late date, a thing which I would have been quick
to do in the beginning of this awful career of mine in London.
No, I couldn't venture it now; I was in too deep; that is, too
deep for me to be risking revelations to so new a friend,
though not clear beyond my depth, as I looked at it.
Because, you see, with all my borrowing, I was carefully
keeping within my means—I mean within my salary. Of
course, I couldn't *know* what my salary was going to be, but
I had a good enough basis for an estimate in the fact that if
I won the bet I was to have *choice* of any situation in that
rich old gentleman's gift, provided I was competent—and I
should certainly prove competent; I hadn't any doubt
about that. And as to be bet, I wasn't worrying about that; I
had always been lucky. Now my estimate of the salary was
six hundred to a thousand a year; say, six hundred for the
first year, and so on up year by year, till I struck the upper
figure by proved merit. At present I was only in debt for my
first year's salary. Everybody had been trying to lend me
money, but I had fought off the most of them on one pretext
or another; so this indebtedness represented only £300 borrowed money, the other £300 represented my keep and my
purchases. I believed my second year's salary would carry
me through the rest of the month if I went on being cautious
and economical, and I intended to look sharply out for that.
My month ended, my employer back from his journey, I
should be all right once more, for I should at once divide
the two years' salary among my creditors by assignment, and
get right down to my work.

It was a lovely dinner-party of fourteen. The Duke and
Duchess of Shoreditch, and their daughter the Lady Anne-
Grace-Eleanor-Celeste-and-so-forth-and-so-forth-de-Bohun, the
Earl and Countess of Newgate, Viscount Cheapside, Lord
and Lady Blatherskite, some untitled people of both sexes,
the minister and his wife and daughter, and his daughter's

visiting friend, an English girl of twenty-two, named Portia Langham, whom I fell in love with in two minutes, and she with me—I could see it without glasses. There was still another guest, an American—but I am a little ahead of my story. While the people were still in the drawing-room, whetting up for dinner, and coldly inspecting the late comers, the servant announced:

"Mr. Lloyd Hastings."

The moment the usual civilities were over, Hastings caught sight of me, and came straight with cordially outstretched hand; then stopped short when about to shake, and said, with an embarrassed look:

"I beg your pardon, sir, I thought I knew you."

"Why, you do know me, old fellow."

"No. Are *you* the—the—"

"Vest-pocket monster? I am, indeed. Don't be afraid to call me by my nickname; I'm used to it."

"Well, well, well, this is a surprise. Once or twice I've seen your own name coupled with the nickname, but it never occurred to me that *you* could be the Henry Adams referred to. Why, it isn't six months since you were clerking away for Blake Hopkins in Frisco on a salary, and sitting up nights on an extra allowance, helping me arrange and verify the Gould and Curry Extension papers and statistics. The idea of your being in London, and a vast millionaire, and a colossal celebrity! Why, it's the Arabian Nights come again. Man, I can't take it in at all; can't realize it; give me time to settle the whirl in my head."

"The fact is, Lloyd, you are no worse off than I am. I can't realize it myself."

"Dear me, it *is* stunning, now isn't it? Why, it's just three months today since we went to the Miners' restaurant—"

"No; the What Cheer."

"Right, it *was* the What Cheer; went there at two in the morning, and had a chop and coffee after a hard six-hours

grind over those Extension papers, and I tried to persuade you
to come to London with me, and offered to get leave of
absence for you and pay all your expenses, and give you
something over if I succeeded in making the sale; and you
would not listen to me, said I wouldn't succeed, and you
couldn't afford to lose the run of business and be no end of
time getting the hang of things again when you got back
home. And yet here you are. How odd it all is! How did
you happen to come, and whatever *did* give you this incredible start?"

"Oh, just an accident. It's a long story—a romance, a body
may say. I'll tell you all about it, but not now."

"When?"

"The end of this month."

"That's more than a fortnight yet. It's too much of a strain
on a person's curiosity. Make it a week."

"I can't. You'll know why, by and by. But how's the trade
getting along?"

His cheerfulness vanished like a breath, and he said with
a sigh:

"You were a true prophet, Hal, a true prophet. I wish I
hadn't come. I don't want to talk about it."

"But you must. You must come and stop with me to-
night, when we leave here, and tell me all about it."

"Oh, may I? Are you in earnest?" and the water showed
in his eyes.

"Yes; I want to hear the whole story, every word."

"I'm so grateful! Just to find a human interest once more,
in some voice and in some eye, in me and affairs of mine,
after what I've been through here—lord! I could go down on
my knees for it!"

He gripped my hand hard, and braced up, and was all
right and lively after that for the dinner—which didn't come
off. No; the usual thing happened, the thing that is always
happening under the vicious and aggravating English sys-

tem—the matter of precedence couldn't be settled, and so
there was no dinner. Englishmen always eat dinner before
they go out to dinner, because *they* know the risks they are
running; but nobody ever warns the stranger, and so he walks
placidly into the trap. Of course, nobody was hurt this time,
because we had all been to dinner, none of us being novices
excepting Hastings, and he having been informed by the minister at the time that he invited him that in deference to the
English custom he had not provided any dinner. Everybody
took a lady and processioned down to the dining-room because it is usual to go through the motions; but there the dis-
pute began. The Duke of Shoreditch wanted to take precedence, and sit at the head of the table, holding that he out-
ranked a minister who represented merely a nation and not a
monarch; but I stood for my rights, and refused to yield. In
the gossip column I ranked all dukes not royal, and said so,
and claimed precedence of this one. It couldn't be settled, of
course, struggle as we might and did, he finally (and in-
judiciously) trying to play birth and antiquity, and I "seeing"
his Conqueror and "raising" him with Adam, whose direct
posterity I was, as shown by my name, while *he* was of a
collateral branch, as shown by *his*, and by his recent Norman
origin; so we all processioned back to the drawing-room again
and had a perpendicular lunch—plate of sardines and a
strawberry, and you group yourself and stand up and eat it.
Here the religion of precedence is not so strenuous; the two
persons of highest rank chuck up a shilling, the one that
wins has first go at his strawberry, and the loser gets the
shilling. The next two chuck up, then the next two, and so on.
After refreshment, tables were brought, and we all played
cribbage, sixpence a game. The English never play any game
for amusement. If they can't make something or lose something—they don't care which—they won't play.

We had a lovely time; certainly two of us had, Miss Langham and I. I was so bewitched with her that I couldn't

count my hands if they went above a double sequence; and when I struck home I never discovered it, and started up the outside row again, and would have lost the game every time, only the girl did the same, she being in just my condition, you see; and consequently neither of us ever got out, or cared to wonder why we didn't; we only just knew we were happy, and didn't wish to know anything else, and didn't want to be interrupted. And I *told* her—I did, indeed— told her I loved her; and she—well, she blushed till her hair turned red, but she liked it; she *said* she did. Oh, there was never such an evening! Every time I pegged I put on a post- script; every time she pegged she acknowledged receipt of it, counting the hands the same. Why, I couldn't even say "Two for his heels" without adding "*My,* how sweet you do look!" and she would say, "Fifteen two, fifteen four, fifteen six, and a pair are eight, and eight are sixteen—*do* you think so?"—peeping out aslant from under her lashes, you know, so sweet and cunning. Oh, it was just *too*-too!

Well, I was perfectly honest and square with her; told her I hadn't a cent in the world but just the million-pound note she'd heard so much talk about, and *it* didn't belong to me, and that started her curiosity; and then I talked low, and told her the whole history right from the start, and it nearly killed her laughing. What in the nation she could find to laugh about *I* couldn't see, but there it was; every half-min- ute some new detail would fetch her, and I would have to stop as much as a minute and a half to give her a chance to settle down again. Why, she laughed herself lame—she did, indeed; I never saw anything like it. I mean I never saw a painful story—a story of a person's troubles and worries and fears—produce just *that* kind of effect before. So I loved her all the more, seeing she could be so cheerful when there wasn't anything to be cheerful about; for I might soon need that kind of wife, you know, the way things looked. Of course, I told her we should have to wait a couple of years, till I could catch up on my salary; but she didn't mind that, only she hoped I would be as careful as possible in the matter of expenses, and not let them run the least risk of trenching on our third year's pay. Then she began to get a little worried, and wondered if we were making any mistake, and starting the salary on a higher figure for the first year than I would get. This was good sense, and it made me feel a little less confident than I had been feeling before; but it gave me a good business idea, and I brought it frankly out.

"Portia, dear, would you mind going with me that day, when I confront those old gentlemen?"

She shrank a little, but said:

"N-o; if my being with you would help hearten you. But —would it be quite proper, do you think?"

"No, I don't know that it would—in fact, I'm afraid it wouldn't; but, you see, there's so *much* dependent upon it that—"

"Then I'll go anyway, proper or improper," she said, with a beautiful and generous enthusiasm. "Oh, I shall be so happy to think I'm helping!"

"Helping, dear? Why, you'll be doing it all. You're so beautiful and so lovely and so winning, that with you there I can pile our salary up till I break those good old fellows, and they'll never have the heart to struggle."

Sho! you should have seen the rich blood mount, and her happy eyes shine!

"You wicked flatterer! There isn't a word of truth in what you say, but still I'll go with you. Maybe it will teach you not to expect other people to look with your eyes."

Were my doubts dissipated? Was my confidence restored? You may judge by this fact: privately I raised my salary to twelve hundred the first year on the spot. But I didn't tell her: I saved it for a surprise.

All the way home I was in the clouds, Hastings talking, I not hearing a word. When he and I entered my parlor, he brought me to myself with his fervent appreciations of my manifold comforts and luxuries.

"Let me just stand here a little and look my fill. Dear me! it's a palace—it's just a palace! And in it everything a body *could* desire, including cozy coal fire and supper standing ready. Henry, it doesn't merely make me realize how rich you are; it makes me realize, to the bone, to the marrow, how poor I am—how poor I am, and how miserable, how defeated, routed, annihilated!"

Plague take it! this language gave me the cold shudders. It scared me broad awake, and made me comprehend that I was standing on a half-inch crust, with a crater underneath. *I* didn't know I had been dreaming—that is, I hadn't been allowing myself to know it for a while back; but *now*—oh, dear! Deep in debt, not a cent in the world, a lovely girl's happiness or woe in my hands, and nothing in front of me but a salary which might never—oh, *would* never—materialize! Oh, oh, oh! I am ruined past hope! nothing can save me!

"Henry, the mere unconsidered drippings of your daily income would—"

"Oh, my daily income! Here, down with this hot Scotch, and cheer up your soul. Here's with you! Or, no—you're hungry; sit down and—"

"Not a bite for me; I'm past it. I can't eat, these days; but I'll drink with you till I drop. Come!"

"Barrel for barrel, I'm with you! Ready? Here we go! Now, then, Lloyd, unreel your story while I brew."

"Unreel it? What, again?"

"Again? What do you mean by that?"

"Why, I mean do you want to hear it *over* again?"

"Do I want to hear it *over* again? This *is* a puzzler. Wait; don't take any more of that liquid. You don't need it."

"Look here, Henry, you alarm me. Didn't I tell you the whole story on the way here?"

"You?"

"Yes, I."

"I'll be hanged if I heard a word of it."

"Henry, this is a serious thing. It troubles me. What did you take up yonder at the minister's?"

Then it all flashed on me, and I owned up like a man.

"I took the dearest girl in this world—prisoner!"

So then he came with a rush, and we shook, and shook, and shook till our hands ached; and he didn't blame me for not having heard a word of a story which had lasted while we walked three miles. He just sat down then, like the patient, good fellow he was, and told it all over again. Synopsized, it amounted to this: He had come to England with what he thought was a grand opportunity; he had an "option" to sell the Gould and Curry Extension for the "locators" of it, and keep all he could get over a million dollars. He had worked hard, had pulled every wire he knew of, had left no honest expedient untried, had spent nearly all the money he had in the world, had not been able to get a solitary capitalist to listen to him, and his option would run out at the end of the month. In a word, he was ruined. Then he jumped up and cried out:

"Henry, you can save me! You can save me, and you're the only man in the universe that can. Will you do it? *Won't* you do it?"

"Tell me how. Speak out, my boy."

"Give me a million and my passage home for my 'option'! Don't, *don't* refuse!"

I was in a kind of agony. I was right on the point of coming out with the words, "Lloyd, I'm a pauper myself—absolutely penniless, and in *debt*." But a white-hot idea came flaming through my head, and I gripped my jaws together, and calmed myself down till I was as cold as a capitalist. Then I said, in a commercial and self-possessed way:

"I will save you, Lloyd—"

"Then I'm already saved! God be merciful to you forever! If ever I—"

"Let me finish, Lloyd. I will save you, but not in that way; for that would not be fair to you, after your hard work, and the risks you've run. I don't need to buy mines; I can keep my capital moving, in a commercial center like London, without that; it's what I'm at, all the time; but here is what I'll do. I know all about that mine, of course; I know it's immense value, and can swear to it if anybody wishes it. You shall sell out inside of the fortnight for three millions cash, using my name freely, and we'll divide, share and share alike."

Do you know, he would have danced the furniture to kindling-wood in his insane joy, and broken everything in the place, if I hadn't tripped him up and tied him.

Then he lay there, perfectly happy, saying:

"I may use your name! Your name—think of it! Man, they'll flock in droves, these rich Londoners; they'll *fight* for that stock! I'm a made man, I'm a made man forever, and I'll never forget you as long as I live!"

In less than twenty-four hours London was abuzz! I hadn't anything to do, day after day, but sit at home, and say to all comers:

"Yes; I told him to refer to me. I know the man, and I know the mine. His character is above reproach, and the mine is worth far more than he asks for it."

Meantime I spent all my evenings at the minister's with Portia. I didn't say a word to her about the mine; I saved it for a surprise. We talked salary; never anything but salary and love; sometimes love, sometimes salary, sometimes love and salary together. And my! the interest the minister's wife and daughter took in our little affair, and the endless ingenuities they invented to save us from interruption, and to keep the minister in the dark and unsuspicious—well, it was just lovely of them!

When the month was up at last, I had a million dollars to my credit in the London and County Bank, and Hastings was fixed in the same way. Dressed at my level best, I drove by the house in Portland Place, judged by the looks of things that my birds were home again, went on toward the minister's and got my precious, and we started back, talking salary with all our might. She was so excited and anxious that it made her just intolerably beautiful. I said:

"Dearie, the way you're looking it's a crime to strike for a salary a single penny under three thousand a year."

"Henry, henry, you'll ruin us!"

"Don't you be afraid. Just keep up those looks and trust to me. It'll all come out right."

So, as it turned out, I had to keep bolstering up *her* courage all the way. She kept pleading with me, and saying:

"Oh, please remember that if we ask for too much we may get no salary at all; and then what will become of us, with no way in the world to earn our living?"

We were ushered in by that same servant, and there they were, the two old gentlemen. Of course, they were surprised to see that wonderful creature with me, but I said:

"It's all right, gentlemen; she is my future stay and helpmate."

And I introduced them to her, and called them by name. It didn't surprise them; they knew I would know enough to consult the directory. They seated us, and were very polite to me, and very solicitous to relieve her from embarrassment, and put her as much at her ease as they could. Then I said:

"Gentlemen, I am ready to report."

"We are glad to hear it," said *my* man, "For now we can decide the bet which my brother Abel and I made. If you have won for me, you shall have any situation in my gift. Have you the million-pound note?"

"Here it is, sir," and I handed it to him.

"I've won!" he shouted, and slapped Abel on the back. "*Now* what do you say, brother?"

"I say he *did* survive, and I've lost twenty thousand pounds. I never would have believed it."

"I've a further report to make," I said, "and a pretty long one. I want you to let me come soon, and detail my whole month's history; and I promise you it's worth hearing. Meantime, take a look at that."

"What, man! Certificate of deposit for £200,000. Is it yours?"

"Mine. I earned it by thirty days' judicious use of that little loan you let me have. And the only use I made of it was to buy trifles and offer the bill in change."

"Come, this is astonishing! It's incredible, man!"

"Never mind, I'll prove it. Don't take my word unsupported."

But now Portia's turn was come to be surprised. Her eyes were spread wide, and she said:

"Henry, is that really your money? Have you been fibbing to me?"

"I have, indeed, dearie. But you'll forgive me, *I* know."

She put up an arch pout, and said:

"Don't you be so sure. You are a naughty thing to deceive me so!"

"Oh, you'll get over it, sweetheart, you'll get over it; it was only fun, you know. Come, let's be going."

"But wait, wait! The situation, you know. I want to give you the situation," said my man.

"Well," I said, "I'm just as grateful as I can be, but really I don't want one."

"But you can have the very choicest one in my gift."

"Thanks again, with all my heart; but I don't even want *that* one."

"Henry, I'm ashamed of you. You don't half thank the good gentleman. May I do it for you?"

"Indeed, you shall, dear, if you can improve it. Let us see you try."

She walked to my man, got up in his lap, put her arm round his neck, and kissed him right on the mouth. Then the two old gentlemen shouted with laughter, but I was dumbfounded, just petrified, as you may say. Portia said:

"Papa, he has said you haven't a situation in your gift that he'd take; and I feel just as hurt as—"

"My darling, is that your papa?"

"Yes; he's my step-papa, and the dearest one that ever was. You understand now, don't you, why I was able to laugh when you told me at the minister's, not knowing my relationships, what trouble and worry papa's and Uncle Abel's scheme was giving you?"

Of course, I spoke right up now, without any fooling, and went straight to the point.

"Oh, my dearest dear sir, I want to take back what I said. You *have* got a situation open that I want."

"Name it."

"Son-in-law."

"Well, well, well! But you know, if you haven't ever served in that capacity, you, of course, can't furnish recommendations of a sort to satisfy the conditions of the contract, and so—"

"Try me—oh, do, I beg of you! Only just try me thirty or forty years, and if—"

"Oh, well, all right; it's but a little thing to ask, take her along."

Happy, we two? There are not words enough in the unabridged to describe it. And when London got the whole history, a day or two later, of my month's adventures with that bank-note, and how they ended, did London talk, and have a good time? Yes.

My Portia's papa took that friendly and hospitable bill back to the Bank of England and cashed it; then the Bank canceled it and made him a present of it, and he gave it to us at our wedding, and it has always hung in its frame in the sacredest place in our home ever since. For it gave me my Portia. But for it I could not have remained in London, would not have appeared at the minister's, never should have met her. And so I always say, "Yes, it's a million-pounder, as you see; but it never made but one purchase in its life, and *then* got the article for only about a tenth part of its value."

Extract from Captain Stormfield's Visit to Heaven

1

Well, when I had been dead about thirty years, I begun to get a little anxious. Mind you, I had been whizzing through space all that time, like a comet. *Like* a comet! Why, Peters, I laid over the lot of them! Of course there warn't any of them going my way, as a steady thing, you know, because they travel in a long circle like the loop of a lasso, whereas I was pointed as straight as a dart for the Hereafter; but I happened on one every now and then that was going my way for an hour or so, and then we had a bit of a brush together. But it was generally pretty one-sided, because I sailed by them the same as if they were standing still. An ordinary comet don't make more than about 200,000 miles a minute. Of course when I came across one of that sort—like

Encke's and Haley's comets, for instance—it warn't anything
but just a flash and a vanish, you see. You couldn't rightly
call it a race. It was as if the comet was a gravel-train and I
was a telegraph despatch. But after I got outside of our astronomical system, I used to flush a comet occasionally that was
something *like*. *We* haven't got any such comets—ours don't
begin. One night I was swinging along at a good round gait,
everything taut and trim, and the wind in my favor—I judged
I was going about a million miles a minute—it might have
been more, it couldn't have been less—when I flushed a most
uncommonly big one about three points off my starboard bow.
By his stern lights I judged he was bearing about northeast-
and-by-north-half-east. Well, it was so near my course that I
wouldn't throw away the chance; so I fell off a point, steadied
my helm, and went for him. You should have heard me whiz,
and seen the electric fur fly! In about a minute and a half I
was fringed out with an electrical nimbus that flamed around
for miles and miles and lit up all space like broad day. The
comet was burning blue in the distance, like a sickly torch,
when I first sighted him, but he begun to grow bigger and
bigger as I crept up on him. I slipped up on him so fast that
when I had gone about a hundred and fifty million miles I
was close enough to be swallowed up in the phosphorescent
glory of his wake, and I couldn't see anything for the glare.
Thinks I, it won't do to run into him, so I shunted to one
side and tore along. By and by I closed up abreast of his
tail. Do you know what it was like? It was like a gnat
closing up on the continent of America. I forged along. By
and by I had sailed along his coast for a little upwards of a
hundred and fifty million miles, and then I could see by the
shape of him that I hadn't even got up to his waistband yet.
Why, Peters, *we* don't know anything about comets, down
here. If you want to see comets that *are* comets, you've got to
go outside of our solar system—where there's room for them,
you understand. My friend, I've seen comets out there that

couldn't even lay down inside the *orbits* of our noblest comets without their tails hanging over.

Well, I boomed along another hundred and fifty million miles, and got up abreast his shoulder, as you may say. I was feeling pretty fine, I tell you; but just then I noticed the officer of the deck come to the side and hoist his glass in my direction. Straight off I heard him sing out—

"Below there, ahoy! Shake her up, shake her up! Heave on a hundred million billion tons of brimstone!"

"Ay—ay, sir!"

"Pipe the starboard watch! All hands on deck!"

"Ay—ay, sir!"

"Send two hundred thousand million men aloft to shake out royals and sky-scrapers!"

"Ay—ay, sir!"

"Hand the stuns'ls! Hang out every rag you've got! Clothe her from stem to rudder-post!"

"Ay—ay, sir!"

In about a second I begun to see I'd woke up a pretty ugly customer, Peters. In less than ten seconds that comet was just a blazing cloud of red-hot canvas. It was piled up into the heavens clean out of sight—the old thing seemed to swell out and occupy all space; the sulphur smoke from the furnaces—oh, well, nobody can describe the way it rolled and tumbled up into the skies, and nobody can half describe the way it smelt. Neither can anybody begin to describe the way that monstrous craft begun to crash along. And such another powwow—thousands of bo's'n's whistles screaming at once, and a crew like the populations of a hundred thousand worlds like ours all swearing at once. Well, I never heard the like of it before.

We roared and thundered along side by side, both doing our level best, because I'd never struck a comet before that could lay over me, and so I was bound to beat this one or break something. I judged I had some reputation in space,

and I calculated to keep it. I noticed I wasn't gaining as fast,
now, as I was before, but still I was gaining. There was a
power of excitement on board the comet. Upwards of a hundred billion passengers swarmed up from below and rushed
to the side and begun to bet on the race. Of course this ca-
reened her and damaged her speed. My, but wasn't the mate
mad! He jumped at that crowd, with his trumpet in his hand,
and sung out—

"Amidships! amidships, you—! * or I'll brain the last idiot
of you!"

Well, sir, I gained and gained, little by little, till at last I
went skimming sweetly by the magnificent old conflagration's
nose. By this time the captain of the comet had been rousted
out, and he stood there in the red glare for'ard, by the mate,
in his shirtsleeves and slippers, his hair all rats' nests and
one suspender hanging, and how sick those two men did
look! I just simply couldn't help putting my thumb to my
nose as I glided away and singing out:

"Ta-ta! ta-ta! Any word to send to your family?"

Peters, it was a mistake. Yes, sir, I've often regretted that
—it was a mistake. You see, the captain had given up the
race, but that remark was too tedious for him—he couldn't
stand it. He turned to the mate, and says he—

"Have we got brimstone enough of our own to make the
trip?"

"Yes, sir."

"Sure?"

"Yes, sir—more than enough."

"How much have we got in cargo for Satan?"

"Eighteen hundred thousand billion quintillions of ka-
zarks."

"Very well, then, let his boarders freeze till the next comet

---

* The Captain could not remember what this word was. He said
it was in a foreign tongue.

comes. Lighten ship! Lively, now, lively, men! Heave the whole cargo overboard!"

Peters, look me in the eye, and be calm. I found out, over there, that a kazark is exactly the bulk of a *hundred and sixty-nine worlds like ours!* They hove all that load overboard. When it fell it wiped out a considerable raft of stars just as clean as if they'd been candles and somebody blowed them out. As for the race, that was at an end. The minute she was lightened the comet swung along by me the same as if I was anchored. The captain stood on the stern, by the after-davits, and put his thumb to his nose and sung out—

"Ta-ta! ta-ta! Maybe *you've* got some message to send your friends in the Everlasting Tropics!"

Then he hove up his other suspender and started for'ard, and inside of three-quarters of an hour his craft was only a pale torch again in the distance. Yes, it was a mistake, Peters —that remark of mine. I don't reckon I'll ever get over being sorry about it. I'd 'a' beat the bully of the firmament if I'd kept my mouth shut.

But I've wandered a little off the track of my tale; I'll get back on my course again. Now you see what kind of speed I was making. So, as I said, when I had been tearing along this way about thirty years I begun to get uneasy. Oh, it was pleasant enough, with a good deal to find out, but then it was kind of lonesome, you know. Besides, I wanted to get somewhere. I hadn't shipped with the idea of cruising forever. First off, I liked the delay, because I judged I was going to fetch up in pretty warm quarters when I got through; but towards the last I begun to feel that I'd rather go to— well, most any place, so as to finish up the uncertainty.

Well, one night—it was always night, except when I was rushing by some star that was occupying the whole universe with its fire and its glare—light enough then, of course, but I necessarily left it behind in a minute or two and plunged

into a solid week of darkness again. The stars ain't so close
together as they look to be. Where was I? Oh yes, one night
I was sailing along, when I discovered a tremendous long
row of blinking lights away on the horizon ahead. As I approached, they begun to tower and swell and look like mighty
furnaces. Says I to myself—

"By George, I've arrived at last—and at the wrong place,
just as I expected!"

Then I fainted. I don't know how long I was insensible, but
it must have been a good while, for, when I came to, the
darkness was all gone and there was the loveliest sunshine
and the balmiest, fragrantest air in its place. And there was
such a marvelous world spread out before me—such a glow-
ing, beautiful, bewitching country. The things I took for
furnaces were gates, miles high, made all of flashing jewels,
and they pierced a wall of solid gold that you couldn't see
the top of, nor yet the end of, in either direction. I was
pointed straight for one of these gates, and a-coming like a
house afire. Now I noticed that the skies were black with
millions of people, pointed for those gates. What a roar they
made, rushing through the air! The ground was as thick as
ants with people, too—billions of them, I judge.

I lit. I drifted up to a gate with a swarm of people, and
when it was my turn the head clerk says, in a businesslike
way—

"Well, quick! Where are you from?"

"San Francisco," says I.

"San Fran—*what?*" says he.

"San Francisco."

He scratched his head and looked puzzled, then he says—
"Is it a planet?"

By George, Peters, think of it! "*Planet?*" says I; "it's a
city. And moreover, it's one of the biggest and finest and—"

"There, there!" says he, "no time here for conversation.

We don't deal in cities here. Where are you from in a *general* way?"

"Oh," I says, "I beg your pardon. Put me down for California."

I had him *again*, Peters! He puzzled a second, then he says, sharp and irritable—

"I don't know any such planet—is it a constellation?"

"Oh, my goodness!" says I. "Constellation, says you? No—it's a State."

"Man, we don't deal in States here. *Will* you tell me where you are from *in general—at large*, don't you understand?"

"Oh, now I get your idea," I says. "I'm from America,—the United States of America."

Peters, do you know I had him *again*? If I hadn't, I'm a clam! His face was as blank as a target after a militia shooting-match. He turned to an under clerk and says—

"Where is America? *What* is America?"

The under clerk answered up prompt and says—

"There ain't any such orb."

"*Orb?*" says I. "Why, what are you talking about, young man? It ain't an orb; it's a country; it's a continent. Columbus discovered it; I reckon likely you've heard of *him*, anyway. America—why, sir, America—"

"Silence!" says the head clerk. "Once for all, where—are—you—*from?*"

"Well," says I, "I don't know anything more to say—unless I lump things, and just say I'm from the world."

"Ah," says he, brightening up, "now that's something like! *What* world?"

Peters, he had *me*, that time. I looked at him, puzzled, he looked at me, worried. Then he burst out—

"Come, come, what world?"

Says I, "Why, *the* world, of course."

"*The* world!" he says. "H'm! there's billions of them! . . . Next!"

That meant for me to stand aside. I done so, and a sky-blue man with seven heads and only one leg hopped into my place. I took a walk. It just occurred to me, then, that all the myriads I had seen swarming to that gate, up to this time, were just like that creature. I tried to run across somebody I was acquainted with, but they were out of acquaintances of mine just then. So I thought the thing all over and finally sidled back there pretty meek and feeling rather stumped, as you may say.

"Well?" said the head clerk.

"Well, sir," I says, pretty humble, "I don't seem to make out which world it is I'm from. But you may know it from this—it's the one the Saviour saved."

He bent his head at the Name. Then he says, gently—

"The worlds He has saved are like to the gates of heaven in number—none can count them. What astronomical system is your world in?—perhaps that may assist."

"It's the one that has the sun in it—and the moon—and Mars"—he shook his head at each name—hadn't ever heard of them, you see—"and Neptune—and Uranus—and Jupiter—"

"Hold on!" says he—"hold on a minute! Jupiter . . . Jupiter . . . Seems to me we had a man from there eight or nine hundred years ago—but people from that system very seldom enter by this gate." All of a sudden he begun to look me so straight in the eye that I thought he was going to bore through me. Then he says, very deliberate, "Did you come *straight here* from your system?"

"Yes, sir," I says—but I blushed the least little bit in the world when I said it.

He looked at me very stern, and says—

"That is not true; and this is not the place for prevarication. You wandered from your course. How did that happen?"

Says I, blushing again—

"I'm sorry, and I take back what I said, and confess. I raced a little with a comet one day—only just the least little bit—only the tiniest lit—"

"So—so," says he—and without any sugar in his voice to speak of.

I went on, and says—

"But I only fell off just a bare point, and I went right back on my course again the minute the race was over."

"No matter—that divergence has made all this trouble. It has brought you to a gate that is billions of leagues from the right one. If you had gone to your own gate they would have known all about your world at once and there would have been no delay. But we will try to accommodate you." He turned to an under clerk and says—

"What system is Jupiter in?"

"I don't remember, sir, but I think there is such a planet in one of the little new systems away out in one of the thinly worlded corners of the universe. I will see."

He got a balloon and sailed up and up and up, in front of a map that was as big as Rhode Island. He went on up till he was out of sight, and by and by he came down and got something to eat and went up again. To cut a long story short, he kept on doing this for a day or two, and finally he came down and said he thought he had found that solar system, but it might be fly-specks. So he got a microscope and went back. It turned out better than he feared. He had rousted out our system, sure enough. He got me to describe our planet and its distance from the sun, and then he says to his chief—

"Oh, I know the one he means, now, sir. It is on the map. It is called the Wart."

"Says I to myself, 'Young man, it wouldn't be wholesome for you to go down *there* and call it the Wart.'"

Well, they let me in, then, and told me I was safe forever and wouldn't have any more trouble.

Then they turned from me and went on with their work, the same as if they considered my case all complete and ship-shape. I was a good deal surprised at this, but I was diffident about speaking up and reminding them. I did so hate to do it, you know; it seemed a pity to bother them, they had so much on their hands. Twice I thought I would give up and let the thing go; so twice I started to leave, but immediately I thought what a figure I should cut stepping out amongst the redeemed in such a rig, and that made me hang back and come to anchor again. People got to eying me—clerks, you know—wondering why I didn't get under way. I couldn't stand this long—it was too uncomfortable. So at last I plucked up courage and tipped the head clerk a signal. He says—

"What! you here yet? What's wanting?"

Says I, in a low voice and very confidential, making a trumpet with my hands at his ear—

"I beg pardon, and you mustn't mind my reminding you, and seeming to meddle, but hain't you forgot something?"

He studied a second, and says—

"Forgot something? . . . No, not that I know of."

"Think," says I.

He thought. Then he says—

"No, I can't seem to have forgot anything. What is it?"

"Look at me," says I, "look me all over."

He done it.

"Well?" says he.

"Well," says I, "you don't notice anything? If I branched out amongst the elect looking like this, wouldn't I attract con-siderable attention?—wouldn't I be a little conspicuous?"

"Well," he says, "I don't see anything the matter. What do you lack?"

"Lack! Why, I lack my harp, and my wreath, and my halo, and my hymn-book, and my palm branch—I lack everything that a body naturally requires up here, my friend."

Puzzled? Peters, he was the worst puzzled man you ever saw. Finally he says—

"Well, you seem to be a curiosity every way a body takes you. I never heard of these things before."

I looked at the man awhile in solid astonishment; then I says—

"Now, I hope you don't take it as an offence, for I don't mean any, but really, for a man that has been in the Kingdom as long as I reckon you have, you do seem to know powerful little about its customs."

"Its customs!" says he. "Heaven is a large place, good friend. Large empires have many and diverse customs. Even small dominions have, as you doubtless know by what you have seen of the matter on a small scale in the Wart. How can you imagine I could ever learn the varied customs of the countless kingdoms of heaven? It makes my head ache to think of it. I know the customs that prevail in those portions inhabited by peoples that are appointed to enter by my own gate—and hark ye, that is quite enough knowledge for one individual to try to pack into his head in the thirty-seven millions of years I have devoted night and day to that study. But the idea of learning the customs of the whole appalling expanse of heaven—O man, how insanely you talk! Now I don't doubt that this odd costume you talk about is the fashion in that district of heaven you belong to, but you won't be conspicuous in this section without it."

I felt all right, if that was the case, so I bade him good-day and left. All day I walked towards the far end of a prodigious hall of the office, hoping to come out into heaven any moment, but it was a mistake. That hall was built on the general heavenly plan—it naturally couldn't be small. At last I got so tired I couldn't go any farther; so I sat down to rest, and began to tackle the queerest sort of strangers and ask for information, but I didn't get any; they couldn't understand my language, and I could not understand theirs. I

got dreadfully lonesome. I was so downhearted and home-
sick I wished a hundred times I never had died. I turned
back, of course. About noon next day, I got back at last and
was on hand at the booking-office once more. Says I to the
head clerk—

"I begin to see that a man's got to be in his own heaven to
be happy."

"Perfectly correct," says he. "Did you imagine the same
heaven would suit all sorts of men?"

"Well, I had that idea—but I see the foolishness of it.
Which way am I to go to get to my district?"

He called the under clerk that had examined the map, and
he gave me general directions. I thanked him and started;
but he says—

"Wait a minute; it is millions of leagues from here. Go
outside and stand on that red wishing-carpet; shut your eyes,
hold your breath, and wish yourself there."

"I'm much obliged," says I; "why didn't you dart me
through when I first arrived?"

"We have a good deal to think of here; it was your place to
think of it and ask for it. Good-by; we probably sha'n't see
you in this region for a thousand centuries or so."

"In that case, o revoor," says I.

I hopped onto the carpet and held my breath and shut my
eyes and wished I was in the booking-office of my own section. The very next instant a voice I knew sung out in a business kind of a way—

"A harp and a hymn-book, pair of wings and a halo, size
13, for Cap'n Eli Stormfield, of San Francisco!—make him out
a clean bill of health, and let him in."

I opened my eyes. Sure enough, it was a Pi Ute Injun I
used to know in Tulare County; mighty good fellow—I remembered being at his funeral, which consisted of him being
burnt and the other Injuns gauming their faces with his ashes
and howling like wild-cats. He was powerful glad to see

me, and you may make up your mind I was just as glad to see him, and felt that I was in the right kind of a heaven at last.

Just as far as your eye could reach, there was swarms of clerks, running and bustling around, tricking out thousands of Yanks and Mexicans and English and Arabs, and all sorts of people in their new outfits; and when they gave me my kit and I put on my halo and I took a look in the glass, I could have jumped over a house for joy, I was so happy. "Now *this* is something like!" says I. "Now," says I, "I'm all right— show me a cloud."

Inside of fifteen minutes I was a mile on my way towards the cloud-banks and about a million people along with me. Most of us tried to fly, but some got crippled and nobody made a success of it. So we concluded to walk, for the present, till we had had some wing practice.

We begun to meet swarms of folks who were coming back. Some had harps and nothing else; some had hymn-books and nothing else; some had nothing at all; all of them looked meek and uncomfortable; one young fellow hadn't anything left but his halo, and he was carrying that in his hand; all of a sudden he offered it to me and says—

"Will you hold it for me a minute?"

Then he disappeared in the crowd. I went on. A woman asked me to hold her palm branch, and then *she* disappeared. A girl got me to hold her harp for her, and by George, *she* disappeared; and so on and so on, till I was about loaded down to the guards. Then comes a smiling old gentleman and asked me to hold *his* things. I swabbed off the perspiration and says, pretty tart—

"I'll have to get you to excuse me, my friend,—*I* ain't no hat-rack."

About this time I begun to run across piles of those traps, lying in the road. I just quietly dumped my extra cargo along with them. I looked around, and, Peters, that whole nation that was following me were loaded down the same as I'd been. The return crowd had got them to hold their things a minute, you see. They all dumped their loads, too, and we went on.

When I found myself perched on a cloud, with a million other people, I never felt so good in my life. Says I, "Now this is according to the promises; I've been having my doubts, but now I *am* in heaven, sure enough." I gave my palm branch a wave or two, for luck, and then I tautened up my harpstrings and struck in. Well, Peters, you can't imagine anything like the row we made. It was grand to listen to, and made a body thrill all over, but there was considerable many tunes going on at once, and that was a drawback to the harmony, you understand; and then there was a lot of Injun tribes, and they kept up such another war-whooping that they kind of took the tuck out of the music. By and by I quit performing, and judged I'd take a rest. There was quite a nice mild old gentleman sitting next me, and I noticed he didn't take a hand; I encouraged him, but he said he was naturally bashful, and was afraid to try before so many people. By and by the old gentleman said he never could seem to enjoy music somehow. The fact was, I was beginning to feel the same way; but I didn't say anything. Him and I had a considerable long silence, then, but of course it warn't noticeable in that place. After about sixteen or seventeen hours, during which I played and sung a little, now and then—always the same tune, because I didn't know any other —I laid down my harp and begun to fan myself with my palm branch. Then we both got to sighing pretty regular. Finally, says he—

"Don't you know any tune but the one you've been pegging at all day?"

"Not another blessed one," says I.

"Don't you reckon you could learn another one?" says he.

"Never," says I; "I've tried to, but I couldn't manage it."

"It's a long time to hang to the one—eternity, you know."

"Don't break my heart," says I; "I'm getting low-spirited enough already."

After another long silence, says he—

"Are you glad to be here?"

Says I, "Old man, I'll be frank with you. This *ain't* just as near my idea of bliss as I thought it was going to be, when I used to go to church."

Says he, "What do you say to knocking off and calling it half a day?"

"That's me," says I. "I never wanted to get off watch so bad in my life."

So we started. Millions were coming to the cloud-bank all the time, happy and hosannahing; millions were leaving it all the time, looking mighty quiet, I tell you. We laid for the new-comers, and pretty soon I'd got them to hold all my things a minute, and then I was a free man again and most outrageously happy. Just then I ran across old Sam Bartlett, who had been dead a long time, and stopped to have a talk with him. Says I—

"Now tell me—is this to go on forever? Ain't there anything else for a change?"

Says he—

"I'll set you right on that point very quick. People take the figurative language of the Bible and the allegories for literal, and the first thing they ask for when they get here is a halo and a harp, and so on. Nothing that's harmless and reasonable is refused a body here, if he asks it in the right spirit. So they are outfitted with these things without a word. They go and sing and play just about one day, and that's the last you'll ever see them in the choir. They don't need anybody to tell them that that sort of thing wouldn't make a heaven—at least not a heaven that a sane man could stand a week and remain sane. That cloud-bank is placed where the noise can't disturb the old inhabitants, and so there ain't any harm in letting everybody get up there and cure himself as soon as he comes.

"Now you just remember this—heaven is as blissful and lovely as it can be; but it's just the busiest place you ever heard of. There ain't any idle people here after the first day. Singing hymns and waving palm branches through all eternity is pretty when you hear about it in the pulpit, but it's as poor a way to put in valuable time as a body could contrive. It would just make a heaven of warbling ignoramuses, don't you see? Eternal Rest sounds comforting in the pulpit, too. Well, you try it once, and see how heavy time will hang on your hands. Why, Stormfield, a man like you, that had been active and stirring all his life, would go mad in six months in a heaven where he hadn't anything to do. Heaven is the very last place to come to *rest* in,—and don't you be afraid to bet on that!"

Says I—

"Sam, I'm as glad to hear it as I thought I'd be sorry. I'm glad I come, now."

Says he—

"Cap'n, ain't you pretty physically tired?"

Says I—

"Sam, it ain't any name for it! I'm dog-tired."

"Just so—just so. You've earned a good sleep, and you'll get it. You've earned a good appetite, and you'll enjoy your dinner. It's the same here as it is on earth—you've got to earn a thing, square and honest, before you enjoy it. You can't enjoy first and earn afterwards. But there's this difference, here: you can choose your own occupation, and all the powers of heaven will be put forth to help you make a success of it, if you do your level best. The shoemaker on earth that had the soul of a poet in him won't have to make shoes here."

"Now that's all reasonable and right," says I. "Plenty of

work, and the kind you hanker after; no more pain, no more suffering—"

"Oh, hold on; there's plenty of pain here—but it don't kill. There's plenty of suffering here, but it don't last. You see, happiness ain't a *thing in itself*—it's only a *contrast* with something that ain't pleasant. That's all it is. There ain't a thing you can mention that is happiness in its own self— it's only so by contrast with the other thing. And so, as soon as the novelty is over and the force of the contrast dulled, it ain't happiness any longer, and you have to get something fresh. Well, there's plenty of pain and suffering in heaven— consequently there's plenty of contrasts, and just no end of happiness."

Says I, "It's the sensiblest heaven I've heard of, yet, Sam, though it's about as different from the one I was brought up on as a live princess is different from her own wax figure."

Along in the first months I knocked around about the Kingdom, making friends and looking at the country, and finally settled down in a pretty likely region, to have a rest before taking another start. I went on making acquaintances and gathering up information. I had a good deal of talk with an old bald-headed angel by the name of Sandy McWilliams. He was from somewhere in New Jersey. I went about with him, considerable. We used to lay around, warm afternoons, in the shade of a rock, on some meadow-ground that was pretty high and out of the marshy slush of his cranberry- farm, and there we used to talk about all kinds of things, and smoke pipes. One day, says I—

"About how old might you be, Sandy?"

"Seventy-two."

"I judged so. How long you been in heaven?"

"Twenty-seven years, come Christmas."

"How old was you when you come up?"

"Why, seventy-two, of course."

"You can't mean it!"

"Why can't I mean it?"

"Because, if you was seventy-two then, you are naturally ninety-nine now."

"No, but I ain't. I stay the same age I was when I come."

"Well," says I, "come to think, there's something just here that I want to ask about. Down below, I always had an idea that in heaven we would all be young, and bright, and spry."

"Well, you *can* be young if you want to. You've only got to wish."

"Well, then, why didn't you wish?"

"I did. They all do. You'll try it, some day, like enough; but you'll get tired of the change pretty soon."

"Why?"

"Well, I'll tell you. Now you've always been a sailor; did you ever try some other business?"

"Yes, I tried keeping grocery, once, up in the mines; but I couldn't stand it; it was too dull—no stir, no storm, no life about it; it was like being part dead and part alive, both at the same time. I wanted to be one thing or t'other. I shut up shop pretty quick and went to sea."

"That's it. Grocery people like it, but you couldn't. You see you wasn't used to it. Well, I wasn't used to being young, and I couldn't seem to take any interest in it. I was strong, and handsome, and had curly hair,—yes, and wings, too!—gay wings like a butterfly. I went to picnics and dances and parties with the fellows, and tried to carry on and talk nonsense with the girls, but it wasn't any use; I couldn't take to it—fact is, it was an awful bore. What I wanted was early to bed and early to rise, and something to *do;* and when my work was done, I wanted to sit quiet, and smoke and think —not tear around with a parcel of giddy young kids. You can't think what I suffered whilst I was young."

"How long was you young?"

"Only two weeks. That was plenty for me. Laws, I was so

lonesome! You see, I was full of the knowledge and experience of seventy-two years; the deepest subject those young folks could strike was only *a-b-c* to me. And to hear them argue—oh, my! it would have been funny, if it hadn't been so pitiful. Well, I was so hungry for the ways and the sober talk I was used to, that I tried to ring in with the old people, but they wouldn't have it. They considered me a conceited young up-start, and gave me the cold shoulder. Two weeks was a-plenty for me. I was glad to get back my bald head again, and my pipe, and my old drowsy reflections in the shade of a rock or a tree."

"Well," says I, "do you mean to say you're going to stand still at seventy-two, forever?"

"I don't know, and I ain't particular. But I ain't going to drop back to twenty-five any more—I know that, mighty well. I know a sight more than I did twenty-seven years ago, and I enjoy learning, all the time, but I don't seem to get any older. That is, bodily—my mind gets older, and stronger, and better seasoned, and more satisfactory."

Says I, "If a man comes here at ninety, don't he ever set himself back?"

"Of course he does. He sets himself back to fourteen; tries it a couple of hours, and feels like a fool; sets himself forward to twenty; it ain't much improvement; tries thirty, fifty, eighty, and finally ninety—finds he is more at home and comfortable at the same old figure he is used to than any other way. Or, if his mind begun to fail him on earth at eighty, that's where he finally sticks up here. He sticks at the place where his mind was last at its best, for there's where his enjoyment is best, and his ways most set and established."

"Does a chap of twenty-five stay always twenty-five, and look it?"

"If he is a fool, yes. But if he is bright, and ambitious and industrious, the knowledge he gains and the experience he has, change his ways and thoughts and likings, and make him find his best pleasure in the company of people above that age; so he allows his body to take on that look of as many added years as he needs to make him comfortable and proper in that sort of society; he lets his body go on taking the look of age, according as he progresses, and by and by he will be bald and wrinkled outside, and wise and deep within."

"Babies the same?"

"Babies the same. Laws, what asses we used to be, on earth, about these things! We said we'd be always young in heaven. We didn't say *how* young—we didn't think of that, perhaps—that is, we didn't all think alike, anyway. When I was a boy of seven, I suppose I thought we'd all be twelve, in heaven; when I was twelve, I suppose I thought we'd all be eighteen or twenty in heaven; when I was forty, I begun to go back; I remember I hoped we'd all be about *thirty* years old in heaven. Neither a man nor a boy ever thinks the age he *has* is exactly the best one—he puts the *right* age a few years older or a few years younger than he is. Then he makes the ideal age the general age of the heavenly people. And he expects everybody to *stick* at that age—stand stock-still—and expects them to enjoy it!— Now just think of the idea of standing still in heaven! Think of a heaven made up entirely of hoop-rolling, marble-playing cubs of seven years!—or of awkward, diffident, sentimental immaturities of nineteen!—or of vigorous people of thirty, healthy-minded, brimming with ambition, but chained hand and foot to that one age and its limitations like so many helpless galley-slaves! Think of the dull sameness of a society made up of people all of one age and one set of looks, habits, tastes and feelings. Think how superior to it earth would be, with its variety of types and faces and ages, and the enlivening attrition of the myriad interests that come into pleasant collision in such a variegated society."

"Look here," says I, "do you know what you're doing?"

"Well, what am I doing?"

"You are making heaven pretty comfortable in one way, but you are playing the mischief with it in another."

"How d'you mean?"

"Well," I says, "take a young mother that's lost her child, and—"

"Sh!" he says. "Look!"

It was a woman. Middle-aged, and had grizzled hair. She was walking slow, and her head was bent down, and her wings hanging limp and droopy; and she looked ever so tired, and was crying, poor thing! She passed along by, with her head down, that way, and the tears running down her face, and didn't see us. Then Sandy said, low and gentle, and full of pity:

"*She's* hunting for her child! No, *found* it, I reckon. Lord, how she's changed! But I recognized her in a minute, though it's twenty-seven years since I saw her. A young mother she was, about twenty-two or four, or along there; and blooming and lovely and sweet—oh, just a flower! And all her heart and all her soul was wrapped up in her child, her little girl, two years old. And it died, and she went wild with grief, just wild! Well, the only comfort she had was that she'd see her child again, in heaven—'never more to part,' she said, and kept on saying it over and over, 'never more to part.' And the words made her happy; yes, they did; they made her joyful; and when I was dying, twenty-seven years ago, she told me to find her child the first thing, and say she was coming—'soon, soon, *very* soon, she hoped and believed!'"

"Why, it's pitiful, Sandy."

He didn't say anything for a while, but sat looking at the ground, thinking. Then he says, kind of mournful:

"And now she's come!"

"Well? Go on."

"Stormfield, maybe she hasn't found the child, but *I* think she has. Looks so to me. I've seen cases before. You see, she's kept that child in her head just the same as it was when she jounced it in her arms a little chubby thing. But here it didn't elect to *stay* a child. No, it elected to grow up, which it did. And in these twenty-seven years it has learned all the deep scientific learning there is to learn, and is studying and studying and learning and learning more and more, all the time, and don't give a damn for anything *but* learning; just learning, and discussing gigantic problems with people like herself."

"Well?"

"Stormfield, don't you see? Her mother knows *cranberries,* and how to tend them, and pick them, and put them up, and market them; and not another blamed thing! Her and her daughter can't be any more company for each other *now* than mud turtle and bird o' paradise. Poor thing, she was looking for a baby to jounce; *I* think she's struck a disappointment."

"Sandy, what will they do—stay unhappy forever in heaven?"

"No, they'll come together and get adjusted by and by. But not this year, and not next. By and by."

2

I had been having considerable trouble with my wings. The day after I helped the choir I made a dash or two with them, but was not lucky. First off, I flew thirty yards, and then fouled an Irishman and brought him down—brought us both down, in fact. Next, I had a collision with a Bishop —and bowled him down, of course. We had some sharp words, and I felt pretty cheap, to come banging into a grave old person like that, with a million strangers looking on and smiling to themselves.

I saw I hadn't got the hang of the steering, and so couldn't rightly tell where I was going to bring up when I started. I went afoot the rest of the day, and let my wings hang. Early next morning I went to a private place to have some practice. I got up on a pretty high rock, and got a good start, and went swooping down, aiming for a bush a little over three hundred yards off; but I couldn't seem to calculate for the wind, which was about two points abaft my beam. I could see I was going considerable to looard of the bush, so I worked my starboard wing slow and went ahead strong on the port one, but it wouldn't answer; I could see I was going to broach to, so I slowed down on both, and lit. I went back to the rock and took another chance at it. I aimed two or three points to starboard of the bush—yes, more than that— enough so as to make it nearly a head-wind. I done well enough, but made pretty poor time. I could see, plain enough, that on a head-wind, wings was a mistake. I could see that a body could sail pretty close to the wind, but he couldn't go in the wind's eye. I could see that if I wanted to go a-visiting any distance from home, and the wind was ahead, I might have to wait days, maybe, for a change; and I could see, too, that these things could not be any use at all in a gale; if you tried to run before the wind, you would make a mess of it, for there isn't any way to shorten sail—like reefing, you know—you have to take it *all* in—shut your feathers down flat to your sides. That would *land* you, of course. You could lay to, with your head to the wind—that is the best you could do, and right hard work you'd find it, too. If you tried any other game, you would founder, sure.

I judge it was about a couple of weeks or so after this that I dropped old Sandy McWilliams a note one day—it was a Tuesday—and asked him to come over and take his manna and quails with me next day; and the first thing he did when he stepped in was to twinkle his eye in a sly way, and say,—

"Well, Cap, what you done with your wings?"

I saw in a minute that there was some sarcasm done up in

that rag somewheres, but I never let on. I only says,—

"Gone to the wash."

"Yes," he says, in a dry sort of way, "they mostly go to
the wash—about this time—I've often noticed it. Fresh angels
are powerful neat. When do you look for 'em back?"

"Day after to-morrow," says I.

He winked at me, and smiled.

Says I,—

"Sandy, out with it. Come—no secrets among friends. I
notice you don't ever wear wings—and plenty others don't.
I've been making an ass of myself—is that it?"

"That is about the size of it. But it is no harm. We all do
it at first. It's perfectly natural. You see, on earth we jumped
to such foolish conclusions as to things up here. In the pictures we always saw the angels with wings on—and that
was all right; but we jumped to the conclusion that that
was their way of getting around—and that was all wrong.
The wings ain't anything but a uniform, that's all. When
they are in the field—so to speak—they always wear them;
you never see an angel going with a message anywhere
without his wings, any more than you would see a military
officer presiding at a court-martial without his uniform, or
a postman delivering letters, or a policeman walking his beat,
in plain clothes. But they ain't to *fly* with! The wings are for
show, not for use. Old experienced angels are like officers of
the regular army—they dress plain, when they are off duty.
New angels are like the militia—never shed the uniform—
always fluttering and floundering around in their wings, butt-
ing people down flapping here, and there, and everywhere,
always imagining they are attracting the admiring eye—well,
they just think they are the very most important people in
heaven. And when you see one of them come sailing around
with one wing tipped up and t'other down, you make up your
mind he is saying to himself: 'I wish Mary Ann in Arkansaw
could see me now. I reckon she'd wish she hadn't shook me.'

No, they're just for show, that's all—only just for show."

"I judge you've got it about right, Sandy," says I.

"Why, look at it yourself," says he. "*You* ain't built for wings—no man is. You know what a grist of years it took you to come here from the earth—and yet you were booming along faster than any cannon-ball could go. Suppose you had to fly that distance with your wings—wouldn't eternity have been over before you got here? Certainly. Well, angels have to go to the earth every day—millions of them—to appear in visions to dying children and good people, you know —it's the heft of their business. They appear with their wings, of course, because they are on official service, and because the dying persons wouldn't know they were angels if they hadn't wings—but do you reckon they fly with them? It stands to reason they don't. The wings would wear out before they got half-way; even the pinfeathers would be gone; the wing frames would be as bare as kite sticks before the paper is pasted on. The distances in heaven are billions of times greater; angels have to go all over heaven every day; could they do it with their wings alone? No, indeed; they wear the wings for style, but they travel any distance in an instant by *wishing*. The wishing-carpet of the Arabian Nights was a sensible idea—but our earthly idea of angels flying these awful distances with their clumsy wings was foolish.

"Our young saints, of both sexes, wear wings all the time —blazing red ones, and blue and green, and gold, and variegated, and rainbowed, and ring-streaked-and-striped ones— and nobody finds fault. It is suitable to their time of life. The things are beautiful, and they set the young people off. They are the most striking and lovely part of their outfit— a halo don't *begin*."

"Well," says I, "I've tucked mine away in the cupboard, and I allow to let them lay there till there's mud."

"Yes—or a reception."

"What's that?"

"Well, you can see one to-night if you want to. There's a barkeeper from Jersey City going to be received."

"Go on—tell me about it."

"This barkeeper got converted at a Moody and Sankey meeting, in New York, and started home on the ferryboat, and there was a collision and he got drowned. He is of a class that thinks all heaven goes wild with joy when a particularly hard lot like him is saved; they think all heaven turns out hosannahing to welcome them; they think there isn't anything talked about in the realms of the blest but their case, for that day. This barkeeper thinks there hasn't been such another stir here in years, as his coming is going to raise.— And I've always noticed this peculiarity about a dead barkeeper—he not only expects all hands to turn out when he arrives, but he expects to be received with a torchlight procession."

"I reckon he is disappointed, then."

"No, he isn't. No man is allowed to be disappointed here. Whatever he wants, when he comes—that is, any reasonable and unsacrilegious thing—he can have. There's always a few millions or billions of young folks around who don't want any better entertainment than to fill up their lungs and swarm out with their torches and have a high time over a barkeeper. It tickles the barkeeper till he can't rest, it makes a charming lark for the young folks, it don't do anybody any harm, it don't cost a rap, and it keeps up the place's reputation for making all comers happy and content."

"Very good. I'll be on hand and see them land the barkeeper."

"It is manners to go in full dress. You want to wear your wings, you know, and your other things."

"Which ones?"

"Halo, and harp, and palm branch, and all that."

"Well," says I, "I reckon I ought to be ashamed of myself,

but the fact is I left them laying around that day I resigned from the choir. I haven't got a rag to wear but this robe and the wings."

"That's all right. You'll find they've been raked up and saved for you. Send for them."

"I'll do it, Sandy. But what was it you was saying about unsacrilegious things, which people expect to get, and will be disappointed about?"

"Oh, there are a lot of such things that people expect and don't get. For instance, there's a Brooklyn preacher by the name of Talmage, who is laying up a considerable disappointment for himself. He says, every now and then in his sermons, that the first thing he does when he gets to heaven, will be to fling his arms around Abraham, Isaac and Jacob, and kiss them and weep on them. There's millions of people down there on earth that are promising themselves the same thing. As many as sixty thousand people arrive here every single day, that want to run straight to Abraham, Isaac and Jacob, and hug them and weep on them. Now mind you, sixty thousand a day is a pretty heavy contract for those old people. If they were a mind to allow it, they wouldn't ever have anything to do, year in and year out, but stand up and be hugged and wept on thirty-two hours in the twenty-four. They would be tired out and as wet as muskrats all the time. What would heaven be, to *them*? It would be a mighty good place to get out of—you know that, yourself. Those are kind and gentle old Jews, but they ain't any fonder of kissing the emotional high-lights of Brooklyn than you be. You mark my words, Mr. T.'s endearments are going to be declined, with thanks. There are limits to the privileges of the elect, even in heaven. Why, if Adam was to show himself to every new-comer that wants to call and gaze at him and strike him for his autograph, he would never have time to do anything else but just that. Talmage has said he is going to give Adam some of his attentions, as well as A., I. and J. But he will have to change his mind about that."

"Do you think Talmage will really come here?"

"Why, certainly, he will; but don't you be alarmed; he will run with his own kind, and there's plenty of them. That is the main charm of heaven—there's all kinds here—which wouldn't be the case if you let the preachers tell it. Anybody can find the sort he prefers, here, and he just lets the others alone, and they let him alone. When the Deity builds a heaven, it is built right, and on a liberal plan."

Sandy sent home for his things, and I sent for mine, and about nine in the evening we begun to dress. Sandy says,—

"This is going to be a grand time for you, Stormy. Like as not some of the patriarchs will turn out."

"No, but will they?"

"Like as not. Of course they are pretty exclusive. They hardly ever show themselves to the common public. I believe they never turn out except for an eleventh-hour convert. They wouldn't do it then, only earthly tradition makes a grand show pretty necessary on that kind of an occasion."

"Do they all turn out, Sandy?"

"Who?—all the patriarchs? Oh, no—hardly ever more than a couple. You will be here fifty thousand years—maybe more —before you get a glimpse of all the patriarchs and prophets. Since I have been here, Job has been to the front once, and once Ham and Jeremiah both at the same time. But the finest thing that has happened in my day was a year or so ago; that was Charles Peace's reception—him they called 'the Bannercross Murderer'—an Englishman. There were four patriarchs and two prophets on the Grand Stand that time—there hasn't been anything like it since Captain Kidd came; Abel was there—the first time in twelve hundred years. A report got around that Adam was coming; well, of course, Abel was enough to bring a crowd, all by himself, but there is nobody that can draw like Adam. It was a false report, but it got around, anyway, as I say, and it will be a long day before I see the like of it again. The reception was in the English department, of course, which is eight hundred and eleven million miles from the New Jersey line. I went, along with a good many of my neighbors, and it was a sight to see, I can tell you. Flocks came from the departments. I saw Esquimaux there, and Tartars, Negroes, Chinamen—people from everywhere. You see a mixture like that in the Grand Choir, the first day you land here, but you hardly ever see it again. There were billions of people; when they were singing or hosannahing, the noise was wonderful; and even when their tongues were still the drumming of the wings was nearly enough to burst your head, for all the sky was as thick as if it was snowing angels. Although Adam was not there, it was a great time anyway, because we had three archangels on the Grand Stand—it is a seldom thing that even one comes out."

"What did they look like, Sandy?"

"Well, they had shining faces, and shining robes, and wonderful rainbow wings, and they stood eighteen feet high, and wore swords, and held their heads up in a noble way, and looked like soldiers."

"Did they have halos?"

"No—anyway, not the hoop kind. The archangels and the upper-class patriarchs wear a finer thing than that. It is a round, solid, splendid glory of gold, that is blinding to look at. You have often seen a patriarch in a picture, on earth, with that thing on—you remember it?—he looks as if he had his head in a brass platter. That don't give you the right idea of it at all—it is much more shining and beautiful."

"Did you talk with those archangels and patriarchs, Sandy?"

"Who—I? Why, what can you be thinking about, Stormy? I ain't worthy to speak to such as they."

"Is Talmage?"

"Of course not. You have got the same mixed-up idea about these things that everybody has down there. I had it once, but I got over it. Down there they talk of the heavenly King—and that is right—but then they go right on speaking as if this was a republic and everybody was on a dead level with everybody else, and privileged to fling his arms around anybody he comes across, and be hail-fellow-well-met with all the elect, from the highest down. How tangled up and absurd that is! How are you going to have a republic under a king? How are you going to have a republic at all, where the head of the government is absolute, holds his place forever, and has no parliament, no council to meddle or make in his affairs, nobody voted for, nobody elected, nobody in the whole universe with a voice in the government, nobody asked to take a hand in its matters, and nobody *allowed* to do it? Fine republic, ain't it?"

"Well, yes—it *is* a little different from the idea I had—but I thought I might go around and get acquainted with the grandees, anyway—not exactly splice the main-brace with them, you know, but shake hands and pass the time of day."

"Could Tom, Dick and Harry call on the Cabinet of Russia and do that?—on Prince Gortschakoff, for instance?"

"I reckon not, Sandy."

"Well, this is Russia—only more so. There's not the shadow of a republic about it anywhere. There are ranks, here. There are viceroys, princes, governors, sub-governors, sub-sub-governors, and a hundred orders of nobility, grading along down from grand-ducal archangels, stage by stage, till the general level is struck, where there ain't any titles. Do you know what a prince of the blood is, on earth?"

"No."

"Well, a prince of the blood don't belong to the royal family exactly, and he don't belong to the mere nobility of the kingdom; he is lower than the one, and higher than t'other. That's about the position of the patriarchs and prophets here.

There's some mighty high nobility here—people that you and I ain't worthy to polish sandals for—and *they* ain't worthy to polish sandals for the patriarchs and prophets. That gives you a kind of an idea of their rank, don't it? You begin to see how high up they are, don't you? Just to get a two-minute glimpse of one of them is a thing for a body to remember and tell about for a thousand years. Why, Captain, just think of this: if Abraham was to set his foot down here by this door, there would be a railing set up around that foot-track right away, and a shelter put over it, and people would flock here from all over heaven, for hundreds and hundreds of years, to look at it. Abraham is one of the parties that Mr. Talmage, of Brooklyn, is going to embrace, and kiss, and weep on, when he comes. He wants to lay in a good stock of tears, you know, or five to one he will go dry before he gets a chance to do it."

"Sandy," says I, "I had an idea that *I* was going to be equal with everybody here, too, but I will let that drop. It don't matter, and I am plenty happy enough anyway."

"Captain, you are happier than you would be, the other way. These old patriarchs and prophets have got ages the start of you; they know more in two minutes than you know in a year. Did you ever try to have a sociable improving-time discussing winds, and currents and variations of compass with an undertaker?"

"I get your idea, Sandy. He couldn't interest me. He would be an ignoramus in such things—he would bore me, and I would bore him."

"You have got it. You would bore the patriarchs when you talked, and when they talked they would shoot over your head. By and by you would say, 'Good morning, your Eminence, I will call again'—but you wouldn't. Did you ever ask the slush-boy to come up in the cabin and take dinner with you?"

"I get your drift again, Sandy. I wouldn't be used to such

grand people as the patriarchs and prophets, and I would be
sheepish and tongue-tied in their company, and mighty glad
to get out of it. Sandy, which is the highest rank, patriarch
or prophet?"

"Oh, the prophets hold over the patriarchs. The newest
prophet, even, is of a sight more consequence than the oldest
patriarch. Yes, sir, Adam himself has to walk behind Shakespeare."

"Was Shakespeare a prophet?"

"Of course he was; and so was Homer, and heaps more.
But Shakespeare and the rest have to walk behind a common tailor from Tennessee, by the name of Billings; and behind a horse-doctor named Sakka, from Afghanistan. Jeremiah, and Billings and Buddha walk together, side by side,
right behind a crowd from planets not in our astronomy;
next come a dozen or two from Jupiter and other worlds;
next come Daniel, and Sakka and Confucius; next a lot from
systems outside of ours; next come Ezekiel, and Mahomet,
Zoroaster, and a knife grinder from ancient Egypt; then there
is a long string, and after them, away down toward the bottom, come Shakespeare and Homer, and a shoemaker named
Marais, from the back settlements of France."

"Have they really rung in Mahomet and all those other
heathens?"

"Yes—they all had their message, and they all get their
reward. The man who don't get his reward on earth, needn't
bother—he will get it here, sure."

"But why did they throw off on Shakespeare, that way,
and put him away down there below those shoemakers and
horse-doctors and knife grinders—a lot of people nobody ever
heard of?"

"That is the heavenly justice of it—they warn't rewarded
according to their deserts, on earth, but here they get their
rightful rank. That tailor Billings, from Tennessee, wrote
poetry that Homer and Shakespeare couldn't begin to come

up to; but nobody would print it, nobody read it but his neighbors, an ignorant lot, and they laughed at it. Whenever the village had a drunken frolic and a dance, they would drag him in and crown him with cabbage leaves, and pretend to bow down to him; and one night when he was sick and nearly starved to death, they had him out and crowned him, and then they rode him on a rail about the village, and everybody followed along, beating tin pans and yelling. Well, he died before morning. He wasn't ever expecting to go to heaven, much less that there was going to be any fuss made over him, so I reckon he was a good deal surprised when the reception broke on him."

"Was you there, Sandy?"

"Bless you, no!"

"Why? Didn't you know it was going to come off?"

"Well, I judge I did. It was the talk of these realms—not for a day, like this barkeeper business, but for twenty years before the man died."

"Why the mischief didn't you go, then?"

"Now how you talk! The like of me go meddling around at the reception of a prophet? A mudsill like me trying to push in and help receive an awful grandee like Edward J. Billings? Why, I should have been laughed at for a billion miles around. I shouldn't ever heard the last of it."

"Well, who did go, then?"

"Mighty few people that you and I will ever get a chance to see, Captain. Not a solitary commoner ever has the luck to see a reception of a prophet, I can tell you. All the nobility, and all the patriarchs and prophets—every last one of them —and all the archangels, and all the princes and governors and viceroys, were there,—and *no* small fry—not a single one. And mind you, I'm not talking about only the grandees from *our* world, but the princes and patriarchs and so on from *all* the worlds that shine in our sky, and from billions more that belong in systems upon systems away outside of the one our sun is in. There were some prophets and patri-

archs there that ours ain't a circumstance to, for rank and il-
lustriousness and all that. Some were from Jupiter and
other worlds in our own system, but the most celebrated were
three poets, Saa, Bo and Soof, from great planets in three different and very remote systems. These three names are common and familiar in every nook and corner of heaven, clear
from one end of it to the other—fully as well known as the
eighty Supreme Archangels, in fact—whereas our Moses, and
Adam, and the rest, have not been heard of outside of our
world's little corner of heaven, except by a few very learned
men scattered here and there—and they always spell their
names wrong, and get the performances of one mixed up with
the doings of another, and they almost always locate them
simply *in our solar system,* and think that is enough without going into little details such as naming the particular
world they are from. It is like a learned Hindoo showing off
how much he knows by saying Longfellow lived in the United
States—as if he lived all over the United States, and as if the
country was so small you couldn't throw a brick there without hitting him. Between you and me, it does gravel me, the
cool way people from those monster worlds outside our system snub our little world, and even our system. Of course
we think a good deal of Jupiter, because our world is only a
potato to it, for size; but then there are worlds in other
systems that Jupiter isn't even a mustard-seed to—like the
planet Goobra, for instance, which you couldn't squeeze inside the orbit of Haley's comet without straining the rivets.
Tourists from Goobra (I mean parties that lived and died
there—natives) come here, now and then, and inquire about
our world, and when they find out it is so little that a streak
of lightning can flash clear around it in the eighth of a second, they have to lean up against something to laugh. Then
they screw a glass into their eye and go to examining *us,* as if
we were a curious kind of foreign bug, or something of that
sort. One of them asked me how long our day was; and when
I told him it was twelve hours long, as a general thing, he

asked me if people where I was from considered it worth
while to get up and wash for such a day as that. That is the
way with those Goobra people—they can't seem to let a
chance go by to throw it in your face that their day is three
hundred and twenty-two of our years long. This young snob
was just of age—he was six or seven thousand of his days old
—say two million of our years—and he had all the puppy
airs that belong to that time of life—that turning-point when
a person has got over being a boy and yet ain't quite a man
exactly. If it had been anywhere else but in heaven, I would
have given him a piece of my mind. Well, anyway, Billings
had the grandest reception that has been seen in thousands of
centuries, and I think it will have a good effect. His name
will be carried pretty far, and it will make our system talked
about, and maybe our world, too, and raise us in the respect
of the general public of heaven. Why, look here—Shakespeare walked backwards before that tailor from Tennessee,
and scattered flowers for him to walk on, and Homer stood
behind his chair and waited on him at the banquet. Of
course that didn't go for much *there*, amongst all those big
foreigners from other systems, as they hadn't heard of Shakespeare or Homer either, but it would amount to considerable
down there on our little earth if they could know about it.
I wish there was something *in* that miserable spiritualism, so
we could send them word. That Tennessee village would set
up a monument to Billings, then, and his autograph would
outsell Satan's. Well, they had grand times at that reception
—a small-fry noble from Hoboken told me all about it—Sir
Richard Duffer, Baronet."

"What, Sandy, a nobleman from Hoboken? How is that?"

"Easy enough. Duffer kept a sausage-shop and never saved
a cent in his life because he used to give all his spare meat
to the poor, in a quiet way. Not tramps,—no, the other sort
—the sort that will starve before they will beg—honest
square people out of work. Dick used to watch hungry-look-
ing men and women and children, and track them home, and

find out all about them from the neighbors, and then feed
them and find them work. As nobody ever *saw* him give anything to anybody, he had the reputation of being mean; he
died with it, too, and everybody said it was a good riddance;
but the minute he landed here, they made him a baronet,
and the very first words Dick the sausage-maker of Hoboken
heard when he stepped upon the heavenly shore were,
'Welcome, Sir Richard Dufferl' It surprised him some, because he thought he had reasons to believe he was pointed
for a warmer climate than this one."

All of a sudden the whole region fairly rocked under the
crash of eleven hundred and one thunder blasts, all let off
at once, and Sandy says,—

"There, that's for the barkeep."

I jumped up and says,—

"Then let's be moving along, Sandy; we don't want to
miss any of this thing, you know."

"Keep your seat," he says; "he is only just telegraphed,
that is all."

"How?"

"That blast only means that he has been sighted from the
signal-station. He is off Sandy Hook. The committees will go
down to meet him, now, and escort him in. There will be ceremonies and delays; they won't be coming up the Bay for a
considerable time, yet. It is several billion milles away, anyway."

"*I* could have been a barkeeper and a hard lot just as well
as not," says I, remembering the lonesome way I arrived,
and how there wasn't any committee nor anything.

"I notice some regret in your voice," says Sandy, "and it is
natural enough; but let bygones be bygones; you went according to your lights, and it is too late now to mend the
thing."

"No, let it slide, Sandy, I don't mind. But you've got a
Sandy Hook *here,* too, have you?"

"We've got everything here, just as it is below. All the States and Territories of the Union, and all the kingdoms of the earth and the islands of the sea are laid out here just as they are on the globe—all the same shape they are down there, and all graded to the relative size, only each State and realm and island is a good many billion times bigger here than it is below. There goes another blast."

"What is that one for?"

"That is only another fort answering the first one. They each fire eleven hundred and one thunder blasts at a single dash—it is the usual salute for an eleventh-hour guest; a hundred for each hour and an extra one for the guest's sex; if it was a woman we would know it by their leaving off the extra gun."

"How do we know there's eleven hundred and one, Sandy, when they all go off at once?—and yet we certainly do know."

"Our intellects are a good deal sharpened up, here, in some ways, and that is one of them. Numbers and sizes and distances are so great, here, that we have to be made so we can *feel* them—our old ways of counting and measuring and ciphering wouldn't ever give us an idea of them, but would only confuse us and oppress us and make our heads ache."

After some more talk about this, I says: "Sandy, I notice that I hardly ever see a white angel; where I run across one white angel, I strike as many as a hundred million copper-colored ones—people that can't speak English. How is that?"

"Well, you will find it the same in any State or Territory of the American corner of heaven you choose to go to. I have shot along, a whole week on a stretch, and gone millions and millions of miles, through perfect swarms of angels, without ever seeing a single white one, or hearing a word I could understand. You see, America was occupied a billion years and more, by Injuns and Aztecs, and that sort of folks, before a white man ever set his foot in it. During the first three hundred years after Columbus's discovery, there wasn't ever more than one good lecture audience of white people, all put together, in America—I mean the whole thing, British Possessions and all; in the beginning of our century there were only 6,000,000 or 7,000,000—say seven; 12,000,000 or 14,000,000 in 1825; say 23,000,000 in 1850; 40,000,000 in 1875. Our death-rate has always been 20 in 1000 per annum. Well, 140,000 died the first year of the century; 280,000 the twenty-fifth year; 500,000 the fiftieth year; about a million the seventy-fifth year. Now I am going to be liberal about this thing, and consider that fifty million whites have died in America from the beginning up to to-day—make it sixty, if you want to; make it a hundred million—it's no difference about a few millions one way or t'other. Well, now, you can see, yourself, that when you come to spread a little dab of people like that over these hundreds of billions of miles of American territory here in heaven, it is like scattering a ten-cent box of homeopathic pills over the Great Sahara and expecting to find them again. You can't expect us to amount to anything in heaven, and we *don't*—now that is the simple fact, and we have got to do the best we can with it. The learned men from other planets and other systems come here and hang around a while, when they are touring around the Kingdom, and then go back to their own section of heaven and write a book of travels, and they give America about five lines in it. And what do they say about us? They say this wilderness is populated with a scattering few hundred thousand billions of red angels, with now and then a curiously complected *diseased* one. You see, they think we whites and the occasional nigger are Injuns that have been bleached out or blackened by some leprous disease or other—for some peculiarly rascally *sin*, mind you. It is a mighty sour pill for us all, my friend—even the modestest of us, let alone the other kind, that think they are going to be received like a long-lost government bond, and hug Abraham into the bargain. I haven't asked you any of the particulars, Captain, but I judge it goes without saying—if my experience is worth anything—that there wasn't much of a hooraw made over you when you arrived—now was there?"

"Don't mention it, Sandy," says I, coloring up a little; "I wouldn't have had the family see it for any amount you are of a mind to name. Change the subject, Sandy, change the subject."

"Well, do you think of settling in the California department of bliss?"

"I don't know. I wasn't calculating on doing anything really definite in that direction till the family come. I thought I would just look around, meantime, in a quiet way, and make up my mind. Besides, I know a good many dead people, and I was calculating to hunt them up and swap a little gossip with them about friends, and old times, and one thing or another, and ask them how they like it here, as far as they have got. I reckon my wife will want to camp in the California range, though, because most all her departed will be there, and she likes to be with folks she knows."

"Don't you let her. You see what the Jersey district of heaven is, for whites; well, the California district is a thousand times worse. It swarms with a mean kind of leather-headed mud-colored angels—and your nearest white neighbors is likely to be a million miles away. *What a man mostly misses, in heaven, is company*—company of his own sort and color and language. I have come near settling in the European part of heaven once or twice on that account."

"Well, why didn't you, Sandy?"

"Oh, various reasons. For one thing, although you *see* plenty of whites there, you can't understand any of them hardly, and so you go about as hungry for talk as you do here. I like to look at a Russian or a German or an Italian—I even like to look at a Frenchman if I ever have the luck to catch him engaged in anything that ain't indelicate—but *looking* don't cure the hunger—what you want is talk."

"Well, there's England, Sandy—the English district of heaven."

"Yes, but it is not so very much better than this end of the heavenly domain. As long as you run across Englishmen born this side of three hundred years ago, you are all right; but the minute you get back of Elizabeth's time the language begins to fog up, and the further back you go the foggier it gets. I had some talk with one Langland and a man by the name of Chaucer—old-time poets—but it was no use, I couldn't quite understand them and they couldn't quite understand me. I have had letters from them since, but it is such broken English I can't make it out. Back of those men's time the English are just simply foreigners, nothing more, nothing less; they talk Danish, German, Norman French, and sometimes a mixture of all three; back of *them*, they talk Latin, and ancient British, Irish, and Gaelic; and then back of these come billions and billions of pure savages that talk a gibberish that Satan himself couldn't understand. The fact is, where you strike one man in the English settlements that you can understand, you wade through awful swarms that talk something you can't make head nor tail of. You see, every country on earth has been overlaid so often, in the course of a billion years, with different kinds of people and different sorts of languages, that this sort of mongrel business was bound to be the result in heaven."

"Sandy," says I, "did you see a good many of the great people history tells about?"

"Yes—plenty. I saw kings and all sorts of distinguished people."

"Do the kings rank just as they did below?"

"No; a body can't bring his rank up here with him. Divine right is a good-enough earthly romance, but it don't go, here. Kings drop down to the general level as soon as they reach the realms of grace. I knew Charles the Second very well—one of the most popular comedians in the English section—draws first rate. There are better, of course—people that were never heard of on earth—but Charles is making a very good reputation indeed, and is considered a rising man. Richard the Lionhearted is in the prize-ring, and coming into considerable favor. Henry the Eighth is a tragedian, and the scenes where he kills people are done to the very life. Henry the Sixth keeps a religious-book stand."

"Did you ever see Napoleon, Sandy?"

"Often—sometimes in the Corsican range, sometimes in the French. He always hunts up a conspicuous place, and goes frowning around with his arms folded and his field-glass under his arm, looking as grand, gloomy and peculiar as his reputation calls for, and very much bothered because he don't stand as high, here, for a soldier, as he expected to."

"Why, who stands higher?"

"Oh, a *lot* of people *we* never heard of before—the shoemaker and horse-doctor and knife-grinder kind, you know—clodhoppers from goodness knows where, that never handled a sword or fired a shot in their lives—but the soldiership was in them, though they never had a chance to show it. But here they take their right place, and Cæsar and Napoleon and Alexander have to take a back seat. The greatest military genius our world ever produced was a bricklayer from somewhere back of Boston—died during the Revolution—by the name of Absalom Jones. Wherever he goes, crowds flock to see him. You see, everybody knows that if he had had a chance he would have shown the world some generalship that would have made all generalship before look like child's play and 'prentice work. But he never got a chance; he tried heaps of times to enlist as a private, but he had lost both thumbs and a couple of front teeth, and the recruiting sergeant wouldn't pass him. However, as I say, everybody knows, now, what he *would* have been, and so they flock by the million to get a glimpse of him whenever they hear he is going to be anywhere. Cæsar, and Hannibal, and Alexander, and Napoleon are all on his staff, and ever so many more great generals; but the public hardly care to look at *them* when *he* is around. Boom! There goes another salute. The barkeeper's off quarantine now."

Sandy and I put on our things. Then we made a wish, and in a second we were at the reception-place. We stood on the edge of the ocean of space, and looked out over the dimness, but couldn't make out anything. Close by us was the Grand Stand—tier on tier of dim thrones rising up toward the zenith. From each side of it spread away the tiers of seats for the general public. They spread away for leagues and leagues—you couldn't see the ends. They were empty and still, and hadn't a cheerful look, but looked dreary, like a theater before anybody comes—gas turned down. Sandy says,—

"We'll sit down here and wait. We'll see the head of the procession come in sight away off yonder pretty soon, now."

Says I,—

"It's pretty lonesome, Sandy; I reckon there's a hitch somewheres. Nobody but just you and me—it ain't much of a display for the barkeeper."

"Don't you fret, it's all right. There'll be one more gunfire—then you'll see."

In a little while we noticed a sort of a lightish flush, away off on the horizon.

"Head of the torchlight procession," says Sandy.

It spread, and got lighter and brighter; soon it had a strong glare like a locomotive headlight; it kept on getting brighter and brighter till it was like the sun peeping above the horizon-line at sea—the big red rays shot high up into the sky.

"Keep your eyes on the Grand Stand and the miles of seats—sharp!" says Sandy, "and listen for the gun-fire."

Just then it burst out, "Boom-boom-boom!" like a million thunder-storms in one, and made the whole heavens rock. Then there was a sudden and awful glare of light all about us, and in that very instant every one of the millions of seats was occupied, and as far as you could see, in both directions, was just a solid pack of people, and the place was all splendidly lit up! It was enough to take a body's breath away. Sandy says,—

"That is the way we do it here. No time fooled away; nobody straggling in after the curtain's up. Wishing is quicker work than traveling. A quarter of a second ago these folks were millions of miles from here. When they heard the last signal, all they had to do was to wish, and here they are."

The prodigious choir struck up,—

> We long to hear thy voice,
> To see thee face to face.

It was noble music, but the uneducated chipped in and spoilt it, just as the congregations used to do on earth.

The head of the procession begun to pass, now, and it was a wonderful sight. It swept along, thick and solid, five hundred thousand angels abreast, and every angel carrying a torch and singing—the whirring thunder of the wings made a body's head ache. You could follow the line of the procession back, and slanting upward into the sky, far away in a glittering snaky rope, till it was only a faint streak in the distance. The rush went on and on, for a long time, and at last, sure enough, along comes the barkeeper, and then everybody rose, and a cheer went up that made the heavens shake, I tell you! He was all smiles, and had his halo tilted over one ear in a cocky way, and was the most satisfied-looking saint I ever saw. While he marched up the steps of the Grand Stand, the choir struck up,—

> The whole wide heaven groans,
> And waits to hear that voice.

There were four gorgeous tents standing side by side in the place of honor, on a broad railed platform in the center of the Grand Stand, with a shining guard of honor round about them. The tents had been shut up all this time. As the

barkeeper climbed along up, bowing and smiling to everybody, and at last got to the platform, these tents were jerked
up aloft all of a sudden, and we saw four noble thrones of
gold, all caked with jewels, and in the two middle ones sat
old white-whiskered men, and in the two others a couple of
the most glorious and gaudy giants, with platter halos and
beautiful armor. All the millions went down on their knees,
and stared, and looked glad, and burst out into a joyful kind
of murmurs. They said,—

"Two archangels!—that is splendid. Who can the others
be?"

The archangels gave the barkeeper a stiff little military
bow; the two old men rose; one of them said, "Moses and
Esau welcome thee!" and then all the four vanished, and the
thrones were empty.

The barkeeper looked a little disappointed, for he was
calculating to hug those old people, I judge; but it was the
gladdest and proudest multitude you ever saw—because they
had seen Moses and Esau. Everybody was saying, "Did you
see them?—I did—Esau's side face was to me, but I saw
Moses full in the face, just as plain as I see you this minute!"

The procession took up the barkeeper and moved on with
him again, and the crowd broke up and scattered. As we
went along home, Sandy said it was a great success, and the
barkeeper would have a right to be proud of it forever. And
he said *we* were in luck, too; said we might attend recep-
tions for forty thousand years to come, and not have a
chance to see a brace of such grand moguls as Moses and
Esau. We found afterwards that we had come near seeing
another patriarch, and likewise a genuine prophet besides,
but at the last moment they sent regrets. Sandy said there
would be a monument put up there, where Moses and Esau
had stood, with the date and circumstances, and all about the
whole business, and travelers would come for thousands of
years and gawk at it, and climb over it, and scribble their
names on it.

The Mysterious Stranger

1

It was in 1590—winter. Austria was far away from the world, and asleep; it was still the Middle Ages in Austria, and promised to remain so forever. Some even set it away back centuries upon centuries and said that by the mental and spiritual clock it was still the Age of Belief in Austria. But they meant it as a compliment, not a slur, and it was so taken, and we were all proud of it. I remember it well, although I was only a boy; and I remember, too, the pleasure it gave me.

Yes, Austria was far from the world, and asleep, and our village was in the middle of that sleep, being in the middle of Austria. It drowsed in peace in the deep privacy of a hilly and woodsy solitude where news from the world hardly ever came to disturb its dreams, and was infinitely content. At its front flowed the tranquil river, its surface painted with

147

cloud-forms and the reflections of drifting arks and stone-
boats; behind it rose the woody steeps to the base of the lofty
precipice; from the top of the precipice frowned a vast castle,
its long stretch of towers and bastions mailed in vines; beyond the river, a league to the left, was a tumbled expanse of
forest-clothed hills cloven by winding gorges where the
sun never penetrated; and to the right a precipice over-
looked the river, and between it and the hills just spoken of
lay a far-reaching plain dotted with little homesteads nested
among orchards and shade trees.

The whole region for leagues around was the hereditary
property of a prince, whose servants kept the castle always
in perfect condition for occupancy, but neither he nor his
family came there oftener than once in five years. When they
came it was as if the lord of the world had arrived, and had
brought all the glories of its kingdoms along; and when they
went they left a calm behind which was like the deep sleep
which follows an orgy.

Eseldorf was a paradise for us boys. We were not over-
much pestered with schooling. Mainly we were trained to be
good Christians; to revere the Virgin, the Church, and the
saints above everything. Beyond these matters we were not
required to know much; and, in fact, not allowed to. Knowledge was not good for the common people, and could make
them discontented with the lot which God had appointed for
them, and God would not endure discontentment with His
plans. We had two priests. One of them, Father Adolf, was
a very zealous and strenuous priest, much considered.

There may have been better priests, in some ways, than
Father Adolf, but there was never one in our commune who
was held in more solemn and awful respect. This was because
he had absolutely no fear of the Devil. He was the only
Christian I have ever known of whom that could be truly
said. People stood in deep dread of him on that account; for
they thought that there must be something supernatural

about him, else he could not be so bold and so confident. All men speak in bitter disapproval of the Devil, but they do it reverently, not flippantly; but Father Adolf's way was very different; he called him by every name he could lay his tongue to, and it made everyone shudder that heard him; and often he would even speak of him scornfully and scoffingly; then the people crossed themselves and went quickly out of his presence, fearing that something fearful might happen.

Father Adolf had actually met Satan face to face more than once, and defied him. This was known to be so. Father Adolf said it himself. He never made any secret of it, but spoke it right out. And that he was speaking true there was proof in at least one instance, for on that occasion he quarreled with the enemy, and intrepidly threw his bottle at him; and there, upon the wall of his study, was the ruddy splotch where it struck and broke.

But it was Father Peter, the other priest, that we all loved best and were sorriest for. Some people charged him with talking around in conversation that God was all goodness and would find a way to save all his poor human children. It was a horrible thing to say, but there was never any absolute proof that Father Peter said it; and it was out of character for him to say it, too, for he was always good and gentle and truthful. He wasn't charged with saying it in the pulpit, where all the congregation could hear and testify, but only outside, in talk; and it is easy for enemies to manufacture *that*. Father Peter had an enemy and a very powerful one, the astrologer who lived in a tumbled old tower up the valley, and put in his nights studying the stars. Every one knew he could foretell wars and famines, though that was not so hard, for there was always a war, and generally a famine somewhere. But he could also read any man's life through the stars in a big book he had, and find lost property, and every one in the village except Father Peter stood in awe of him. Even Father Adolf, who had defied the Devil, had a wholesome respect for the astrologer when he came through our village wearing his tall, pointed hat and his long, flowing robe with stars on it, carrying his big book, and a staff which was known to have magic power. The bishop himself sometimes listened to the astrologer, it was said, for, besides studying the stars and prophesying, the astrologer made a great show of piety, which would impress the bishop, of course.

But Father Peter took no stock in the astrologer. He denounced him openly as a charlatan—a fraud with no valuable knowledge of any kind, or powers beyond those of an ordinary and rather inferior human being, which naturally made the astrologer hate Father Peter and wish to ruin him. It was the astrologer, as we all believed, who originated the story about Father Peter's shocking remark and carried it to the bishop. It was said that Father Peter had made the remark to his niece, Marget, though Marget denied it and implored the bishop to believe her and spare her old uncle from poverty and disgrace. But the bishop wouldn't listen. He suspended Father Peter indefinitely, though he wouldn't go so far as to excommunicate him on the evidence of only one witness; and now Father Peter had been out a couple of years, and our other priest, Father Adolf, had his flock.

Those had been hard years for the old priest and Marget. They had been favorites, but of course that changed when they came under the shadow of the bishop's frown. Many of their friends fell away entirely, and the rest became cool and distant. Marget was a lovely girl of eighteen when the trouble came, and she had the best head in the village, and the most in it. She taught the harp, and earned all her clothes and pocket money by her own industry. But her scholars fell off one by one now; she was forgotten when there were dances and parties among the youth of the village; the young fellows stopped coming to the house, all except Wilhelm Meidling—and he could have been spared; she and her uncle were sad and forlorn in their neglect and disgrace, and the

sunshine was gone out of their lives. Matters went worse and
worse, all through the two years. Clothes were wearing out,
bread was harder and harder to get. And now, at last, the
very end was come. Solomon Isaacs had lent all the money
he was willing to put on the house, and gave notice that to-
morrow he would foreclose.

2

Three of us boys were always together, and had been so
from the cradle, being fond of one another from the beginning, and this affection deepened as the years went on—Nikolaus Bauman, son of the principal judge of the local court;
Seppi Wohlmeyer, son of the keeper of the principal inn, the
Golden Stag, which had a nice garden, with shade trees
reaching down to the riverside, and pleasure boats for hire;
and I was the third—Theodor Fischer, son of the church
organist, who was also leader of the village musicians, teacher
of the violin, composer, tax-collector of the commune, sexton,
and in other ways a useful citizen, and respected by all. We
knew the hills and the woods as well as the birds knew them;
for we were always roaming them when we had leisure—at
least, when we were not swimming or boating or fishing, or
playing on the ice or sliding down hill.

And we had the run of the castle park, and very few had
that. It was because we were pets of the oldest servingman
in the castle—Felix Brandt; and often we went there,
nights, to hear him talk about old times and strange things,
and to smoke with him (he taught us that) and to drink
coffee; for he had served in the wars, and was at the siege of
Vienna; and there, when the Turks were defeated and
driven away, among the captured things were bags of coffee,
and the Turkish prisoners explained the character of it and
how to make a pleasant drink out of it, and now he always
kept coffee by him, to drink himself and also to astonish the

ignorant with. When it stormed he kept us all night; and while it thundered and lightened outside he told us about ghosts and horrors of every kind, and of battles and murders and mutilations, and such things, and made it pleasant and cozy inside; and he told these things from his own experience largely. He had seen many ghosts in his time, and witches and enchanters, and once he was lost in a fierce storm at midnight in the mountains, and by the glare of the lightning had seen the Wild Huntsman rage on the blast with his specter dogs chasing after him through the driving cloud-rack. Also he had seen an incubus once, and several times he had seen the great bat that sucks the blood from the necks of people while they are asleep, fanning them softly with its wings and so keeping them drowsy till they die.

He encouraged us not to fear supernatural things, such as ghosts, and said they did no harm, but only wandered about because they were lonely and distressed and wanted kindly notice and compassion; and in time we learned not to be afraid, and even went down with him in the night to the haunted chamber in the dungeons of the castle. The ghost appeared only once, and it went by very dim to the sight and floated noiseless through the air, and then disappeared; and we scarcely trembled, he had taught us so well. He said it came up sometimes in the night and woke him by passing its clammy hand over his face, but it did him no hurt; it only wanted sympathy and notice. But the strangest thing was that he had seen angels—actual angels out of heaven—and had talked with them. They had no wings, and wore clothes, and talked and looked and acted just like any natural person, and you would never know them for angels except for the wonderful things they did which a mortal could not do, and the way they suddenly disappeared while you were talking with them, which was also a thing which no mortal could do. And he said they were pleasant and cheerful, not gloomy and melancholy, like ghosts.

It was after that kind of a talk one May night that we got up next morning and had a good breakfast with him and then went down and crossed the bridge and went away up into the hills on the left to a woody hill-top which was a favorite place of ours, and there we stretched out on the grass in the shade to rest and smoke and talk over these strange things, for they were in our minds yet, and impressing us. But we couldn't smoke, because we had been heedless and left our flint and steel behind.

Soon there came a youth strolling toward us through the trees, and he sat down and began to talk in a friendly way, just as if he knew us. But we did not answer him, for he was a stranger and we were not used to strangers and were shy of them. He had new and good clothes on, and was handsome and had a winning face and a pleasant voice, and was easy and graceful and unembarrassed, not slouchy and awkward and diffident, like other boys. We wanted to be friendly with him, but didn't know how to begin. Then I thought of the pipe, and wondered if it would be taken as kindly meant if I offered it to him. But I remembered that we had no fire, so I was sorry and disappointed. But he looked up bright and pleased, and said:

"Fire? Oh, that is easy; I will furnish it."

I was so astonished I couldn't speak; for I had not said anything. He took the pipe and blew his breath on it, and the tobacco glowed red, and spirals of blue smoke rose up. We jumped up and were going to run, for that was natural; and we did run a few steps, although he was yearningly pleading for us to stay, and giving us his word that he would not do us any harm, but only wanted to be friends with us and have company. So we stopped and stood, and wanted to go back, being full of curiosity and wonder, but afraid to venture. He went on coaxing, in his soft, persuasive way;

and when we saw that the pipe did not blow up and nothing happened, our confidence returned by little and little, and presently our curiosity got to be stronger than our fear, and we ventured back—but slowly, and ready to fly at any alarm.

He was bent on putting us at ease, and he had the right art; one could not remain doubtful and timorous where a person was so earnest and simple and gentle, and talked so alluringly as he did; no, he won us over, and it was not long before we were content and comfortable and chatty, and glad we had found this new friend. When the feeling of constraint was all gone we asked him how he had learned to do that strange thing, and he said he hadn't learned it at all; it came natural to him—like other things—other curious things.

"What ones?"

"Oh, a number; I don't know how many."

"Will you let us see you do them?"

"Do—please!" the others said.

"You won't run away again?"

"No—indeed we won't. Please do. Won't you?"

"Yes, with pleasure; but you mustn't forget your promise, you know."

We said we wouldn't, and he went to a puddle and came back with water in a cup which he had made out of a leaf, and blew upon it and threw it out, and it was a lump of ice the shape of the cup. We were astonished and charmed, but not afraid any more; we were very glad to be there, and asked him to go on and do some more things. And he did. He said he would give us any kind of fruit we liked, whether it was in season or not. We all spoke at once;

"Orange!"

"Apple!"

"Grapes!"

"They are in your pockets," he said, and it was true. And

they were of the best, too, and we ate them and wished we
had more, though none of us said so.

"You will find them where those came from," he said, "and
everything else your appetites call for; and you need not
name the thing you wish; as long as I am with you, you
have only to wish and find."

And he said true. There was never anything so wonderful
and so interesting. Bread, cakes, sweets, nuts—whatever one
wanted, it was there. He ate nothing himself, but sat and
chatted, and did one curious thing after another to amuse us.
He made a tiny toy squirrel out of clay, and it ran up a
tree and sat on a limb overhead and barked down at us.
Then he made a dog that was not much larger than a mouse,
and it treed the squirrel and danced about the tree, excited
and barking, and was as alive as any dog could be. It frightened the squirrel from tree to tree and followed it up until
both were out of sight in the forest. He made birds out of
clay and set them free, and they flew away, singing.

At last I made bold to ask him to tell us who he was.

"An angel," he said, quite simply, and set another bird
free and clapped his hands and made it fly away.

A kind of awe fell upon us when we heard him say that,
and we were afraid again; but he said we need not be troubled, there was no occasion for us to be afraid of an angel,
and he liked us, anyway. He went on chatting as simply and
unaffectedly as ever; and while he talked he made a crowd
of little men and women the size of your finger, and they
went diligently to work and cleared and leveled off a space
a couple of yards square in the grass and began to build a
cunning little castle in it, the women mixing the mortar and
carrying it up the scaffoldings in pails on their heads, just as
our work-women have always done, and the men laying the
courses of masonry—five hundred of these toy people swarming briskly about and working diligently and wiping the sweat
off their faces as natural as life. In the absorbing interest of

watching those five hundred little people make the castle grow step by step and course by course, and take shape and symmetry, that feeling and awe soon passed away and we were quite comfortable and at home again. We asked if we might make some people, and he said yes, and told Seppi to make some cannon for the walls, and told Nikolaus to make some halberdiers, with breastplates and greaves and helmets, and I was to make some cavalry, with horses, and in allotting these tasks he called us by our names, but did not say how he knew them. Then Seppi asked him what his own name was, and he said, tranquilly, "Satan," and held out a chip and caught a little woman on it who was falling from the scaffolding and put her back where she belonged, and said, "She is an idiot to step backward like that and not notice what she is about."

It caught us suddenly, that name did, and our work dropped out of our hands and broke to pieces—a cannon, a halberdier, and a horse. Satan laughed, and asked what was the matter. I said, "Nothing, only it seemed a strange name for an angel." He asked why.

"Because it's—it's—well, it's his name, you know."

"Yes—he is my uncle."

He said it placidly, but it took our breath for a moment and made our hearts beat. He did not seem to notice that, but mended our halberdiers and things with a touch, handing them to us finished, and said, "Don't you remember?—he was an angel himself, once."

"Yes—it's true," said Seppi; "I didn't think of that."

"Before the Fall he was blameless."

"Yes," said Nikolaus, "he was without sin."

"It is a good family—ours," said Satan; "there is not a better. He is the only member of it that has ever sinned."

I should not be able to make any one understand how exciting it all was. You know that kind of quiver that trembles around through you when you are seeing something so strange and enchanting and wonderful that it is just a fearful joy to be alive and look at it; and you know how you gaze, and your lips turn dry and your breath comes short, but you wouldn't be anywhere but there, not for the world. I was bursting to ask one question—I had it on my tongue's end and could hardly hold it back—but I was ashamed to ask it; it might be a rudeness. Satan set an ox down that he had been making, and smiled up at me and said:

"It wouldn't be a rudeness, and I should forgive it if it was. Have I seen him? Millions of times. From the time that I was a little child a thousand years old I was his second favorite among the nursery angels of our blood and lineage—to use a human phrase—yes, from that time until the Fall, eight thousand years, measured as you count time."

"Eight—thousand!"

"Yes." He turned to Seppi, and went on as if answering something that was in Seppi's mind: "Why, naturally I look like a boy, for that is what I am. With us what you call time is a spacious thing; it takes a long stretch of it to grow an angel to full age." There was a question in my mind, and he turned to me and answered it, "I am sixteen thousand years old—counting as you count." Then he turned to Nikolaus and said: "No, the Fall did not affect me nor the rest of the relationship. It was only he that I was named for who ate of the fruit of the tree and then beguiled the man and the woman with it. We others are still ignorant of sin; we are not able to commit it; we are without blemish, and shall abide in that estate always. We—" Two of the little workmen were quarreling, and in buzzing little bumblebee voices they were cursing and swearing at each other; now came blows and blood; then they locked themselves together in a life-and-death struggle. Satan reached out his hand and crushed the life out of them with his fingers, threw them away, wiped the red from his fingers on his handkerchief, and went on talking where he had left off: "We cannot do wrong;

neither have we any disposition to do it, for we do not know
what it is."

It seemed a strange speech, in the circumstances, but we
barely noticed that, we were so shocked and grieved at the
wanton murder he had committed—for murder it was, that
was its true name, and it was without palliation or excuse,
for the men had not wronged him in any way. It made us
miserable, for we loved him, and had thought him so noble
and so beautiful and gracious, and had honestly believed he
was an angel; and to have him do this cruel thing—ah, it
lowered him so, and we had had such pride in him. He went
right on talking, just as if nothing had happened, telling
about his travels, and the interesting things he had seen in
the big worlds of our solar systems and of other solar systems
far away in the remotenesses of space, and about the customs
of the immortals that inhabit them, somehow fascinating us,
enchanting us, charming us in spite of the pitiful scene that
was now under our eyes, for the wives of the little dead men
had found the crushed and shapeless bodies and were crying
over them, and sobbing and lamenting, and a priest was
kneeling there with his hands crossed upon his breast, praying; and crowds and crowds of pitying friends were massed
about them, reverently uncovered, with their bare heads
bowed, and many with the tears running down—a scene which
Satan paid no attention to until the small noise of the weeping and praying began to annoy him, then he reached out
and took the heavy board seat out of our swing and brought
it down and mashed all those people into the earth just
as if they had been flies, and went on talking just the same.

An angel, and kill a priest! An angel who did not know
how to do wrong, and yet destroys in cold blood hundreds
of helpless poor men and women who had never done him
any harm! It made us sick to see that awful deed, and to
think that none of those poor creatures was prepared except
the priest, for none of them had ever heard a mass or seen a

church. And we were witnesses; we had seen these murders done and it was our duty to tell, and let the law take
its course.

But he went on talking right along, and worked his en-
chantments upon us again with that fatal music of his voice.
He made us forget everything; we could only listen to him,
and love him, and be his slaves, to do with us as he would.
He made us drunk with the joy of being with him, and
of looking into the heaven of his eyes, and of feeling the
ecstasy that thrilled along our veins from the touch of his
hand.

3

The Stranger had seen everything, he had been everywhere, he knew everything, and he forgot nothing. What another must study, he learned at a glance; there were no
difficulties for him. And he made things live before you when
he told about them. He saw the world made; he saw Adam
created; he saw Samson surge against the pillars and bring
the temple down in ruins about him; he saw Cæsar's death;
he told of the daily life in heaven; he had seen the damned
writhing in the red waves of hell; and he made us see all
these things, and it was as if we were on the spot and looking at them with our own eyes. And we felt them, too, but
there was no sign that they were anything to him beyond
mere entertainments. Those visions of hell, those poor babes
and women and girls and lads and men shrieking and sup-
plicating in anguish—why, we could hardly bear it, but he
was as bland about it as if it had been so many imitation
rats in an artificial fire.

And always when he was talking about men and women
here on the earth and their doings—even their grandest and
sublimest—we were secretly ashamed, for his manner showed
that to him they and their doings were of paltry poor con-

sequence; often you would think he was talking about flies,
if you didn't know. Once he even said, in so many words,
that our people down here were quite interesting to him,
notwithstanding they were so dull and ignorant and trivial
and conceited, and so diseased and rickety, and such a
shabby, poor, worthless lot all around. He said it in a quite
matter-of-course way and without bitterness, just as a person
might talk about bricks or manure or any other thing that
was of no consequence and hadn't feelings. I could see he
meant no offense, but in my thoughts I set it down as not
very good manners.

"Manners!" he said. "Why, it is merely the truth, and truth
is good manners; manners are a fiction. The castle is done.
Do you like it?"

Any one would have been obliged to like it. It was lovely
to look at, it was so shapely and fine, and so cunningly perfect in all its particulars, even to the little flags waving
from the turrets. Satan said we must put the artillery in
place now, and station the halberdiers and display the cavalry. Our men and horses were a spectacle to see, they were
so little like what they were intended for; for, of course, we
had no art in making such things. Satan said they were the
worst he had seen; and when he touched them and made
them alive, it was just ridiculous the way they acted, on
account of their legs not being of uniform lengths. They
reeled and sprawled around as if they were drunk, and en-
dangered everybody's lives around them, and finally fell over
and lay helpless and kicking. It made us all laugh, though
it was a shameful thing to see. The guns were charged with
dirt, to fire a salute, but they were so crooked and so badly
made that they all burst when they went off, and killed
some of the gunners and crippled the others. Satan said we
would have a storm now, and an earthquake, if we liked, but
we must stand off a piece, out of danger. We wanted to
call the people away, too, but he said never mind them;

they were of no consequence, and we could make more, some time or other, if we needed them.

A small storm-cloud began to settle down black over the castle, and the miniature lightning and thunder began to play, and the ground to quiver, and the wind to pipe and wheeze, and the rain to fall, and all the people flocked into the castle for shelter. The cloud settled down blacker and blacker, and one could see the castle only dimly through it; the lightning blazed out flash upon flash and pierced the castle and set it on fire, and the flames shone out red and fierce through the cloud, and the people came flying out, shrieking, but Satan brushed them back, paying no attention to our begging and crying and imploring; and in the midst of the howling of the wind and volleying of the thunder the magazine blew up, the earthquake rent the ground wide, and the castle's wreck and ruin tumbled into the chasm, which swallowed it from sight, and closed upon it, with all that innocent life, not one of the five hundred poor creatures escaping. Our hearts were broken; we could not keep from crying.

"Don't cry," Satan said; "they were of no value."

"But they are gone to hell!"

"Oh, it is no matter; we can make plenty more."

It was of no use to try to move him; evidently he was wholly without feeling, and could not understand. He was full of bubbling spirits, and as gay as if this were a wedding instead of a fiendish massacre. And he was bent on making us feel as he did, and of course his magic accomplished his desire. It was no trouble to him; he did whatever he pleased with us. In a little while we were dancing on that grave, and he was playing to us on a strange, sweet instrument which he took out of his pocket; and the music— but there is no music like that, unless perhaps in heaven, and that was where he brought it from, he said. It made one mad, for pleasure; and we could not take our eyes from him, and the looks that went out of our eyes came from our hearts, and their dumb speech was worship. He brought the dance from heaven, too, and the bliss of paradise was in it.

Presently he said he must go away on an errand. But we could not bear the thought of it, and clung to him, and pleaded with him to stay; and that pleased him, and he said so, and said he would not go yet, but would wait a little while and we would sit down and talk a few minutes longer; and he told us Satan was only his real name, and he was to be known by it to us alone, but he had chosen another one to be called by in the presence of others; just a common one, such as people have—Philip Traum.

It sounded so odd and mean for such a being! But it was his decision, and we said nothing; his decision was sufficient.

We had seen wonders this day; and my thoughts began to run on the pleasure it would be to tell them when I got home, but he noticed those thoughts, and said:

"No, all these matters are a secret among us four. I do not mind your trying to tell them, if you like, but I will protect your tongues, and nothing of the secret will escape from them."

It was a disappointment, but it couldn't be helped, and it cost us a sigh or two. We talked pleasantly along, and he was always reading our thoughts and responding to them, and it seemed to me that this was the most wonderful of all the things he did, but he interrupted my musings and said:

"No, it would be wonderful for you, but it is not wonderful for me. I am not limited like you. I am not subject to human conditions. I can measure and understand your human weaknesses, for I have studied them; but I have none of them. My flesh is not real, although it would seem firm to your touch; my clothes are not real; I am a spirit. Father

Peter is coming." We looked around, but did not see any one. "He is not in sight yet, but you will see him presently."

"Do you know him, Satan?"

"No."

"Won't you talk with him when he comes? He is not ignorant and dull, like us, and he would so like to talk with you. Will you?"

"Another time, yes, but not now. I must go on my errand after a little. There he is now; you can see him. Sit still, and don't say anything."

We looked up and saw Father Peter approaching through the chestnuts. We three were sitting together in the grass, and Satan sat in front of us in the path. Father Peter came slowly along with his head down, thinking, and stopped within a couple of yards of us and took off his hat and got out his silk handkerchief, and stood there mopping his face and looking as if he were going to speak to us, but he didn't. Presently he muttered, "I can't think what brought me here; it seems as if I were in my study a minute ago—but I suppose I have been dreaming along for an hour and have come all this stretch without noticing; for I am not myself in these troubled days." Then he went mumbling along to himself and walked straight through Satan, just as if nothing were there. It made us catch our breath to see it. We had the impulse to cry out, the way you nearly always do when a startling thing happens, but something mysteriously restrained us and we remained quiet, only breathing fast. Then the trees hid Father Peter after a little, and Satan said:

"It is as I told you—I am only a spirit."

"Yes, one perceives it now," said Nikolaus, "but we are not spirits. It is plain he did not see you, but were we invisible, too? He looked at us, but he didn't seem to see us."

"No, none of us was visible to him, for I wished it so."

It seemed almost too good to be true, that we were actually

seeing these romantic and wonderful things, and that it was not a dream. And there he sat, looking just like anybody—so natural and simple and charming, and chatting along again the same as ever, and—well, words cannot make you understand what we felt. It was an ecstasy; and an ecstasy is a thing that will not go into words; it feels like music, and one cannot tell about music so that another person can get the feeling of it. He was back in the old ages once more now, and making them live before us. He had seen so much, so much! It was just a wonder to look at him and try to think how it must seem to have such experience behind one.

But it made you seem sorrowfully trivial, and the creature of a day, and such a short and paltry day, too. And he didn't say anything to raise up your drooping pride—no, not a word. He always spoke of men in the same old indifferent way—just as one speaks of bricks and manure-piles and such things; you could see that they were of no consequence to him, one way or the other. He didn't mean to hurt us, you could see that; just as we don't mean to insult a brick when we disparage it; a brick's emotions are nothing to us; it never occurs to us to think whether it has any or not.

Once when he was bunching the most illustrious kings and conquerors and poets and prophets and pirates and beggars together—just a brick-pile—I was shamed into putting in a word for man, and asked him why he made so much difference between men and himself. He had to struggle with that a moment; he didn't seem to understand how I could ask such a strange question. Then he said:

"The difference between man and me? The difference between a mortal and an immortal? between a cloud and a spirit?" He picked up a wood-louse that was creeping along a piece of bark: "What is the difference between Cæsar and this?"

I said, "One cannot compare things which by their nature and by the interval between them are not comparable."

"You have answered your own question," he said. "I will expand it. Man is made of dirt—I saw him made. I am not made of dirt. Man is a museum of diseases, a home of impurities; he comes to-day and is gone to-morrow; he begins as dirt and departs as stench; I am of the aristocracy of the Imperishables. And man has the *Moral Sense*. You understand? He has the *Moral Sense*. That would seem to be difference enough between us, all by itself."

He stopped there, as if that settled the matter. I was sorry, for at that time I had but a dim idea of what the Moral Sense was. I merely knew that we were proud of having it, and when he talked like that about it, it wounded me, and I felt as a girl feels who thinks her dearest finery is being admired and then overhears strangers making fun of it. For a while we were all silent, and I, for one, was depressed. Then Satan began to chat again, and soon he was sparkling along in such a cheerful and vivacious vein that my spirits rose once more. He told some very cunning things that put us in a gale of laughter; and when he was telling about the time that Samson tied the torches to the foxes' tails and set them loose in the Philistines' corn, and Samson sitting on the fence slapping his thighs and laughing, with the tears running down his cheeks, and lost his balance and fell off the fence, the memory of that picture got him to laughing, too, and we did have a most lovely and jolly time. By and by he said:

"I am going on my errand now."

"Don't!" we all said. "Don't go; stay with us. You won't come back."

"Yes, I will; I give you my word."

"When? To-night? Say when."

"It won't be long. You will see."

"We like you."

"And I you. And as a proof of it I will show you something fine to see. Usually when I go I merely vanish; but now I will dissolve myself and let you see me do it."

He stood up, and it was quickly finished. He thinned away and thinned away until he was a soap-bubble, except that he kept his shape. You could see the bushes through him as clearly as you see things through a soap-bubble, and all over him played and flashed the delicate iridescent colors of the bubble, and along with them was that thing shaped like a window-sash which you always see on the globe of the bubble. You have seen a bubble strike the carpet and lightly bound along two or three times before it bursts. He did that. He sprang—touched the grass—bounded—floated along—touched again—and so on, and presently exploded—puff! and in his place was vacancy.

It was a strange and beautiful thing to see. We did not say anything, but sat wondering and dreaming and blinking; and finally Seppi roused up and said, mournfully sighing:

"I suppose none of it has happened."

Nikolaus sighed and said about the same.

I was miserable to hear them say it, for it was the same cold fear that was in my own mind. Then we saw poor old Father Peter wandering along back, with his head bent down, searching the ground. When he was pretty close to us he looked up and saw us, and said, "How long have you been here, boys?"

"A little while, Father."

"Then it is since I came by, and maybe you can help me. Did you come up by the path?"

"Yes, Father."

"That is good. I came the same way. I have lost my wallet. There wasn't much in it, but a very little is much to me, for it was all I had. I suppose you haven't seen anything of it?"

"No, Father, but we will help you hunt."

"It is what I was going to ask you. Why, here it is!"

We hadn't noticed it; yet there it lay, right where Satan stood when he began to melt—if he did melt and it wasn't a delusion. Father Peter picked it up and looked very much surprised.

"It is mine," he said, "but not the contents. This is fat; mine was flat; mine was light; this is heavy." He opened it; it was stuffed as full as it could hold with gold coins. He let us gaze our fill; and of course we did gaze, for we had never seen so much money at one time before. All our mouths came open to say "Satan did it!" but nothing came out. There it was, you see—we couldn't tell what Satan didn't want told; he had said so himself.

"Boys, did you do this?"

It made us laugh. And it made him laugh, too, as soon as he thought what a foolish question it was.

"Who has been here?"

Our mouths came open to answer, but stood so for a moment, because we couldn't say "Nobody," for it wouldn't be true, and the right word didn't seem to come; then I thought of the right one, and said it:

"Not a human being."

"That is so," said the others, and let their mouths go shut.

"It is not so," said Father Peter, and looked at us very severely. "I came by here a while ago, and there was no one here, but that is nothing; some one has been here since. I don't mean to say that the person didn't pass here before you came, and I don't mean to say you saw him, but some one did pass, that I know. On your honor—you saw no one?"

"Not a human being."

"That is sufficient; I know you are telling me the truth."

He began to count the money on the path, we on our knees eagerly helping to stack it in little piles.

"It's eleven hundred ducats odd!" he said. "Oh dear! if it were only mine—and I need it so!" and his voice broke and his lips quivered.

"It is yours, sir!" we all cried out at once, "every heller!"

"No—it isn't mine. Only four ducats are mine; the rest
. . . !" He fell to dreaming, poor old soul, and caressing
some of the coins in his hands, and forgot where he was,
sitting there on his heels with his old gray head bare; it was
pitiful to see. "No," he said, waking up, "it isn't mine. I
can't account for it. I think some enemy . . . it must be a trap."

Nikolaus said: "Father Peter, with the exception of the astrologer you haven't a real enemy in the village—nor Marget,
either. And not even a half-enemy that's rich enough to
chance eleven hundred ducats to do you a mean turn. I'll ask
you if that's so or not?"

He couldn't get around that argument, and it cheered him
up. "But it isn't mine, you see—it isn't mine, in any case."

He said it in a wistful way, like a person that wouldn't be
sorry, but glad, if anybody would contradict him.

"It is yours, Father Peter, and we are witness to it. Aren't
we, boys?"

"Yes, we are—and we'll stand by it, too."

"Bless your hearts, you do almost persuade me; you do, indeed. If I had only a hundred-odd ducats of it! The house is
mortgaged for it, and we've no home for our heads if we
don't pay to-morrow. And that four ducats is all we've got
in the—"

"It's yours, every bit of it, and you've got to take it—we
are bail that it's all right. Aren't we, Theodor? Aren't we,
Seppi?"

We two said yes, and Nikolaus stuffed the money back into
the shabby old wallet and made the owner take it. So he said
he would use two hundred of it, for his house was good
enough security for that, and would put the rest at interest
till the rightful owner came for it; and on our side we must
sign a paper showing how he got the money—a paper to show
to the villagers as proof that he had not got out of his troubles
dishonestly.

4

It made immense talk next day, when Father Peter paid
Solomon Isaacs in gold and left the rest of the money with
him at interest. Also, there was a pleasant change; many
people called at the house to congratulate him, and a number
of cool old friends became kind and friendly again; and, to
top all, Marget was invited to a party.

And there was no mystery; Father Peter told the whole circumstance just as it happened, and said he could not account for it, only it was the plain hand of Providence, so far
as he could see.

One or two shook their heads and said privately it looked
more like the hand of Satan; and really that seemed a surprisingly good guess for ignorant people like that. Some came
slyly buzzing around and tried to coax us boys to come out
and "tell the truth;" and promised they wouldn't ever tell,
but only wanted to know for their own satisfaction, because
the whole thing was so curious. They even wanted to buy
the secret, and pay money for it; and if we could have invented something that would answer—but we couldn't; we
hadn't the ingenuity, so we had to let the chance go by, and
it was a pity.

We carried that secret around without any trouble, but
the other one, the big one, the splendid one, burned the very
vitals of us, it was so hot to get out and we so hot to let
it out and astonish people with it. But we had to keep it
in; in fact, it kept itself in. Satan said it would, and it
did. We went off every day and got to ourselves in the woods
so that we could talk about Satan, and really that was the
only subject we thought of or cared anything about; and day
and night we watched for him and hoped he would come, and
we got more and more impatient all the time. We hadn't any
interest in the other boys any more, and wouldn't take part

in their games and enterprises. They seemed so tame, after
Satan; and their doings so trifling and commonplace after
his adventures in antiquity and the constellations, and his
miracles and meltings and explosions, and all that.

During the first day we were in a state of anxiety on
account of one thing, and we kept going to Father Peter's
house on one pretext or another to keep track of it. That
was the gold coin; we were afraid it would crumble and turn
to dust, like fairy money. If it did— But it didn't. At the
end of the day no complaint had been made about it, so after
that we were satisfied that it was real gold, and dropped
the anxiety out of our minds.

There was a question which we wanted to ask Father
Peter, and finally we went there the second evening, a
little diffidently, after drawing straws, and I asked it as
casually as I could, though it did not sound as casual as
I wanted, because I didn't know how:

"What is the Moral Sense, sir?"

He looked down, surprised, over his great spectacles, and
said, "Why, it is the faculty which enables us to distinguish
good from evil."

It threw some light, but not a glare, and I was a little
disappointed, also to some degree embarrassed. He was waiting for me to go on, so, in default of anything else to say,
I asked, "Is it valuable?"

"Valuable? Heavens! lad, it is the one thing that lifts man
above the beasts that perish and makes him heir to immortality!"

This did not remind me of anything further to say, so
I got out, with the other boys, and we went away with that
indefinite sense you have often had of being filled but
not fatted. They wanted me to explain, but I was tired.

We passed out through the parlor, and there was Marget
at the spinnet teaching Marie Lueger. So one of the deserting
pupils was back; and an influential one, too; the others

would follow. Marget jumped up and ran and thanked us
again, with tears in her eyes—this was the third time—for
saving her and her uncle from being turned into the street,
and we told her again we hadn't done it; but that was her
way, she never could be grateful enough for anything a
person did for her; so we let her have her say. And as we
passed through the garden, there was Wilhelm Meidling
sitting there waiting, for it was getting toward the edge of
the evening, and he would be asking Marget to take a walk
along the river with him when she was done with the lesson.
He was a young lawyer, and succeeding fairly well and
working his way along, little by little. He was very fond of
Marget, and she of him. He had not deserted along with the
others, but had stood his ground all through. His faithfulness
was not lost on Marget and her uncle. He hadn't so very
much talent, but he was handsome and good, and these are a
kind of talents themselves and help along. He asked us how
the lesson was getting along, and we told him it was about
done. And maybe it was so; we didn't know anything about
it, but we judged it would please him, and it did, and didn't
cost us anything.

5

On the fourth day comes the astrologer from his crumbling
old tower up the valley, where he had heard the news, I
reckon. He had a private talk with us, and we told him what
we could, for we were mightily in dread of him. He sat
there studying and studying awhile to himself; then he
asked:

"How many ducats did you say?"

"Eleven hundred and seven, sir."

Then he said, as if he were talking to himself: "It is ver-y
singular. Yes . . . very strange. A curious coincidence." Then
he began to ask questions, and went over the whole ground

from the beginning, we answering. By and by he said:
"Eleven hundred and six ducats. It is a large sum."

"Seven," said Seppi, correcting him.

"Oh, seven, was it? Of course a ducat more or less isn't
of consequence, but you said eleven hundred and six before."

It would not have been safe for us to say he was mistaken, but we knew he was. Nikolaus said, "We ask pardon
for the mistake, but we meant to say seven."

"Oh, it is no matter, lad; it was merely that I noticed the
discrepancy. It is several days, and you cannot be expected
to remember precisely. One is apt to be inexact when there
is no particular circumstance to impress the count upon the
memory."

"But there was one, sir," said Seppi, eagerly.

"What was it, my son?" asked the astrologer, indifferently.

"First, we all counted the piles of coin, each in turn, and
all made it the same—eleven hundred and six. But I had
slipped one out, for fun, when the count began, and now I
slipped it back and said, 'I think there is a mistake—there
are eleven hundred and seven; let us count again.' We did,
and of course I was right. They were astonished; then I told
how it came about."

The astrologer asked us if this was so, and we said it was.

"That settles it," he said. "I know the thief now. Lads,
the money was stolen."

Then he went away, leaving us very much troubled, and
wondering what he could mean. In about an hour we found
out; for by that time it was all over the village that Father
Peter had been arrested for stealing a great sum of money
from the astrologer. Everybody's tongue was loose and going.
Many said it was not in Father Peter's character and must
be a mistake; but the others shook their heads and said misery
and want could drive a suffering man to almost anything.
About one detail there were no differences; all agreed that

Father Peter's account of how the money came into his hands
was just about unbelievable—it had such an impossible look.
They said it might have come into the astrologer's hands in
some such way, but into Father Peter's, never! Our characters
began to suffer now. We were Father Peter's only witnesses;
how much did he probably pay us to back up his fantastic
tale? People talked that kind of talk to us pretty freely and
frankly, and were full of scoffings when we begged them to
believe really we had told only the truth. Our parents were
harder on us than any one else. Our fathers said we were
disgracing our families, and they commanded us to purge
ourselves of our lie, and there was no limit to their anger
when we continued to say we had spoken true. Our mothers
cried over us and begged us to give back our bribe and get
back our honest names and save our families from shame,
and come out and honorably confess. And at last we were
so worried and harassed that we tried to tell the whole
thing, Satan and all—but no, it wouldn't come out. We were
hoping and longing all the time that Satan would come and
help us out of our trouble, but there was no sign of him.

Within an hour after the astrologer's talk with us, Father
Peter was in prison and the money sealed up and in the
hands of the officers of the law. The money was in a bag, and
Solomon Isaacs said he had not touched it since he had
counted it; his oath was taken that it was the same money,
and that the amount was eleven hundred and seven ducats.
Father Peter claimed trial by the ecclesiastical court, but our
other priest, Father Adolf, said an ecclesiastical court hadn't
jurisdiction over a suspended priest. The bishop upheld him.
That settled it; the case would go to trial in the civil court.
The court would not sit for some time to come. Wilhelm
Meidling would be Father Peter's lawyer and do the best he
could, of course, but he told us privately that a weak case
on his side and all the power and prejudice on the other made
the outlook bad.

So Marget's new happiness died a quick death. No friends came to condole with her, and none were expected; an unsigned note withdrew her invitation to the party. There would be no scholars to take lessons. How could she support herself? She could remain in the house, for the mortgage was paid off, though the government and not poor Solomon Isaacs had the mortgage-money in its grip for the present. Old Ursula, who was cook, chambermaid, housekeeper, laundress, and everything else for Father Peter, and had been Marget's nurse in earlier years, said God would provide. But she said that from habit, for she was a good Christian. She meant to help in the providing, to make sure, if she could find a way.

We boys wanted to go and see Marget and show friendliness for her, but our parents were afraid of offending the community and wouldn't let us. The astrologer was going around inflaming everybody against Father Peter, and saying he was an abandoned thief and had stolen eleven hundred and seven gold ducats from him. He said he knew he was a thief from that fact, for it was exactly the sum he had lost and which Father Peter pretended he had "found."

In the afternoon of the fourth day after the catastrophe old Ursula appeared at our house and asked for some washing to do, and begged my mother to keep this secret, to save Marget's pride, who would stop this project if she found it out, yet Marget had not enough to eat and was growing weak. Ursula was growing weak herself, and showed it; and she ate of the food that was offered her like a starving person, but could not be persuaded to carry any home, for Marget would not eat charity food. She took some clothes down to the stream to wash them, but we saw from the window that handling the bat was too much for her strength; so she was called back and a trifle of money offered her, which she was afraid to take lest Marget should suspect; then she took it, saying she would explain that she found it in the road.

To keep it from being a lie and damning her soul, she got me to drop it while she watched; then she went along by there and found it, and exclaimed with surprise and joy, and picked it up and went her way. Like the rest of the village, she could tell every-day lies fast enough and without taking any precautions against fire and brimstone on their account; but this was a new kind of lie, and it had a dangerous look because she hadn't had any practice in it. After a week's practice it wouldn't have given her any trouble. It is the way we are made.

I was in trouble, for how would Marget live? Ursula could not find a coin in the road every day—perhaps not even a second one. And I was ashamed, too, for not having been near Marget, and she so in need of friends; but that was my parents' fault, not mine, and I couldn't help it.

I was walking along the path, feeling very downhearted, when a most cherry and tingling freshening-up sensation went rippling through me, and I was too glad for any words, for I knew by that sign that Satan was by. I had noticed it before. Next moment he was alongside of me and I was telling him all my trouble and what had been happening to Marget and her uncle. While we were talking we turned a curve and saw old Ursula resting in the shade of a tree, and she had a lean stray kitten in her lap and was petting it. I asked her where she got it, and she said it came out of the woods and followed her; and she said it probably hadn't any mother or any friends and she was going to take it home and take care of it. Satan said:

"I understand you are very poor. Why do you want to add another mouth to feed? Why don't you give it to some rich person?"

Ursula bridled at this and said: "Perhaps you would like to have it. You must be rich, with your fine clothes and quality airs." Then she sniffed and said: "Give it to the rich—the idea! The rich don't care for anybody but them-

selves; it's only the poor that have feeling for the poor, and
help them. The poor and God. God will provide for this kitten."

"What makes you think so?"

Ursula's eyes snapped with anger. "Because I know it!"
she said. "Not a sparrow falls to the ground without His
seeing it."

"But it falls, just the same. What good is seeing it fall?"

Old Ursula's jaws worked, but she could not get any word
out for the moment, she was so horrified. When she got her
tongue, she stormed out, "Go about your business, you
puppy, or I will take a stick to you!"

I could not speak, I was so scared. I knew that with his
notions about the human race Satan would consider it a
matter of no consequence to strike her dead, there being
"plenty more;" but my tongue stood still, I could give her no
warning. But nothing happened; Satan remained tranquil
—tranquil and indifferent. I suppose he could not be insulted
by Ursula any more than the king could be insulted by a
tumble-bug. The old woman jumped to her feet when she
made her remark, and did it as briskly as a young girl. It had
been many years since she had done the like of that. That
was Satan's influence; he was a fresh breeze to the weak and
the sick, wherever he came. His presence affected even the
lean kitten, and it skipped to the ground and began to chase
a leaf. This surprised Urusla, and she stood looking at the
creature and nodding her head wonderingly, her anger quite
forgotten.

"What's come over it?" she said. "Awhile ago it could
hardly walk."

"You have not seen a kitten of that breed before," said
Satan.

Ursula was not proposing to be friendly with the mocking
stranger, and she gave him an ungentle look and retorted:
"Who asked you to come here and pester me, I'd like to

know? And what do you know about what I've seen and what I haven't seen?"

"You haven't seen a kitten with the hair-spines on its tongue pointing to the front, have you?"

"No—nor you, either."

"Well, examine this one and see."

Ursula was become pretty spry, but the kitten was spryer, and she could not catch it, and had to give it up. Then Satan said:

"Give it a name and maybe it will come."

Ursula tried several names, but the kitten was not interested.

"Call it Agnes. Try that."

The creature answered to the name and came. Ursula examined its tongue. "Upon my word, it's true!" she said. "I have not seen this kind of a cat before. Is it yours?"

"No."

"Then how did you know its name so pat?"

"Because all cats of that breed are named Agnes; they will not answer to any other."

Ursula was impressed. "It is the most wonderful thing!" Then a shadow of trouble came into her face, for her superstitions were aroused, and she reluctantly put the creature down, saying: "I suppose I must let it go; I am not afraid— no, not exactly that, though the priest—well, I've heard people—indeed, many people . . . And, besides, it is quite well now and can take care of itself." She sighed, and turned to go, murmuring: "It is such a pretty one, too, and would be such company—and the house is so sad and lonesome these troubled days . . . Miss Marget so mournful and just a shadow, and the old master shut up in jail."

"It seems a pity not to keep it," said Satan.

Ursula turned quickly—just as if she were hoping some one would encourage her.

"Why?" she asked, wistfully.

"Because this breed brings luck."

"Does it? Is it true? Young man, do you know it to be true? How does it bring luck?"

"Well, it brings money, anyway."

Ursula looked disappointed. "Money? A cat bring money? The idea! You could never sell it here; people do not buy cats here; one can't even give them away." She turned to go.

"I don't mean sell it. I mean have an income from it. This kind is called the Lucky Cat. Its owner finds four silver groschen in his pocket every morning."

I saw the indignation rising in the old woman's face. She was insulted. This boy was making fun of her. That was her thought. She thrust her hands into her pockets and straightened up to give him a piece of her mind. Her temper was all up, and hot. Her mouth came open and let out three words of a bitter sentence, then it fell silent, and the anger in her face turned to surprise or wonder or fear, or something, and she slowly brought out her hands from her pockets and opened them and held them so. In one was my piece of money, in the other lay four silver groschen. She gazed a little while, perhaps to see if the groschen would vanish away; then she said, fervently:

"It's true—it's true—and I'm ashamed and beg forgiveness, O dear master and benefactor!" And she ran to Satan and kissed his hand, over and over again, according to the Austrian custom.

In her heart she probably believed it was a witch-cat and an agent of the Devil; but no matter, it was all the more certain to be able to keep its contract and furnish a daily good living for the family, for in matters of finance even the piousest of our peasants would have more confidence in an arrangement with the Devil than with an archangel. Ursula started homeward, with Agnes in her arms, and I said I wished I had her privilege of seeing Marget.

Then I caught my breath, for we were there. There in the parlor, and Marget standing looking at us, astonished. She was feeble and pale, but I knew that those conditions would not last in Satan's atmosphere, and it turned out so. I introduced Satan—that is, Philip Traum—and we sat down and talked. There was no constraint. We were simple folk, in our village, and when a stranger was a pleasant person we were soon friends. Marget wondered how we got in without her hearing us. Traum said the door was open, and we walked in and waited until she should turn around and greet us. This was not true; no door was open; we entered through the walls or the roof or down the chimney, or somehow; but no matter, what Satan wished a person to believe, the person was sure to believe, and so Marget was quite satisfied with that explanation. And then the main part of her mind was on Traum, anyway; she couldn't keep her eyes off him, he was so beautiful. That gratified me, and made me proud. I hoped he would show off some, but he didn't. He seemed only interested in being friendly and telling lies. He said he was an orphan. That made Marget pity him. The water came into her eyes. He said he had never known his mamma; she passed away while he was a young thing; and said his papa was in shattered health, and had no property to speak of— in fact, none of any earthly value—but he had an uncle in business down in the tropics, and he was very well off and had a monopoly, and it was from this uncle that he drew his support. The very mention of a kind uncle was enough to remind Marget of her own, and her eyes filled again. She said she hoped their two uncles would meet, some day. It made me shudder. Philip said he hoped so, too; and that made me shudder again.

"Maybe they will," said Marget. "Does your uncle travel much?"

"Oh yes, he goes all about; he has business everywhere."

And so they went on chatting, and poor Marget forgot

her sorrow for one little while, anyway. It was probably the only really bright and cheery hour she had known lately. I saw she liked Philip, and I knew she would. And when he told her he was studying for the ministry I could see that she liked him better than ever. And then, when he promised to get her admitted to the jail so that she could see her uncle, that was the capstone. He said he would give the guards a little present, and she must always go in the evening after dark, and say nothing, "but just show this paper and pass in, and show it again when you come out"—and he scribbled some queer marks on the paper and gave it to her, and she was ever so thankful, and right away was in a fever for the sun to go down; for in that old, cruel time prisoners were not allowed to see their friends, and sometimes they spent years in the jails without ever seeing a friendly face. I judged that the marks on the paper were an enchantment, and that the guards would not know what they were doing, nor have any memory of it afterward; and that was indeed the way of it. Ursula put her head in at the door now and said:

"Supper's ready, miss." Then she saw us and looked frightened, and motioned me to come to her, which I did, and she asked if we had told about the cat. I said no, and she was relieved, and said please don't; for if Miss Marget knew, she would think it was an unholy cat and would send for a priest and have its gifts all purified out of it, and then there wouldn't be any more dividends. So I said we wouldn't tell, and she was satisfied. Then I was beginning to say good-by to Marget, but Satan interrupted and said, ever so politely —well, I don't remember just the words, but anyway he as good as invited himself to supper, and me, too. Of course Marget was miserably embarrassed, for she had no reason to suppose there would be half enough for a sick bird. Ursula heard him, and she came straight into the room, not a bit pleased. At first she was astonished to see Marget looking so fresh and rosy, and said so; then she spoke up in her native tongue, which was Bohemian, and said—as I learned afterward—"Send him away, Miss Marget; there's not victuals enough."

Before Marget could speak, Satan had the word, and was talking back to Ursula in her own language—which was a surprise to her, and for her mistress, too. He said, "Didn't I see you down the road awhile ago?"

"Yes, sir."

"Ah, that pleases me; I see you remember me." He stepped to her and whispered: "I told you it is Lucky Cat. Don't be troubled; it will provide."

That sponged the slate of Ursula's feelings clean of its anxieties, and a deep, financial joy shone in her eyes. The cat's value was augmenting. It was getting full time for Marget to take some sort of notice of Satan's invitation, and she did it in the best way, the honest way that was natural to her. She said she had little to offer, but that we were welcome if we would share it with her.

We had supper in the kitchen, and Ursula waited at table. A small fish was in the frying-pan, crisp and brown and tempting, and one could see that Marget was not expecting such respectable food as this. Ursula brought it, and Marget divided it between Satan and me, declining to take any of it herself; and was beginning to say she did not care for fish to-day, but she did not finish the remark. It was because she noticed that another fish had appeared in the pan. She looked surprised, but did not say anything. She probably meant to inquire of Ursula about this later. There were other surprises: flesh and game and wines and fruits—things which had been strangers in that house lately; but Marget made no exclamations, and now even looked unsurprised, which was Satan's influence, of course. Satan talked right along, and was entertaining, and made the time pass pleasantly and cheerfully; and although he told a good many

lies, it was no harm in him, for he was only an angel and did
not know any better. They do not know right from wrong; I
knew this, because I remembered what he had said about it.
He got on the good side of Ursula. He praised her to Marget,
confidentially, but speaking just loud enough for Ursula to
hear. He said she was a fine woman, and he hoped some day
to bring her and his uncle together. Very soon Ursula was
mincing and simpering around in a ridiculous girly way,
and smoothing out her gown and prinking at herself like a
foolish old hen, and all the time pretending she was not
hearing what Satan was saying. I was ashamed, for it showed
us to be what Satan considered us, a silly race and trivial.
Satan said his uncle entertained a great deal, and to have a
clever woman presiding over the festivities would double the
attractions of the place.

"But your uncle is a gentleman, isn't he?" asked Marget.

"Yes," said Satan indifferently; "some even call him a
Prince, out of compliment, but he is not bigoted; to him per-
sonal merit is everything, rank nothing."

My hand was hanging down by my chair; Agnes came
along and licked it; by this act a secret was revealed. I
started to say, "It is all a mistake; this is just a common, ordinary cat; the hair-needles on her tongue point inward,
not outward." But the words did not come, because they
couldn't. Satan smiled upon me, and I understood.

When it was dark Marget took food and wine and fruit,
in a basket, and hurried away to the jail, and Satan and
I walked toward my home. I was thinking to myself that I
should like to see what the inside of the jail was like; Satan
overheard the thought, and the next moment we were in the
jail. We were in the torture-chamber, Satan said. The rack
was there, and the other instruments, and there was a smoky
lantern or two hanging on the walls and helping to make the
place look dim and dreadful There were people there—and
executioners—but as they took no notice of us, it meant

that we were invisible. A young man lay bound, and Satan said he was suspected of being a heretic, and the executioners were about to inquire into it. They asked the man to confess to the charge, and he said he could not, for it was not true. Then they drove splinter after splinter under his nails, and he shrieked with the pain. Satan was not distrubed, but I could not endure it, and had to be whisked out of there. I was faint and sick, but the fresh air revived me, and we walked toward my home. I said it was a brutal thing.

"No, it was a human thing. You should not insult the brutes by such a misuse of that word; they have not deserved it," and he went on talking like that. "It is like your paltry race—always lying, always claiming virtues which it hasn't got, always denying them to the higher animals, which alone possess them. No brute ever does a cruel thing—that is the monopoly of those with the Moral Sense. When a brute inflicts pain he does it innocently; it is not wrong; for him there is no such thing as wrong. And he does not inflict pain for the pleasure of inflicting it—only man does that. Inspired by that mongrel Moral Sense of his! A sense whose function is to distinguish between right and wrong, with liberty to choose which of them he will do. Now what advantage can he get out of that? He is always choosing, and in nine cases out of ten he prefers the wrong. There shouldn't be any wrong; and without the Moral Sense there couldn't be any. And yet he is such an unreasoning creature that he is not able to perceive that the Moral Sense degrades him to the bottom layer of animated beings and is a shameful possession. Are you feeling better? Let me show you something."

6

In a moment we were in a French village. We walked through a great factory of some sort, where men and women and little children were toiling in heat and dirt and a fog of dust; and they were clothed in rags, and drooped at their work, for they were worn and half starved, and weak and drowsy. Satan said:

"It is some more Moral Sense. The proprietors are rich, and very holy; but the wage they pay to these poor brothers and sisters of theirs is only enough to keep them from dropping dead with hunger. The work-hours are fourteen per day, winter and summer—from six in the morning till eight at night— little children and all. And they walk to and from the pigsties which they inhabit—four miles each way, through mud and slush, rain, snow, sleet, and storm, daily, year in and year out. They get four hours of sleep. They kennel together, three families in a room, in unimaginable filth and stench; and disease comes, and they die off like flies. Have they committed a crime, these mangy things? No. What have they done, that they are punished so? Nothing at all, except getting themselves born into your foolish race. You have seen how they treat a misdoer there in the jail; now you see how they treat the innocent and the worthy. Is your race logical? Are these ill-smelling innocents better off than that heretic? Indeed, no; his punishment is trivial compared with theirs. They broke him on the wheel and smashed him to rags and pulp after we left, and he is dead now, and free of your precious race; but these poor slaves here—why, they have been dying for years, and some of them will not escape from life for years to come. It is the Moral Sense which teaches the factory proprietors the difference between right and wrong —you perceive the result. They think themselves better than dogs. Ah, you are such an illogical, unreasoning race! And paltry—oh, unspeakably!"

Then he dropped all seriousness and just overstrained himself making fun of us, and deriding our pride in our war-like deeds, our great heroes, our imperishable fames, our mighty kings, our ancient aristocracies, our venerable history

—and laughed and laughed till it was enough to make a person sick to hear him; and finally he sobered a little and said, "But, after all, it is not all ridiculous; there is a sort of pathos about it when one remembers how few are your days, how childish your pomps, and what shadows you are!"

Presently all things vanished suddenly from my sight, and I knew what it meant. The next moment we were walking along in our village; and down toward the river I saw the twinkling lights of the Golden Stag. Then in the dark I heard a joyful cry:

"He's come again!"

It was Seppi Wohlmeyer. He had felt his blood leap and his spirits rise in a way that could mean only one thing, and he knew Satan was near, although it was too dark to see him. He came to us, and we walked along together, and Seppi poured out his gladness like water. It was as if he were a lover and had found his sweetheart who had been lost. Seppi was a smart and animated boy, and had enthusiasm and expression, and was a contrast to Nikolaus and me. He was full of the last new mystery, now—the disappearance of Hans Oppert, the village loafer. People were beginning to be curious about it, he said. He did not say anxious—curious was the right word, and strong enough. No one had seen Hans for a couple of days.

"Not since he did that brutal thing, you know," he said.

"What brutal thing?" It was Satan that asked.

"Well, he is always clubbing his dog, which is a good dog, and his only friend, and is faithful, and loves him, and does no one any harm; and two days ago he was at it again, just for nothing—just for pleasure—and the dog was howling and begging, and Theodor and I begged, too, but he threatened us, and struck the dog again with all his might and knocked one of his eyes out, and he said to us, 'There, I hope you are satisfied now; that's what you have got for him by your damned meddling'—and he laughed, the heart-

less brute." Seppi's voice trembled with pity and anger. I
guessed what Satan would say, and he said it.

"There is that misused word again—that shabby slander.
Brutes do not act like that, but only men."

"Well, it was inhuman, anyway."

"No, it wasn't, Seppi; it was human—quite distinctly
human. It is not pleasant to hear you libel the higher animals by attributing to them dispositions which they are free
from, and which are found nowhere but in the human heart.
None of the higher animals is tainted with the disease called
the Moral Sense. Purify your language, Seppi; drop those
lying phrases out of it."

He spoke pretty sternly—for him—and I was sorry I
hadn't warned Seppi to be more particular about the word he
used. I knew how he was feeling. He would not want to offend Satan; he would rather offend all his kin. There was an
uncomfortable silence, but relief soon came, for that poor
dog came along now, with his eye hanging down, and went
straight to Satan, and began to moan and mutter brokenly,
and Satan began to answer in the same way, and it was plain
that they were talking together in the dog language. We all
sat down in the grass, in the moonlight, for the clouds were
breaking away now, and Satan took the dog's head in his
lap and put the eye back in its place, and the dog was comfortable, and he wagged his tail and licked Satan's hand,
and looked thankful and said the same; I knew he was
saying it, though I did not understand the words. Then the
two talked together a bit, and Satan said:

"He says his master was drunk."

"Yes, he was," said we.

"And an hour later he fell over the precipice there beyond
the Cliff Pasture."

"We know the place; it is three miles from here."

"And the dog has been often to the village, begging people

to go there, but he was only driven away and not listened to."

We remembered it, but hadn't understood what he wanted.

"He only wanted help for the man who had misused him, and he thought only of that, and has had no food nor sought any. He has watched by his master two nights. What do you think of your race? Is heaven reserved for it, and this dog ruled out, as your teachers tell you? Can your race add anything to this dog's stock of morals and magnanimities?" He spoke to the creature, who jumped up, eager and happy, and apparently ready for orders and impatient to execute them. "Get some men; go with the dog—he will show you that carrion; and take a priest along to arrange about insurance, for death is near."

With the last word he vanished, to our sorrow and disappointment. We got the men and Father Adolf, and we saw the man die. Nobody cared but the dog; he mourned and grieved, and licked the dead face, and could not be comforted. We buried him where he was, and without a coffin, for he had no money, and no friend but the dog. If we had been an hour earlier the priest would have been in time to send that poor creature to heaven, but now he was gone down into the awful fires, to burn forever. It seemed such a pity that in a world where so many people have difficulty to put in their time, one little hour could not have been spared for this poor creature who needed it so much, and to whom it would have made the difference between eternal joy and eternal pain. It gave an appalling idea of the value of an hour, and I thought I could never waste one again without remorse and terror. Seppi was depressed and grieved, and said it must be so much better to be a dog and not run such awful risks. We took this one home with us and kept him for our own. Seppi had a very good thought as we were walking along, and it cheered us up and made us feel much better. He said the dog had forgiven the man that had wronged him so, and maybe God would accept that absolution.

There was a very dull week, now, for Satan did not come, nothing much was going on, and we boys could not venture to go and see Marget, because the nights were moonlit and our parents might find us out if we tried. But we came across Ursula a couple of times taking a walk in the meadows beyond the river to air the cat, and we learned from her that things were going well. She had natty new clothes on and bore a prosperous look. The four groschen a day were arriving without a break, but were not being spent for food and wine and such things—the cat attended to all that.

Marget was enduring her forsakenness and isolation fairly well, all things considered, and was cheerful by help of Wilhelm Meidling. She spent an hour or two every night in the jail with her uncle, and had fattened him up with the cat's contributions. But she was curious to know more about Philip Traum, and hoped I would bring him again. Ursula was curious about him herself, and asked a good many questions about his uncle. It made the boys laugh, for I had told them the nonsense Satan had been stuffing her with. She got no satisfaction out of us, our tongues being tied.

Ursula gave us a small item of information: money being plenty now, she had taken on a servant to help about the house and run errands. She tried to tell it in a commonplace, matter-of-course way, but she was so set up by it and so vain of it that her pride in it leaked out pretty plainly. It was beautiful to see her veiled delight in this grandeur, poor old thing, but when we heard the name of the servant we wondered if she had been altogether wise; for although we were young, and often thoughtless, we had fairly good perception on some matters. This boy was Gottfried Narr, a dull, good creature, with no harm in him and nothing against him personally; still, he was under a cloud, and properly so, for it had not been six months since a social blight had mildewed the family—his grandmother had been burned as a witch. When that kind of a malady is in the blood it does not always come out with just one burning. Just now was not a good time for Ursula and Marget to be having dealings with a member of such a family, for the witch-terror had risen higher during the past year than it had ever reached in the memory of the oldest villagers. The mere mention of a witch was almost enough to frighten us out of out wits. This was natural enough, because of late years there were more kinds of witches than there used to be; in old times it had been only old women, but of late years they were of all ages—even children of eight and nine; it was getting so that anybody might turn out to be a familiar of the Devil—age and sex hadn't anything to do with it. In our little region we had tried to extirpate the witches, but the more of them we burned the more of the breed rose up in their places.

Once, in a school for girls only ten miles away, the teachers found that the back of one of the girls was all red and inflamed, and they were greatly frightened, believing it to be the Devil's marks. The girl was scared, and begged them not to denounce her, and said it was only fleas; but of course it would not do to let the matter rest there. All the girls were examined, and eleven out of the fifty were badly marked, the rest less so. A commission was appointed, but the eleven only cried for their mothers and would not confess. Then they were shut up, each by herself, in the dark, and put on black bread and water for ten days and nights; and by that time they were haggard and wild and their eyes were dry and they did not cry any more, but only sat and mumbled, and would not take the food. Then one of them confessed, and said they had often ridden through the air on broomsticks to the witches' Sabbath, and in a bleak place high up in the mountains had danced and drunk and caroused with several hundred other witches and the Evil One, and all had conducted themselves in a scandalous way

and had reviled the priests and blasphemed God. That is
what she said—not in narrative form, for she was not able to
remember any of the details without having them called to
her mind one after the other; but the commission did that,
for they knew just what questions to ask, they being all
written down for the use of witch-commissioners two centuries before. They asked, "Did you do so and so?" and she
always said yes, and looked weary and tired, and took no
interest in it. And so when the other ten heard that this one
confessed, they confessed, too, and answered yes to the questions. Then they were burned at the stake all together, which
was just and right; and everybody went from all the country-
side to see it. I went, too; but when I saw that one of them
was a bonny, sweet girl I used to play with, and looked so
pitiful there chained to the stake, and her mother crying
over her and devouring her with kisses and clinging around
her neck, and saying, "Oh, my God! oh, my God!" it was
too dreadful, and I went away.

It was bitter cold weather when Gottfried's grandmother
was burned. It was charged that she had cured bad head-
aches by kneading the person's head and neck with her fingers—as she said—but really by the Devil's help, as everybody knew. They were going to examine her, but she stopped
them, and confessed straight off that her power was from
the Devil. So they appointed to burn her next morning,
early, in our market-square. The officer who was to prepare
the fire was there first, and prepared it. She was there next—
brought by the constables, who left her and went to fetch
another witch. Her family did not come with her. They might
be reviled, maybe stoned, if the people were excited. I came,
and gave her an apple. She was squatting at the fire, warming
herself and waiting; and her old lips and hands were blue
with the cold. A stranger came next. He was a traveler, passing through; and he spoke to her gently, and, seeing nobody
but me there to hear, said he was sorry for her. And he asked

if what she confessed was true, and she said no. He looked surprised and still more sorry then, and asked her: "Then why did you confess?"

"I am old and very poor," she said, "and I work for my living. There was no way but to confess. If I hadn't they might have set me free. That would ruin me, for no one would forget that I had been suspected of being a witch, and so I would get no more work, and wherever I went they would set the dogs on me. In a little while I would starve. The fire is best; it is soon over. You have been good to me, you two, and I thank you."

She snuggled closer to the fire, and put out her hands to warm them, the snow-flakes descending soft and still on her old gray head and making it white and whiter. The crowd was gathering now, and an egg came flying and struck her in the eye, and broke and ran down her face. There was a laugh at that.

I told Satan all about the eleven girls and the old woman, once, but it did not effect him. He only said it was the human race, and what the human race did was of no consequence. And he said he had seen it made; and it was not made of clay; it was made of mud—part of it was, anyway. I knew what he meant by that—the Moral Sense. He saw the thought in my head, and it tickled him and made him laugh. Then he called a bullock out of a pasture and petted it and talked with it, and said:

"There—he wouldn't drive children mad with hunger and fright and loneliness, and then burn them for confessing to things invented for them which had never happened. And neither would he break the hearts of innocent, poor old women and make them afraid to trust themselves among their own race; and he would not insult them in their death-agony. For he is not besmirched with the Moral Sense, but is as the angels are, and knows no wrong, and never does it."

Lovely as he was, Satan could be cruelly offensive when he

chose; and he always chose when the human race was
brought to his attention. He always turned up his nose at it,
and never had a kind word for it.

Well, as I was saying, we boys doubted if it was a good
time for Ursula to be hiring a member of the Narr family. We
were right. When the people found it out they were naturally
indignant. And, moreover, since Marget and Ursula hadn't
enough to eat themselves, where was the money coming from
to feed another mouth? That is what they wanted to know;
and in order to find out they stopped avoiding Gottfried and
began to seek his society and have sociable conversa-
tions with him. He was pleased—not thinking any harm and
not seeing the trap—and so he talked innocently along, and
was no discreeter than a cow.

"Money!" he said; "they've got plenty of it. They pay me
two groschen a week, besides my keep. And they live on the
fat of the land, I can tell you; the prince himself can't beat
their table."

This astonishing statement was conveyed by the astrologer
to Father Adolf on a Sunday morning when he was returning
from mass. He was deeply moved, and said:

"This must be looked into."

He said there must be witchcraft at the bottom of it, and
told the villagers to resume relations with Marget and Ursula in a private and unostentatious way, and keep both eyes
open. They were told to keep their own counsel, and not
rouse the suspicions of the household. The villagers were
at first a bit reluctant to enter such a dreadful place, but the
priest said they would be under his protection while there,
and no harm could come to them, particularly if they carried
a trifle of holy water along and kept their beads and crosses
handy. This satisfied them and made them willing to go; envy
and malice made the baser sort even eager to go.

And so poor Marget began to have company again, and was
as pleased as a cat. She was like 'most anybody else—just

human, and happy in her prosperities and not averse from showing them off a little; and she was humanly grateful to have the warm shoulder turned to her and be smiled upon by her friends and the village again; for of all the hard things to bear, to be cut by your neighbors and left in contemptuous solitude is maybe the hardest.

The bars were down, and we could all go there now, and we did—our parents and all—day after day. The cat began to strain herself. She provided the top of everything for those companies, and in abundance—among them many a dish and many a wine which they had not tasted before and which they had not even heard of except at second-hand from the prince's servants. And the tableware was much above ordinary, too.

Marget was troubled at times, and pursued Ursula with questions to an uncomfortable degree; but Ursula stood her ground and stuck to it that it was Providence, and said no word about the cat. Marget knew that nothing was impossible to Providence, but she could not help having doubts that this effort was from there, though she was afraid to say so, lest disaster come of it. Witchcraft occurred to her, but she put the thought aside, for this was before Gottfried joined the household, and she knew Ursula was pious and a bitter hater of witches. By the time Gottfried arrived Providence was established, unshakably intrenched, and getting all the gratitude. The cat made no murmur, but went on composedly improving in style and prodigality by experience.

In any community, big or little, there is always a fair proportion of people who are not malicious or unkind by nature, and who never do unkind things except when they are overmastered by fear, or when their self-interest is greatly in danger, or some such matter as that. Eseldorf had its proportion of such people, and ordinarily their good and gentle influence was felt, but these were not ordinary times—on account of the witch-dread—and so we did not seem to have

any gentle and compassionate hearts left, to speak of. Every
person was frightened at the unaccountable state of things
at Marget's house, not doubting that witchcraft was at the
bottom of it, and fright frenzied their reason. Naturally there
were some who pitied Marget and Ursula for the danger that
was gathering about them, but naturally they did not say
so; it would not have been safe. So the others had it all their
own way, and there was none to advise the ignorant girl and
the foolish woman and warn them to modify their doings.
We boys wanted to warn them, but we backed down when it
came to the pinch, being afraid. We found that we were not
manly enough nor brave enough to do a generous action
when there was a chance that it could get us into trouble.
Neither of us confessed this poor spirit to the others, but did
as other people would have done—dropped the subject and
talked about something else. And I knew we all felt mean,
eating and drinking Marget's fine things along with those
companies of spies, and petting her and complimenting her
with the rest, and seeing with self-reproach how foolishly
happy she was, and never saying a word to put her on her
guard. And, indeed, she was happy, and as proud as a princess, and so grateful to have friends again. And all the time
these people were watching with all their eyes and reporting
all they saw to Father Adolf.

But he couldn't make head or tail of the situation. There
must be an enchanter somewhere on the premises, but who
was it? Marget was not seen to do any jugglery, nor was Ursula, nor yet Gottfried; and still the wines and dainties never
ran short, and a guest could not call for a thing and not get
it. To produce these effects was usual enough with witches
and enchanters—that part of it was not new; but to do it
without any incantations, or even any rumblings or earth-
quakes or lightnings or apparitions—that was new, novel,
wholly irregular. There was nothing in the books like this.
Enchanted things were always unreal. Gold turned to dirt

in an unenchanted atmosphere, food withered away and
vanished. But this test failed in the present case. The spies
brought samples: Father Adolf prayed over them, exorcised
them, but it did no good; they remained sound and real,
they yielded to natural decay only, and took the usual time
to do it.

Father Adolf was not merely puzzled, he was also exas-
perated; for these evidences very nearly convinced him—
privately—that there was no witchcraft in the matter. It did
not wholly convince him, for this could be a new kind of
witchcraft. There was a way to find out as to this: if this
prodigal abundance of provender was not brought in from the
outside, but produced on the premises, there was witchcraft,
sure.

7

Marget announced a party, and invited forty people; the
date for it was seven days away. This was a fine opportunity. Marget's house stood by itself, and it could be easily
watched. All the week it was watched night and day. Marget's
household went out and in as usual, but they carried nothing
in their hands, and neither they nor others brought anything
to the house. This was ascertained. Evidently rations for
forty people were not being fetched. If they were furnished
any sustenance it would have to be made on the premises. It
was true that Marget went out with a basket every evening,
but the spies ascertained that she always brought it back
empty.

The guests arrived at noon and filled the place. Father
Adolf followed; also, after a little, the astrologer, without invitation. The spies had informed him that neither at the back
nor the front had any parcels been brought in. He entered,
and found the eating and drinking going on finely, and everything progressing in a lively and festive way. He glanced

around and perceived that many of the cooked delicacies
and all of the native and foreign fruits were of a perishable
character, and he also recognized that these were fresh and
perfect. No apparitions, no incantations, no thunder. That
settled it. This was witchcraft. And not only that, but of a
new kind—a kind never dreamed of before. It was a prodigious power, an illustrious power; he resolved to discover its
secret. The announcement of it would resound throughout the
world, penetrate to the remotest lands, paralyze all the na-
tions with amazement—and carry his name with it, and make
him renowned forever. It was a wonderful piece of luck, a
splendid piece of luck; the glory of it made him dizzy.

All the house made room for him; Marget politely seated
him; Ursula ordered Gottfried to bring a special table for
him. Then she decked it and furnished it, and asked for his
orders.

"Bring me what you will," he said.

The two servants brought supplies from the pantry, together with white wine and red—a bottle of each. The astrologer, who very likely had never seen such delicacies before,
poured out a beaker of red wine, drank it off, poured another, then began to eat with a grand appetite.

I was not expecting Satan, for it was more than a week
since I had seen or heard of him, but now he came in—I
knew it by the feel, though people were in the way and I
could not see him. I heard him apologizing for intruding;
and he was going away, but Marget urged him to stay, and he
thanked her and stayed. She brought him along, introducing
him to the girls, and to Meidling, and to some of the elders;
and there was quite a rustle of whispers: "It's the young
stranger we hear so much about and can't get sight of, he is
away so much." "Dear, dear, but he is beautiful—what is his
name?" "Philip Traum." "Ah, it fits him!" (You see, "Traum"
is German for "Dream.") "What does he do?" "Studying for
the ministry, they say." "His face is his fortune—he'll be a

cardinal some day." "Where is his home?" "Away down somewhere in the tropics, they say—has a rich uncle down there."
And so on. He made his way at once; everybody was anxious
to know him and talk with him. Everybody noticed how cool
and fresh it was, all of a sudden, and wondered at it, for they
could see that the sun was beating down the same as before,
outside, and the sky was clear of clouds, but no one guessed
the reason, of course.

The astrologer had drunk his second beaker; he poured
out a third. He set the bottle down, and by accident over-
turned it. He seized it before much was spilled, and held it
up to the light, saying, "What a pity—it is royal wine." Then
his face lighted with joy or triumph, or something, and he
said, "Quick! Bring a bowl."

It was brought—a four-quart one. He took up that two-
pint bottle and began to pour; went on pouring, the red
liquor gurgling and gushing into the white bowl and rising
higher and higher up its sides, everybody staring and holding his breath—and presently the bowl was full to the brim.

"Look at the bottle," he said, holding it up; "it is full
yet!" I glanced at Satan, and in that moment he vanished.
Then Father Adolf rose up, flushed and excited, crossed himself, and began to thunder in his great voice, "This house
is bewitched and accursed!" People began to cry and shriek
and crowd toward the door. "I summon this detected household to—"

His words were cut off short. His face became red, then
purple, but he could not utter another sound. Then I saw
Satan, a transparent film, melt into the astrologer's body;
then the astrologer put up his hand, and apparently in his
own voice said, "Wait—remain where you are." All stopped
where they stood. "Bring a funnel!" Ursula brought it, trembling and scared, and he stuck it in the bottle and took up
the great bowl and began to pour the wine back, the people
gazing and dazed with astonishment, for they knew the

bottle was already full before he began. He emptied the whole of the bowl into the bottle, then smiled out over the room, chuckled, and said, indifferently: "It is nothing—anybody can do it! With my powers I can even do much more."

A frightened cry burst out everywhere. "Oh, my God, he is possessed!" and there was a tumultuous rush for the door which swiftly emptied the house of all who did not belong in it except us boys and Meidling. We boys knew the secret, and would have told it if we could, but we couldn't. We were very thankful to Satan for furnishing that good help at the needful time.

Marget was pale, and crying; Meidling looked kind of petrified; Ursula the same; but Gottfried was the worst—he couldn't stand, he was to weak and scared. For he was of a witch family, you know, and it would be bad for him to be suspected. Agnes came loafing in, looking pious and unaware, and wanted to rub up against Ursula and be petted, but Ursula was afraid of her and shrank away from her, but pretending she was not meaning any incivility, for she knew very well it wouldn't answer to have strained relations with that kind of a cat. But we boys took Agnes and petted her, for Satan would not have befriended her if he had not had a good opinion of her, and that was indorsement enough for us. He seemed to trust anything that hadn't the Moral Sense.

Outside, the guests, panic-stricken, scattered in every direction and fled in a pitiable state of terror; and such a tumult as they made with their running and sobbing and shrieking and shouting that soon all the village came flocking from their houses to see what had happened, and they thronged the street and shouldered and jostled one another in excitement and fright; and then Father Adolf appeared, and they fell apart in two walls like the cloven Red Sea, and presently down this lane the astrologer came striding and mumbling, and where he passed the lanes surged back in packed masses, and fell silent with awe, and their eyes stared and their breasts heaved, and several women fainted; and when he was gone by the crowd swarmed together and followed him at a distance, talking excitedly and asking questions and finding out the facts. Finding out the facts and passing them on to others, with improvements—improvements which soon enlarged the bowl of wine to a barrel, and made the one bottle hold it all and yet remain empty to the last.

When the astrologer reached the market-square he went straight to a juggler, fantastically dressed, who was keeping three brass balls in the air, and took them from him and faced around upon the approaching crowd and said: "This poor clown is ignorant of his art. Come forward and see an expert perform."

So saying, he tossed the balls up one after another and set them whirling in a slender bright oval in the air, and added another, then another and another, and soon—no one seeing whence he got them—adding, adding, adding, the oval lengthening all the time, his hands moving so swiftly that they were just a web or a blur and not distinguishable as hands; and such as counted said there were now a hundred balls in the air. The spinning great oval reached up twenty feet in the air and was a shining and glinting and and wonderful sight. Then he folded his arms and told the balls to go on spinning without his help—and they did it. After a couple of minutes he said, "There, that will do," and the oval broke and came crashing down, and the balls scattered abroad and rolled every whither. And wherever one of them came the people fell back in dread, and no one would touch it. It made him laugh, and he scoffed at the people and called them cowards and old women. Then he turned and saw the tight-rope, and said foolish people were daily wasting their money to see a clumsy and ignorant varlet degrade that beautiful art; now they should see the work of a master. With that he made a spring into the air and lit firm on his

feet on the rope. Then he hopped the whole length of it back
and forth on one foot, with his hands clasped over his eyes;
and next he began to throw somersaults, both backward and
forward, and threw twenty-seven.

The people murmured, for the astrologer was old, and always before had been halting of movement and at times
even lame, but he was nimble enough now and went on with
his antics in the liveliest manner. Finally he sprang lightly
down and walked away, and passed up the road and around
the corner and disappeared. Then that great, pale silent,
solid crowd drew a deep breath and looked into one another's faces as if they said: "Was it real? Did you see it,
or was it only I—and was I dreaming?" Then they
broke into a low murmur of talking, and fell apart in couples,
and moved toward their homes, still talking in that awed
way, with faces close together and laying a hand on an arm
and making other such gestures as people make when they
have been deeply impressed by something.

We boys followed behind our fathers, and listened, catch-
ing all we could of what they said; and when they sat
down in our house and continued their talk they still had us
for company. They were in a sad mood, for it was certain,
they said, that disaster for the village must follow this awful
visitation of witches and devils. Then my father remembered
that Father Adolf had been struck dumb at the moment of his
denunciation.

"They have not ventured to lay their hands upon an
anointed servant of God before," he said; "and how they
could have dared it this time I cannot make out, for he wore
his crucifix. Isn't it so?"

"Yes," said the others, "we saw it."

"It is serious, friends, it is very serious. Always before, we
had a protection. It has failed."

The others shook, as with a sort of chill, and muttered
those words over—"It has failed." "God has forsaken us."

"It is true," said Seppi Wohlmeyer's father; "there is nowhere to look for help."

"The people will realize this," said Nikolaus's father, the judge, "and despair will take away their courage and their energies. We have indeed fallen upon evil times."

He sighed, and Wohlmeyer said, in a troubled voice: "The report of it all will go about the country, and our village will be shunned as being under the displeasure of God. The Golden Stag will know hard times."

"True, neighbor," said my father; "all of us will suffer—all in repute, many in estate. And, good God!—"

"What is it?"

"That can come—to finish us!"

"Name it—*um Gottes Willen!*"

"The Interdict!"

It smote like a thunderclap, and they were like to swoon with the terror of it. Then the dread of this calamity roused their energies, and they stopped brooding and began to consider ways to avert it. They discussed this, that, and the other way, and talked till the afternoon was far spent, then confessed that at present they could arrive at no decision. So they parted sorrowfully, with oppressed hearts which were filled with bodings.

While they were saying their parting words I slipped out and set my course for Marget's house to see what was happening there. I met many people, but none of them greeted me. It ought to have been surprising, but it was not, for they were so distraught with fear and dread that they were not in their right minds, I think; they were white and haggard, and walked like persons in a dream, their eyes open but seeing nothing, their lips moving but uttering nothing, and worriedly clasping and unclasping their hands without knowing it.

At Marget's it was like a funeral. She and Wilhelm sat together on the sofa, but said nothing, and not even holding hands. Both were steeped in gloom, and Marget's eyes were red from the crying she had been doing. She said:

"I have been begging him to go, and come no more, and so save himself alive. I cannot bear to be his murderer. This house is bewitched, and no inmate will escape the fire. But he will not go, and he will be lost with the rest."

Wilhelm said he would not go; if there was danger for her, his place was by her, and there he would remain. Then she began to cry again, and it was all so mournful that I wished I had stayed away. There was a knock, now, and Satan came in, fresh and cheery and beautiful, and brought that winy atmosphere of his and changed the whole thing. He never said a word about what had been happening, nor about the awful fears which were freezing the blood in the hearts of the community, but began to talk and rattle on about all manner of gay and pleasant things; and next about music—an artful stroke which cleared away the remnant of Marget's depression and brought her spirits and her interests broad awake. She had not heard any one talk so well and so knowingly on that subject before and she was so uplifted by it and so charmed that what she was feeling lit up her face and came out in her words; and Wilhelm noticed it and did not look as pleased as he ought to have done. And next Satan branched off into poetry, and recited some, and did it well, and Marget was charmed again; and again Wilhelm was not as pleased as he ought to have been, and this time Marget noticed it and was remorseful.

I fell asleep to pleasant music that night—the patter of rain upon the panes and the dull growling of distant thunder. Away in the night Satan came and roused me and said: "Come with me. Where shall we go?"

"Anywhere—so it is with you."

Then there was a fierce glare of sunlight, and he said, "This is China."

That was a grand surprise, and made me sort of drunk

with vanity and gladness to think I had come so far—so much, much farther than anybody else in our village, including Bartel Sperling, who had such a great opinion of his travels. We buzzed around over that empire for more than half an hour, and saw the whole of it. It was wonderful, the spectacles we saw; and some were beautiful, others too horrible to think about. For instance— However, I may go into that by and by, and also why Satan chose China for this excursion instead of another place; it would interrupt my tale to do it now. Finally we stopped flitting and lit.

We sat upon a mountain commanding a vast landscape of mountain-range and gorge and valley and plain and river, with cities and villages slumbering in the sunlight, and a glimpse of blue sea on the farther verge. It was a tranquil and dreamy picture, beautiful to the eye and restful to the spirit. If we could only make a change like that whenever we wanted to, the world would be easier to live in than it is, for change of scene shifts the mind's burdens to the other shoulder and banishes old, shop-worn wearinesses from mind and body both.

We talked together, and I had the idea of trying to reform Satan and persuade him to lead a better life. I told him about all those things he had been doing, and begged him to be more considerate and stop making people unhappy. I said I knew he did not mean any harm, but that he ought to stop and consider the possible consequences of a thing before launching it in that impulsive and random way of his; then he would not make so much trouble. He was not hurt by this plain speech; he only looked amused and surprised, and said:

"What? I do random things? Indeed. I never do. I stop and consider possible consequences? Where is the need? I know what the consequences are going to be—always."

"Oh, Satan, then how could you do these things?"

"Well, I will tell you, and you must understand if you

can. You belong to a singular race. Every man is a suffering-machine and a happiness-machine combined. The two functions work together harmoniously, with a fine and delicate precision, on the give-and-take principle. For every happiness turned out in one department the other stands ready to modify it with a sorrow or a pain—maybe a dozen. In most cases the man's life is about equally divided between happiness and unhappiness. When this is not the case the unhappiness predominates—always; never the other. Sometimes a man's make and disposition are such that his misery-machine is able to do nearly all the business. Such a man goes through life almost ignorant of what happiness is. Everything he touches, everything he does, brings a misfortune upon him. You have seen such people? To that kind of a person life is not an advantage, is it? It is only a disaster. Sometimes for an hour's happiness a man's machinery makes him pay years of misery. Don't you know that? It happens every now and then. I will give you a case or two presently. Now the people of your village are nothing to me—you know that, don't you?"

I did not like to speak out too flatly, so I said I had suspected it.

"Well, it is true that they are nothing to me. It is not possible that they should be. The difference between them and me is abysmal, immeasurable. They have no intellect."

"No intellect?"

"Nothing that resembles it. At a future time I will examine what man calls his mind and give you the details of that chaos, then you will see and understand. Men have nothing in common with me—there is no point of contact; they have foolish little feelings and foolish little vanities and impertinences and ambitions; their foolish little life is but a laugh, a sigh, and extinction; and they have no sense. Only the Moral Sense. I will show you what I mean. Here is a red spider, not so big as a pin's head. Can you imagine an elephant being interested in him—caring whether he is happy

or isn't, or whether he is wealthy or poor, or whether his
sweetheart returns his love or not, or whether his mother is
sick or well, or whether he is looked up to in society or
not, or whether his enemies will smite him or his
friends desert him, or whether his hopes will suffer blight or
his political ambitions fail, whether he shall die in the bosom
of his family or neglected and despised in a foreign land?
These things can never be important to the elephant; they
are nothing to him; he cannot shrink his sympathies to the
microscopic size of them. Man is to me as the red spider
is to the elephant. The elephant has nothing against the spider
—he cannot get down to that remote level; I have nothing
against man. The elephant is indifferent; I am indifferent. The
elephant would not take the trouble to do the spider an ill
turn; if he took the notion he might do him a good turn, if it
came in his way and cost nothing. I have done men good
service, but no ill turns.

"The elephant lives a century, the red spider a day; in
power, intellect, and dignity the one creature is separated
from the other by a distance which is simply astronomical.
Yet in these, as in all qualities, man is immeasurably further
below me than is the wee spider below the elephant.

"Man's mind clumsily and tediously and laboriously patches
little trivialities together and gets a result—such as it is. My
mind creates! Do you get the force of that? Creates anything
it desires—and in a moment. Creates without material. Creates
fluids, solids, colors—anything, everything—out of the airy
nothing which is called Thought. A man imagines a silk
thread, imagines a machine to make it, imagines a picture,
then by weeks of labor embroiders it on canvas with the
thread. I think the whole thing, and in a moment it is before
you—created.

"I think a poem, music, the record of a game of chess—
anything—and it is there. This is the immortal mind—nothing is beyond its reach. Nothing can obstruct my vision; the
rocks are transparent to me, and darkness is daylight. I do

not need to open a book; I take the whole of its contents into my mind at a single glance, through the cover; and in a million years I could not forget a single word of it, or its place in the volume. Nothing goes on in the skull of man, bird, fish, insect, or other creature which can be hidden from me. I pierce the learned man's brain with a single glance, and the treasures which cost him threescore years to accumulate are mine; he can forget, and he does forget, but I retain.

"Now, then, I perceive by your thoughts that you are understanding me fairly well. Let us proceed. Circumstances might so fall out that the elephant could like the spider—supposing he can see it—but he could not love it. His love is for his own kind—for his equals. An angel's love is sublime, adorable, divine, beyond the imagination of man—infinitely beyond it! But it is limited to his own august order. If it fell upon one of your race for only an instant, it would consume its object to ashes. No, we cannot love men, but we can be harmlessly indifferent to them; we can also like them, sometimes. I like you and the boys, I like Father Peter, and for your sakes I am doing all these things for the villagers."

He saw that I was thinking a sarcasm, and he explained his position.

"I have wrought well for the villagers, though it does not look like it on the surface. Your race never know good fortune from ill. They are always mistaking the one for the other. It is because they cannot see into the future. What I am doing for the villagers will bear good fruit some day; in some cases to themselves; in others, to unborn generations of men. No one will ever know that I was the cause, but it will be none the less true, for all that. Among you boys you have a game: you stand a row of bricks on end a few inches apart; you push a brick, it knocks its neighbor over, the neighbor knocks over the next brick—and so on till all the row is prostrate. That is human life. A child's first act knocks over the initial brick, and the rest will follow inexorably. If you could see into the future, as I can, you would see everything that was going to happen to that creature; for nothing can change the order of its life after the first event has determined it. That is, nothing will change it, because each act unfailingly begets an act, that act begets another, and so on to the end, and the seer can look forward down the line and see just when each act is to have birth, from cradle to grave."

"Does God order the career?"

"Foreordain it? No. The man's circumstances and enviroment order it. His first act determines the second and all that follow after. But suppose, for argument's sake, that the man should skip one of these acts; an apparently trifling one, for instance; suppose that it had been appointed that on a certain day, at a certain hour and minute and second and fraction of a second he should go to the well, and he didn't go. That man's career would change utterly, from that moment; thence to the grave it would be wholly different from the career which his first act as a child had arranged for him. Indeed, it might be that if he had gone to the well he would have ended his career on a throne, and that omitting to do it would set him upon a career that would lead to beggary and a pauper's grave. For instance: if at any time—say in boyhood—Columbus had skipped the triflingest little link in the chain of acts projected and made inevitable by his first childish act, it would have changed his whole subsequent life, and he would have become a priest and died obscure in an Italian village, and America would not have been discovered for two centuries afterward. I know this. To skip any one of the billion acts in Columbus's chain would have wholly changed his life. I have examined his billion of possible careers, and in only one of them occurs the discovery of America. You people do not suspect that all of your acts are of one size and importance, but it is true; to snatch at an appointed fly is as big with fate for you as in any other appointed act—"

"As the conquering of a continent, for instance?"

"Yes. Now, then, no man ever does drop a link—the thing has never happened! Even when he is trying to make up his mind as to whether he will do a thing or not, that itself is a link, an act, and has its proper place in his chain; and when he finally decides an act, that also was the thing which he was absolutely certain to do. You see, now, that a man will never drop a link in his chain. He cannot. If he made up his mind to try, that project would itself be an unavoidable link—a thought bound to occur to him at that precise moment, and made certain by the first act of his babyhood."

It seemed so dismal!

"He is prisoner for life," I said sorrowfully, "and cannot get free."

"No, of himself he cannot get away from the consequences of his first childish act. But I can free him."

I looked up wistfully.

"I have changed the careers of a number of your villagers."

I tried to thank him, but found it difficult, and let it drop.

"I shall make some other changes. You know that little Lisa Brandt?"

"Oh yes, everybody does. My mother says she is so sweet and so lovely that she is not like any other child. She says she will be the pride of the village when she grows up; and its idol, too, just as she is now."

"I shall change her future."

"Make it better?" I asked.

"Yes. And I will change the future of Nikolaus."

I was glad, this time, and said, "I don't need to ask about his case; you will be sure to do generously by him."

"It is my intention."

Straight off I was building that great future of Nicky's in my imagination, and had already made a renowned general of him and hofmeister at the court, when I noticed that Satan was waiting for me to get ready to listen again. I was ashamed of having exposed my cheap imaginings to him, and was expecting some sarcasms, but it did not happen. He proceeded with his subject:

"Nicky's appointed life is sixty-two years."

"That's grand!" I said.

"Lisa's, thirty-six. But, as I told you, I shall change their lives and those ages. Two minutes and a quarter from now Nikolaus will wake out of his sleep and find the rain blowing in. It was appointed that he should turn over and go to sleep again. But I have appointed that he shall get up and close the window first. That trifle will change his career entirely. He will rise in the morning two minutes later than the chain of his life had appointed him to rise. By consequence, thenceforth nothing will ever happen to him in accordance with the details of the old chain." He took out his watch and sat looking at it a few moments then said: "Nikolaus has risen to close the window. His life is changed, his new career has begun. There will be consequences."

It made me feel creepy; it was uncanny.

"But for this change certain things would happen twelve days from now. For instance, Nikolaus would save Lisa from drowning. He would arrive on the scene at exactly the right moment—four minutes past ten, the long-ago appointed instant of time—and the water would be shoal, the achievement easy and certain. But he will arrive some seconds too late, now; Lisa will have struggled into deeper water. He will do his best, but both will drown."

"Oh, Satan! oh, dear Satan!" I cried, with the tears rising in my eyes, "save them! Don't let it happen, I can't bear to lose Nikolaus, he is my loving playmate and friend; and think of Lisa's poor mother!"

I clung to him and begged and pleaded, but he was not moved. He made me sit down again, and told me I must hear him out.

"I have changed Nikolaus's life, and this has changed Lisa's. If I had not done this, Nikolaus would save Lisa, then he would catch cold from his drenching; one of your race's fantastic and desolating scarlet fevers would follow, with pathetic aftereffects; for forty-six years he would lie in his bed a paralytic log, deaf, dumb, blind, and praying night and day for the blessed relief of death. Shall I change his life back?"

"Oh no! Oh, not for the world! In charity and pity leave it as it is."

"It is best so. I could not have changed any other link in his life and done him so good a service. He had a billion possible careers, but not one of them was worth living; they were charged full with miseries and disasters. But for my intervention he would do his brave deed twelve days from now—a deed begun and ended in six minutes—and get for all reward those forty-six years of sorrow and suffering I told you of. It is one of the cases I was thinking of awhile ago when I said that sometimes an act which brings the actor an hour's happiness and self-satisfaction is paid for—or punished—by years of suffering."

I wondered what poor little Lisa's early death would save her from. He answered the thought:

"From ten years of pain and slow recovery from an accident, and then from nineteen years' pollution, shame, depravity, crime, ending with death at the hands of the executioner. Twelve days hence she will die; her mother would save her life if she could. Am I not kinder than her mother?"

"Yes—oh, indeed yes; and wiser."

"Father Peter's case is coming on presently. He will be acquitted, through unassailable proofs of his innocence."

"Why, Satan, how can that be? Do you really think it?"

"Indeed, I know it. His good name will be restored, and the rest of his life will be happy."

"I can believe it. To restore his good name will have that effect."

"His happiness will not proceed from that cause. I shall change his life that day, for his good. He will never know his good name has been restored."

In my mind—and modestly—I asked for particulars, but Satan paid no attention to my thought. Next, my mind wandered to the astrologer, and I wondered where he might be.

"In the moon," said Satan, with a fleeting sound which I believed was a chuckle. "I've got him on the cold side of it, too. He doesn't know where he is, and is not having a pleasant time; still, it is good enough for him, a good place for his star studies. I shall need him presently; then I shall bring him back and possess him again. He has a long and cruel and odious life before him, but I will change that, for I have no feeling against him and am quite willing to do him a kindness. I think I shall get him burned."

He had such strange notions of kindness! But angels are made so, and do not know any better. Their ways are not like our ways; and, besides, human beings are nothing to them; they think they are only freaks. It seems to me odd that he should put the astrologer so far away; he could have dumped him in Germany just as well, where he would be handy.

"Far away?" said Satan. "To me no place is far away; distance does not exist for me. The sun is less than a hundred million miles from here, and the light that is falling upon us has taken eight minutes to come; but I can make that flight, or any other, in a fraction of time so minute that it cannot be measured by a watch. I have but to think the journey, and it is accomplished."

I held out my hand and said, "The light lies upon it; think it into a glass of wine, Satan."

He did it. I drank the wine.

"Break the glass," he said.

I broke it.

"There—you see it is real. The villagers thought the brass balls were magic stuff and as perishable as smoke. They were afraid to touch them. You are a curious lot—your race. But come along; I have business. I will put you to bed."

Said and done. Then he was gone; but his voice came back
to me through the rain and darkness saying, "Yes, tell Seppi,
but no other."

It was the answer to my thought.

8

Sleep would not come. It was not because I was proud of
my travels and excited about having been around the big
world to China, and feeling contemptuous of Bartel Sperling, "the traveler," as he called himself, and looked down
upon us others because he had been to Vienna once and was
the only Eseldorf boy who had made such a journey and seen
the world's wonders. At another time that would have kept
me awake, but it did not affect me now. No, my mind was
filled with Nikolaus, my thoughts ran upon him only, and the
good days we had seen together at romps and frolics in the
woods and the fields and the river in the long summer days,
and skating and sliding in the winter when our parents
thought we were in school. And now he was going out of
this young life, and the summers and winters would come
and go, and we others would rove and play as before, but his
place would be vacant; we should see him no more. To-
morrow he would not suspect, but would be as he had
always been, and it would shock me to hear him laugh, and
see him do lightsome and frivolous things, for to me he would
be a corpse, with waxen hands and dull eyes, and I should
see the shroud around his face; and next day he would not
suspect, nor the next, and all the time his handful of days
would be wasting swiftly away and that awful thing coming nearer and nearer, his fate closing steadily around him
and no one knowing it but Seppi and me. Twelve days—
only twelve days. It was awful to think of. I noticed that in
my thoughts I was not calling him by his familiar names,
Nick and Nicky, but was speaking of him by his full name,
and reverently, as one speaks of the dead. Also, as incident

after incident of our comradeship came thronging into my
mind out of the past, I noticed that they were mainly
cases where I had wronged him or hurt him, and they rebuked
me and reproached me, and my heart was wrung with
remorse, just as it is when we remember our unkindnesses to
friends who have passed beyond the veil, and we wish we
could have them back again, if only for a moment, so that
we could go on our knees to them and say, "Have pity, and
forgive."

Once when we were nine years old he went a long errand
of nearly two miles from the fruiterer, who gave him a splendid big apple for reward, and he was flying home with it,
almost beside himself with astonishment and delight, and
I met him, and he let me look at the apple, not thinking of
treachery, and I ran off with it, eating it as I ran, he
following me and begging; and when he overtook me I
offered him the core, which was all that was left; and I
laughed. Then he turned away, crying, and said he had meant
to give it to his little sister. That smote me, for she was
slowly getting well of a sickness, and it would have been a
proud moment for him, to see her joy and surprise and have
her caresses. But I was ashamed to say I was ashamed,
and only said something rude and mean, to pretend I did
not care, and he made no reply in words, but there was a
wounded look in his face as he turned away toward his home
which rose before me many times in after years, in the night,
and reproached me and made me ashamed again. It had
grown dim in my mind, by and by, then it disappeared; but
it was back now, and not dim.

Once at school, when we were eleven, I upset my ink and
spoiled four copy-books, and was in danger of severe punishment; but I put it upon him, and he got the whipping.

And only last year I had cheated him in a trade, giving him
a large fish-hook which was partly broken through for three
small sound ones. The first fish he caught broke the hook,
but he did not know I was blamable, and he refused to take

back one of the small hooks which my conscience forced me to offer him, but said, "A trade is a trade; the hook was bad, but that was not your fault."

No, I could not sleep. These little, shabby wrongs upbraided me and tortured me, and with a pain much sharper than one feels when the wrongs have been done to the living. Nikolaus was living, but no matter; he was to me as one already dead. The wind was still moaning about the eaves, the rain still pattering upon the panes.

In the morning I sought out Seppi and told him. It was down by the river. His lips moved, but he did not say anything, he only looked dazed and stunned, and his face turned very white. He stood like that a few moments, the tears welling into his eyes, then he turned away and I locked my arm in his and we walked along thinking, but not speaking. We crossed the bridge and wandered through the meadows and up among the hills and the woods, and at last the talk came and flowed freely, and it was all about Nikolaus and was a recalling of life we had lived with him. And every now and then Seppi said, as if to himself:

"Twelve days!—less than twelve days."

We said we must be with him all the time; we must have all of him we could; the days were precious now. Yet we did not go to seek him. It would be like meeting the dead, and we were afraid. We did not say it, but that was what we were feeling. And so it gave us a shock when we turned a curve and came upon Nikolaus face to face. He shouted, gaily:

"Hi-hi! What is the matter? Have you seen a ghost?"

We couldn't speak, but there was no occasion; he was willing to talk for us all, for he had just seen Satan and was in high spirits about it. Satan had told him about our trip to China, and he had begged Satan to take him on a journey, and Satan had promised. It was to be a far journey, and wonderful and beautiful; and Nikolaus had begged him to take us, too, but he said no, he would take us some day, maybe, but not now. Satan would come for him on the 13th, and Nikolaus was already counting the hours, he was so impatient.

That was the fatal day. We were already counting the hours, too.

We wandered many a mile, always following paths which had been our favorites from the days when we were little, and always we talked about the old times. All the blitheness was with Nikolaus; we others could not shake off our depression. Our tone toward Nikolaus was so strangely gentle and tender and yearning that he noticed it, and was pleased; and we were constantly doing him deferential little offices of courtesy, and saying, "Wait, let me do that for you," and that pleased him, too. I gave him seven fish-hooks—all I had —and made him take them; and Seppi gave him his new knife and a humming-top painted red and yellow—atonements for swindles practised upon him formerly, as I learned later, and probably no longer remembered by Nikolaus now. These things touched him, and he could not have believed that we loved him so; and his pride in it and gratefulness for it cut us to the heart, we were so underserving of them. When we parted at last, he was radiant, and said he had never had such a happy day.

As we walked along homeward, Seppi said, "We always prized him, but never so much as now, when we are going to lose him."

Next day and every day we spent all our spare time with Nikolaus; and also added to it time which we (and he) stole from work and other duties, and this cost the three of us some sharp scoldings, and some threats of punishment. Every morning two of us woke with a start and a shudder, saying, as the days flew along, "Only ten days left;" "only nine days left;" "only eight;" "only seven." Always it was narrowing. Always Nikolaus was gay and happy, and always puzzled because we were not. He wore his invention to the bone trying to invent ways to cheer us up, but it was only a hollow success; he could see that our jollity had no heart in it, and that the laughs we broke into came up against some obstruction or other and suffered damage and decayed into a sigh. He tried to find out what the matter was, so that he could help us out of our trouble or make it lighter by sharing it with us; so we had to tell many lies to deceive him and appease him.

But the most distressing thing of all was that he was always making plans, and often they went beyond the 13th! Whenever that happened it made us groan in spirit. All his mind was fixed upon finding some way to conquer our depression and cheer us up; and at last, when he had but three days to live, he fell upon the right ideas, and was jubilant over it—a boys-and-girls' frolic and dance in the woods, up there where we first met Satan, and this was to occur on the 14th. It was ghastly, for that was his funeral day. We couldn't venture to protest; it would only have brought a "Why?" which we could not answer. He wanted us to help him invite his guests, and we did it—one can refuse nothing to a dying friend. But it was dreadful, for really we were inviting them to his funeral.

It was an awful eleven days; and yet, with a lifetime stretching back between to-day and then, they are still a grateful memory to me, and beautiful. In effect they were days of companionship with one's sacred dead, and I have known no comradeship that was so close or so precious. We clung to the hours and the minutes, counting them as they wasted away, and parting with them with that pain and bereavement which a miser feels who sees his hoard filched from him coin by coin by robbers and is helpless to prevent it.

When the evening of the last day came we stayed out too long; Seppi and I were in fault for that; we could not bear to part with Nikolaus; so it was very late when we left him at his door. We lingered near awhile, listening; and that happened which we were fearing. His father gave him the promised punishment, and we heard his shrieks. But we listened only a moment, then hurried away, remorseful for this thing which we had caused. And sorry for the father, too; our thought being, "If he only knew—if he only knew!"

In the morning Nikolaus did not meet us at the appointed place, so we went to his home to see what the matter was. His mother said:

"His father is out of all patience with these goings-on, and will not have any more of it. Half the time when Nick is needed he is not to be found; then it turns out that he has been gadding around with you two. His father gave him a flogging last night. It always grieved me before, and many's the time I have begged him off and saved him, but this time he appealed to me in vain, for I was out of patience myself."

"I wish you had saved him just this one time," I said, my voice trembling a little; "it would ease a pain in your heart to remember it some day."

She was ironing at the time, and her back was partly toward me. She turned about with a startled or wondering look in her face and said, "What do you mean by that?"

I was not prepared, and didn't know anything to say; so it was awkward, for she kept looking at me; but Seppi was alert and spoke up:

"Why, of course it would be pleasant to remember, for the very reason we were out so late was that Nikolaus got to telling how good you are to him, and how he never got whipped when you were by to save him; and he was so full of it, and we were so full of the interest of it, that none of us noticed how late it was getting."

"Did he say that? Did he?" and she put her apron to her eyes.

"You can ask Theodor—he will tell you the same."

"It is a dear, good lad, my Nick," she said. "I am sorry I let him get whipped; I will never do it again. To think —all the time I was sitting here last night, fretting and angry

at him, he was loving me and praising me! Dear, dear, if
we could only know! Then we shouldn't ever go wrong;
but we are only poor, dumb beasts groping around and making mistakes. I shan't ever think of last night without a
pang."

She was like all the rest; it seemed as if nobody could open
a mouth, in these wretched days, without saying something
that made us shiver. They were "groping around," and did
not know what true, sorrowfully true things they were saying by accident.

Seppi asked if Nikolaus might go out with us.

"I am sorry," she answered, "but he can't. To punish him
further, his father doesn't allow him to go out of the house
to-day."

We had a great hope! I saw it in Seppi's eyes. We
thought, "If he cannot leave the house, he cannot be drowned
Seppi asked, to make sure:

"Must he stay in all day, or only the morning?"

"All day. It's such a pity, too; it's a beautiful day, and he
is so unused to being shut up. But he is busy planning his
party, and maybe that is company for him. I do hope he
isn't too lonesome."

Seppi saw that in her eye which emboldened him to ask
if we might go up and help him pass his time.

"And welcome!" she said, right heartily. "Now I call that
real friendship, when you might be abroad in the fields
and the woods, having a happy time. You are good boys,
I'll allow that, though you don't always find satisfactory ways
of improving it. Take these cakes—for yourselves—and give
him this one, from his mother."

The first thing we noticed when we entered Nikolaus's
room was the time—a quarter to ten. Could that be correct?
Only such a few minutes to live! I felt a contraction at my
heart. Nikolaus jumped up and gave us a glad welcome. He
was in good spirits over his plannings for his party and had
not been lonesome.

"Sit down," he said, "and look at what I've been doing. And I've finished a kite that you will say is a beauty. It's drying, in the kitchen; I'll fetch it."

He had been spending his penny savings in fanciful trifles of various kinds, to go as prizes in the games, and they were marshaled with fine and showy effect upon the table. He said:

"Examine them at your leisure while I get mother to touch up the kite with her iron if it isn't dry enough yet."

Then he tripped out and went clattering down-stairs, whistling.

We did not look at the things; we couldn't take any interest in anything but the clock. We sat staring at it in silence, listening to the ticking, and every time the minute-hand jumped we nodded recognition—one minute fewer to cover in the race for life or for death. Finally Seppi drew a deep breath and said:

"Two minutes to ten. Seven minutes more and he will pass the death-point. Theodor, he is going to be saved! He's going to—"

"Hush! I'm on needles. Watch the clock and keep still."

Five minutes more. We were panting with the strain and the excitement. Another three minutes, and there was a footstep on the stair.

"Saved!" And we jumped up and faced the door.

The old mother entered, bringing the kite. "Isn't it a beauty?" she said. "And, dear me, how he has slaved over it—ever since daylight, I think, and only finished it awhile before you came." She stood it against the wall, and stepped back to take a view of it. "He drew the pictures his own self, and I think they are very good. The church isn't so very good, I'll have to admit, but look at the bridge—any one can recognize the bridge in a minute. He asked me to bring it up. . . . Dear me! it's seven minutes past ten, and I—"

"But where is he?"

"He? Oh, he'll be here soon; he's gone out a minute."

"Gone out?"

"Yes. Just as he came down-stairs little Lisa's mother came in and said the child had wandered off somewhere, and as she was a little uneasy I told Nikolaus to never mind about his father's orders—go and look her up. . . . Why, how white you two do look! I do believe you are sick. Sit down; I'll fetch something. That cake has disagreed with you. It is a little heavy, but I thought—"

She disappeared without finishing her sentence, and we hurried at once to the back window and looked toward the river. There was a great crowd at the other end of the bridge, and people were flying toward that point from every direction.

"Oh, it is all over—poor Nikolaus! Why, oh, why did she let him get out of the house!"

"Come away," said Seppi, half sobbing, "come quick—we can't bear to meet her; in five minutes she will know."

But we were not to escape. She came upon us at the foot of the stairs, with her cordials in her hands, and made us come in and sit down and take the medicine. Then she watched the effect, and it did not satisfy her; so she made us wait longer and kept upbraiding herself for giving us the unwholesome cake.

Presently the thing happened which we were dreading. There was a sound of tramping and scarping outside, and a crowd came solemnly in, with heads uncovered, and laid the two drowned bodies on the bed.

"Oh, my God!" that poor mother cried out, and fell on her knees, and put her arms about her dead boy and began to cover the wet face with kisses. "Oh, it was I that sent him, and I have been his death. If I had obeyed, and kept him in the house, this would not have happened. And I am rightly punished; I was cruel to him last night, and him begging me, his own mother, to be his friend."

And so she went on and on, and all the women cried, and pitied her, and tried to comfort her, but she could not

forgive herself and could not be comforted, and kept on saying if she had not sent him out he would be alive and
well now, and she was the cause of his death.

It shows how foolish people are when they blame themselves for anything they have done. Satan knows, and he
said nothing happens that your first act hasn't arranged to
happen and made inevitable; and so, of your own motion
you can't ever alter the scheme or do a thing that will break
a link. Next we heard screams, and Frau Brandt came wildly
plowing and plunging through the crowd with her dress in
disorder and hair flying loose, and flung herself upon her dead
child with moans and kisses and pleadings and endearments; and by and by she rose up almost exhausted with her
outpourings of passionate emotion, and clenched her fist
and lifted it toward the sky, and her tear-drenched face grew
hard and resentful, and she said:

"For nearly two weeks I have had dreams and presenti-
ments and warnings that death was going to strike what
was most precious to me, and day and night and night and
day I have groveled in the dirt before Him, praying Him to
have pity on my innocent child and save it from harm—and
here is His answer!"

Why, He had saved it from harm—but she did not know.

She wiped the tears from her eyes and cheeks, and stood
awhile gazing down at the child and caressing its face and its
hair with her hands; then she spoke again in that bitter tone:
"But in His hard heart is no compassion. I will never pray
again."

She gathered her dead child to her bosom and strode away,
the crowd falling back to let her pass, and smitten dumb by
the awful words they had heard. Ah, that poor woman! It
is as Satan said, we do not know good fortune from bad,
and are always mistaking the one for the other. Many a time
since I have heard people pray to God to spare the life of sick
persons, but I have never done it.

Both funerals took place at the same time in our little

church next day. Everybody was there, including the party guests. Satan was there, too; which was proper, for it was on account of his efforts that the funerals had happened. Nikolaus had departed this life without absolution, and a collection was taken up for masses, to get him out of purgatory. Only two-thirds of the required money was gathered, and the parents were going to try to borrow the rest, but Satan furnished it. He told us privately that there was no purgatory, but he had contributed in order that Nikolaus's parents and their friends might be saved from worry and distress. We thought it very good of him, but he said money did not cost him anything.

At the graveyard the body of little Lisa was seized for debt by a carpenter to whom the mother owed fifty groschen for work done the year before. She had never been able to pay this and was not able now. The carpenter took the corpse home and kept it four days in his cellar, the mother weeping and imploring about his house all the time; then he buried it in his brother's cattle-yard, without religious ceremonies. It drove the mother wild with grief and shame, and she forsook her work and went daily about the town, cursing the carpenter and blaspheming the laws of the emperor and the church, and it was pitiful to see. Seppi asked Satan to interfere, but he said the carpenter and the rest were members of the human race and were acting quite neatly for that species of animal. He would interfere if he found a horse acting in such a way, and we must inform him when we came across that kind of horse doing that kind of a human thing, so that he could stop it. We believed this was sarcasm, for of course there wasn't any such horse.

But after a few days we found that we could not abide that poor woman's distress, so we begged Satan to examine her several possible careers, and see if he could not change her, to her profit, to a new one. He said the longest of her careers as they now stood gave her forty-two years to live, and her shortest one twenty-nine, and that both were charged with grief and hunger and cold and pain. The only improvement he could make would be to enable her to skip a certain three minutes from now; and he asked us if he should do it. This was such a short time to decide in that we went to pieces with nervous excitement, and before we could pull ourselves together and ask for particulars he said the time would be up in a few more seconds; so then we gasped out, "Do it!"

"It is done," he said; "she was going around a corner; I have turned her back; it has changed her career."

"Then what will happen, Satan?"

"It is happening now. She is having words with Fischer, the weaver. In his anger Fischer will straightway do what he would not have done but for this accident. He was present when she stood over her child's body and uttered those blasphemies."

"What will he do?"

"He is doing it now—betraying her. In three days she will go to the stake."

We could not speak; we were frozen with horror, for if we had not meddled with her career she would have been spared this awful fate. Satan noticed these thoughts, and said:

"What you are thinking is strictly human-like—that is to say, foolish. The woman is advantaged. Die when she might, she would go to heaven. By this prompt death she gets twenty nine years more of heaven than she is entitled to, and escapes twenty-nine years of misery here."

A moment before we were bitterly making up our minds that we would ask no more favors of Satan for friends of ours, for he did not seem to know any way to do a person a kindness but by killing him; but the whole aspect of the case was changed now, and we were glad of what we had done and full of happiness in the thought of it.

After a little I began to feel troubled about Fischer, and asked, timidly "Does this episode change Fischer's life-scheme, Satan?"

"Change it? Why, certainly. And radically. If he had not met Frau Brandt awhile ago he would die next year, thirty-four years of age. Now he will live to be ninety, and have a pretty prosperous and comfortable life of it, as human lives go."

We felt a great joy and pride in what we had done for Fischer, and were expecting Satan to sympathize with this feeling; but he showed no sign and this made us uneasy. We waited for him to speak, but he didn't; so, to assuage our solicitude we had to ask him if there was any defect in Fischer's good luck. Satan considered the question a moment, then said, with some hesitation:

"Well, the fact is, it is a delicate point. Under his several former possible life-careers he was going to heaven."

We were aghast. "Oh, Satan! and under this one—"

"There, don't be so distressed. You were sincerely trying to do him a kindness; let that comfort you."

"Oh, dear, dear, that cannot comfort us. You ought to have told us what we were doing, then we wouldn't have acted so."

But it made no impression on him. He had never felt a pain or a sorrow, and did not know what they were, in any really informing way. He had no knowledge of them except theoretically—that is to say, intellectually. And of course that is no good. One can never get any but a loose and ignorant notion of such things except by experience. We tried our best to make him comprehend the awful thing that had been done and how we were compromised by it, but he couldn't seem to get hold of it. He said he did not think it important where Fischer went to; in heaven he would not be missed, there were "plenty there." We tried to make him see that he was missing the point entirely; that Fischer, and not other people, was the proper one to decide about the importance of it; but it all went for nothing; he said he did not care for Fischer—there were plenty more Fischers.

The next minute Fischer went by on the other side of the

way, and it made us sick and faint to see him, remembering the doom that was upon him, and we the cause of it. And how unconscious he was that anything had happened to him! You could see by his elastic step and his alert manner that he was well satisfied with himself for doing that hard turn for poor Frau Brandt. He kept glancing back over his shoulder expectantly. And, sure enough, pretty soon Frau Brandt followed after, in charge of the officers and wearing jingling chains. A mob was in her wake, jeering and shouting, "Blasphemer and heretic!" and some among them were neighbors and friends of her happier days. Some were trying to strike her, and the officers were not taking as much trouble as they might to keep them from it.

"Oh, stop them, Satan!" It was out before we remembered that he could not interrupt them for a moment without changing their whole after-lives. He puffed a little puff toward them with his lips and they began to reel and stagger and grab at the empty air; then they broke apart and fled in every direction, shrieking, as if in intolerable pain. He had crushed a rib of each of them with that little puff. We could not help asking if their life-chart was changed.

"Yes, entirely. Some have gained years, some have lost them. Some few will profit in various ways by the change, but only that few."

We did not ask if we had brought poor Fischer's luck to any of them. We did not wish to know. We fully believed in Satan's desire to do us kindness, but we were losing confidence in his judgment. It was at this time that our growing anxiety to have him look over our life-charts and suggest improvements began to fade out and give place to other interests.

For a day or two the whole village was a chattering turmoil over Frau Brandt's case and over the mysterious calamity that had overtaken the mob, and at her tiral the place was crowded. She was easily convicted of her blasphemies, for she uttered those terrible words again and said she would not

take them back. When warned that she was imperilimg her
life, she said they could take it in welcome, she did not want
it, she would rather live with the professional devils in per-
dition than with these imitators in the village. They accused
her of breaking all those ribs by witchcraft, and asked her if
she was not a witch? She answered scornfully:

"No. If I had that power would any of you holy hypo-
crites be alive fine minutes? No; I would strike you all dead.
Pronounce your sentence and let me go; I am tired of your
society."

So they found her guilty, and she was excommunicated and
cut off from the joys of heaven and doomed to the fires of
hell; then she was clothed in a coarse robe and delivered to
the secular arm, and conducted to the market-place, the bell
solemnly tolling the while. We saw her chained to the stake,
and saw the first film of blue smoke rise on the still air.
Then her hard face softened, and she looked upon the packed
crowd in front of her and said, with gentleness:

"We played together once, in long-agone days when we
were innocent little creatures. For the sake of that, I forgive
you."

We went away then, and did not see the fires consume her,
but we heard the shrieks, although we put our fingers in our
ears. When they ceased we knew she was in heaven, notwithstanding the excommunication; and we were glad of
her death and not sorry that we had brought it about.

One day, a little while after this, Satan appeared again. We
were always watching out for him, for life was never very
stagnant when he was by. He came upon us at that place in
the woods where we had first met him. Being boys, we wanted
to be entertained; we asked him to do a show for us.

"Very well," he said; "would you like to see a history of
the progress of the human race?—its development of that
product which it calls civilization?"

We said we should.

So, with a thought, he turned the place into the Garden of

Eden, and we saw Abel praying by his altar; then Cain
came walking toward him with his club, and did not seem to
see us, and would have stepped on my foot if I had not drawn
it in. He spoke to his brother in a language which we did not
understand; then he grew violent and threatening, and we
knew what was going to happen, and turned away our heads
for the moment; but we heard the crash of the blows and
heard the shrieks and the groans; then there was silence, and
we saw Abel lying in his blood and gasping out his life,
and Cain standing over him und looking down at him,
vengeful and unrepentant.

Then the vision vanished, and was followed by a long
series of unknown wars, murders, and massacres. Next we
had the Flood, and the Ark tossing around in the stormy
waters, with lofty mountains in the distance showing veiled
and dim through the rain. Satan said:

"The progress of your race was not satisfactory. It is to
have another chance now."

The scene changed, and we saw Noah overcome with
wine.

Next, we had Sodom and Gomorrah, and "the attempt to
discover two or three respectable persons there," as Satan
described it. Next, Lot and his daughters in the cave.

Next came the Hebraic wars, and we saw the victors massacre the survivors and their cattle, and save the young girls
alive and distribute them around.

Next we had Jael; and saw her slip into the tent and drive
the nail into the temple of her sleeping guest; and we
were so close that when the blood gushed out it trickled in
a little, red stream to our feet, and we could have stained our
hands in it if we had wanted to.

Next we had Egyptian wars, Greek wars, Roman wars,
hideous drenchings of the earth with blood; and we saw the
treacheries of the Romans toward the Carthaginians, and the
sickening spectacle of the massacre of those brave people.
Also we saw Cæsar invade Britain—"not that those barbar-

ians had done him any harm, but because he wanted their land, and desired to confer the blessings of civilization upon their widows and orphans," as Satan explained.

Next, Christianity was born. Then ages of Europe passed in review before us, and we saw Christianity and Civilization march hand in hand through those ages, "leaving famine and death and desolation in their wake, and other signs of the progress of the human race," as Satan observed.

And always we had wars, and more wars, and still other wars—all over Europe, all over the world. "Sometimes in the private interest of royal families," Satan said, "sometimes to crush a weak nation; but never a war started by the aggressor for any clean purpose—there is no such war in the history of the race.

"Now," said Satan, "you have seen your progress down to the present, and you must confess that it is wonderful—in its way. We must now exhibit the future."

He showed us slaughters more terrible in their destruction of life, more devastating in their engines of war, than any we had seen.

"You perceive," he said, "that you have made continual progress. Cain did his murder with a club; the Hebrews did their murders with javelins and swords; the Greeks and Romans added protective armor and the fine arts of military organization and generalship; the Christian has added guns and gunpowder; a few centuries from now he will have so greatly improved the deadly effectiveness of his weapons of slaughter that all men will confess that without Christian civilization war must have remained a poor and trifling thing to the end of time."

Then he began to laugh in the most unfeeling way, and make fun of the human race, although he knew that what he had been saying shamed us and wounded us. No one but an angel could have acted so; but suffering is nothing to them; they do not know what it is, except by hearsay.

More than once Seppi and I had tried in a humble and dif-

fident way to convert him, and as he had remained silent
we had taken his silence as a sort of encouragement; necessarily, then, this talk of his was a disappointment to us, for
it showed that we had made no deep impression upon him.
The thought made us sad, and we knew then how the mis-
sionary must feel when he has been cherishing a glad hope
and has seen it blighted. We kept our grief to ourselves,
knowing that this was not the time to continue our work.

Satan laughed his unkind laugh to a finish; then he said:
"It is a remarkable progress. In five or six thousand years
five or six high civilizations have risen, flourished, commanded the wonder of the world, then faded out and disappeared; and not one of them except the latest ever invented
any sweeping and adequate way to kill people. They all did
their best—to kill being the chiefest ambition of the human
race and the earliest incident in its history—but only the Christian civilization has scored a triumph to be proud of.
Two of three centuries from now it will be recognized that
all the competent killers are Christians; then the pagan
world will go to school to the Christian—not to acquire his
religion, but his guns. The Turk and the Chinaman will buy
those to kill missionaries and converts with."

By this time his theater was at work agian, and before our
eyes nation after nation drifted by, during two or three centuries, a mighty procession, an endless procession, raging,
struggling, wallowing through seas of blood, smothered
in battle-smoke through which the flags glinted and the red
jets from the cannon darted; and always we heard the thunder of the guns and the cries of the dying.

"And what does it amount to?" said Satan, with his evil
chuckle. "Nothing at all. You gain nothing; you always come
out where you went in. For a million years the race had gone
on monotonously propagating itself and monotonously re-
performing this dull nonsense—to what end? No wisdom
can guess! Who gets a profit out of it? Nobody but a parcel
of usurping little monarchs and nobilities who despise you;

would feel defiled if you touched them; would shut the door
in your face if you proposed to call; whom you slave for,
fight for, die for, and are not ashamed of it, but proud; whose
existence is a perpetual insult to you and you are afraid to
resent it; who are mendicants supported by your alms, yet
assume toward you the airs of benefactor toward beggar; who
address you in the language of master to slave, and are answered in the language of slave to master; who are worshiped
by you with your mouth, while in your heart—if you have
one—you despise yourselves for it. The first man was a
hypocrite and a coward, qualities which have not yet
failed in his line; it is the foundation upon which all civilizations have been built. Drink to their perpetuation! Drink
to their augmentation! Drink to—" Then he saw by our faces
how much we were hurt, and he cut his sentence short and
stopped chuckling, and is manner changed. He said, gently:
"No, we will drink one another's health, and let civilization
go. The wine which has flown to our hands out of space by
desire is earthly, and good enough for that other toast; but
throw away the glasses; we will drink this one in wine
which has not visited this world before."

We obeyed, and reached up and received the new cups
as they descended. They were shapely and beautiful goblets,
but they were not made of any material that we were acquainted with. They seemed to be in motion, they seemed
to be alive; and certainly the colors in them were in motion.
They were very brilliant and sparkling, and of every
tint, and they were never still, flowed to and fro in rich
tides which met and broke and flashed out dainty explosions
of enchanting color. I think it was most like opals washing
about in waves and flashing out their splendid fires. But there
is nothing to compare the wine with. We drank it, and felt
a strange and witching ecstasy as of heaven go stealing
through us, and Seppi's eyes filled and he said worshipingly:

"We shall be there some day, and then—"

He glanced furtively at Satan, and I think he hoped Satan

would say, "Yes, you will be there some day," but Satan seemed to be thinking about something else, and said nothing. This made me feel ghastly, for I knew he had heard; nothing, spoken or unspoken, ever escaped him. Poor Seppi looked distressed, and did not finish his remark. The goblets rose and clove their way into the sky, a triplet of radiant sundogs, and disappeared. Why didn't they stay? It seemed a bad sign, and depressed me. Should I ever see mine again? Would Seppi ever see his?

9

It was wonderful, the mastery Satan had over time and distance. For him they did not exist. He called them human inventions, and said they were artificialities. We often went to the most distant parts of the globe with him, and stayed weeks and months, and yet were gone only a fraction of a second, as a rule. You could prove it by the clock. One day when our people were in such awful distress because the witch commission were afraid to proceed against the astrologer and Father Peter's household, or against any, indeed, but the poor and the friendless, they lost patience and took to witch-hunting on their own score, and began to chase a born lady who was known to have the habit of curing people by devilish arts, such as bathing them, washing them, and nourishing them instead of bleeding them and purging them through the ministrations of a barber-surgeon in the proper way. She came flying down, with the howling and cursing mob after her, and tried to take refuge in houses, but the doors were shut in her face. They chased her more than half an hour, we following to see, and at last she was exhausted and fell, and they caught her. They dragged her to a tree and threw a rope over the limb, and began to make a noose in it, some holding her, meantime, and she crying and begging, and her young daughter looking on and weeping, but afraid to say or do anything.

They hanged the lady, and I threw a stone at her, although in my heart I was sorry for her; but all were throwing stones and each was watching his neighbor, and if I had not done as the others did, it would have been noticed and spoken of. Satan burst out laughing.

All that were near by turned upon him, astonished and not pleased. It was an ill time to laugh, for his free and scoffing ways and his supernatural music had brought him under suspicion all over the town and turned many privately against him. The big blacksmith called attention to him now, raising his voice so that all should hear, and said:

"What are you laughing at? Answer! Moreover, please explain to the company why you threw no stone."

"Are you sure I did not throw a stone?"

"Yes. You needn't try to get out of it; I had my eye on you."

"And I—I noticed you!" shouted two others.

"Three witnesses," said Satan: "Mueller, the blacksmith; Klein, the butcher's man; Pfeiffer, the weaver's journeyman. Three very ordinary liars. Are there any more?"

"Never mind whether there are others or not, and never mind about what you consider us—three's enough to settle your matter for you. You'll prove that you threw a stone, or it shall go hard with you."

"That's so!" shouted the crowd, and surged up as closely as they could to the center of interest.

"And first you will answer that other question," cried the blacksmith, pleased with himself for being mouthpiece to the public and hero of the occasion. "What are you laughing at?"

Satan smiled and answered, pleasantly: "To see three cowards stoning a dying lady when they were so near death themselves."

You could see the superstitious crowd shrink and catch their breath, under the sudden shock. The blacksmith, with a show of bravado, said:

"Pooh! What do you know about it?"

"I? Everything. By profession I am a fortuneteller, and I read the hands of you three—and some others—when you lifted them to stone the woman. One of you will die to-morrow week; another of you will die to-night; the third has but five minutes to live—and yonder is the clock!"

It made a sensation. The faces of the crowd blanched, and turned mechanically toward the clock. The butcher and the weaver seemed smitten with an illness, but the blacksmith braced up and said, with spirit:

"It is not long to wait for prediction number one. If it fails, young master, you will not live a whole minute after, I promise you that."

No one said anything; all watched the clock in a deep stillness which was impressive. When four and a half minutes were gone the blacksmith gave a sudden gasp and clapped his hands upon his heart, saying, "Give me breath! Give me room!" and began to sink down. The crowd surged back, no one offering to support him, and he fell lumbering to the ground and was dead. The people stared at him, then at Satan, then at one another; and their lips moved, but no words came. Then Satan said:

"Three saw that I threw no stone. Perhaps there are others; let them speak."

It struck a kind of panic into them, and, although no one answered him, many began to violently accuse one another saying, "You said he didn't throw," and getting for reply, "It is a lie, and I will make you eat it!" And so in a moment they were in a raging and noisy turmoil, and beating and banging one another; and in the midst was the only indifferent one—the dead lady hanging from her rope, her troubles forgotten, her spirit at peace.

So we walked away, and I was not at ease, but was saying to myself, "He told them he was laughing at them, but it was a lie—he was laughing at me."

That made him laugh again, and he said, "Yes, I was

laughing at you, because, in fear of what others might report about you, you stoned the woman when your heart revolted at the act—but I was laughing at the others, too."

"Why?"

"Because their case was yours."

"How is that?"

"Well, there were sixty-eight people there, and sixty-two of them had no more desire to throw a stone than you had."

"Satan!"

"Oh, it's true. I know your race. It is made up of sheep. It is governed by minorities, seldom or never by majorities. It suppresses its feelings and its beliefs and follows the hand-full that makes the most noise. Sometimes the noisy handful is right, sometimes wrong; but no matter, the crowd follows it. The vast majority of the race, whether savage or civilized, are secretly kind-hearted and shrink from inflicting pain, but in the presence of the aggressive and pitiless minority they don't dare to assert themselves. Think of it! One kind-hearted creature spies upon another, and sees to it that he loyally helps in iniquities which revolt both of them. Speaking as an expert, I know that ninety-nine out of a hundred of your race were strongly against the killing of witches when that foolishness was first agitated by a handful of pious lunatics in the long ago. And I know that even to-day, after ages of transmitted prejudice and silly teaching, only one person in twenty puts any real heart into the harrying of a witch. And yet apparently everybody hates witches and wants them killed. Some day a handful will rise up on the other side and make the most noise—perhaps even a single daring man with a big voice and a determined front will do it—and in a week all the sheep will wheel and follow him, and witch-hunting will come to a sudden end.

"Monarchies, aristocracies, and religions are all based upon that large defect in your race—the individual's distrust of his neighbor, and his desire, for safety's or comfort's sake, to stand well in his neighbor's eye. These institutions will always remain, and always flourish, and always oppress you, affront you, and degrade you, because you will always be and remain slaves of minorities. There was never a country where the majority of the people were in their secret hearts loyal to any of these institutions."

I did not like to hear our race called sheep, and said I did not think they were.

"Still, it is true, lamb," said Satan. "Look at you in war—what mutton you are, and how ridiculous!"

"In war? How?"

"There has never been a just one, never an honorable one —on the part of the instigator of the war. I can see a million years ahead, and this rule will never change in so many as half a dozen instances. The loud little handful—as usual—will shout for the war. The pulpit will—warily and cautiously—object—at first; the great, big, dull bulk of the nation will rub its sleepy eyes and try to make out why there should be a war, and will say, earnestly and indignantly, 'It is unjust and dishonorable, and there is no necessity for it.' Then the handful will shout louder. A few fair men on the other side will argue and reason against the war with speech and pen, and at first will have a hearing and be applauded; but it will not last long; those others will outshout them, and presently the anti-war audiences will thin out and lose popularity. Before long you will see this curious thing: the speakers stoned from the platform, and free speech strangled by hordes of furious men who in their secret hearts are still at one with those stoned speakers—as earlier—but do not dare to say so. And now the whole nation—pulpit an all—will take up the war-cry, and shout itself hoarse, and mob any honest man who ventures to open his mouth; and presently such mouths will cease to open. Next the statesmen will invent cheap lies, putting the blame upon the nation that is attacked, and every man will be glad of those conscience-soothing falsities, and will diligently study them, and refuse

to examine any refutations of them; and thus he will by and
by convince himself that the war is just, and will thank God
for the better sleep he enjoys after this process of grotesque self-deception."

10

Days and days went by now, and no Satan. It was dull
without him. But the astrologer, who had returned from
his excursion to the moon, went about the village, braving
public opinion, and getting a stone in the middle of his
back now and then when some witch-hater got a safe chance
to throw it and dodge out of sight. Meantime two influences
had been working well for Marget. That Satan, who was
quite indifferent to her, had stopped going to her house after
a visit or two had hurt her pride, and she had set herself
the task of banishing him from her heart. Reports of Wilhelm Meidling's dissipation brought to her from time to time
by old Ursula had touched her with remorse, jealousy of
Satan being the cause of it; and so now, these two matters
working upon her together, she was getting a good
profit out of the combination—her interest in Satan was
steadily cooling, her interest in Wilhelm as steadily warming. All that was needed to complete her conversion was
that Wilhelm should brace up and do something that should
cause favorable talk and incline the public toward him again.

The opportunity came now. Marget sent and asked him
to defend her uncle in the approaching trial, and he was
greatly pleased, and stopped drinking and began his preparations with diligence. With more diligence than hope, in
fact, for it was not a promising case. He had many inter-
views in his office with Seppi and me, and threshed out our
testimony pretty thoroughly, thinking to find some valuable
grains among the chaff, but the harvest was poor of course.

If Satan would only come! That was my constant thought.
He could invent some way to win the case; for he had said

it would be won, so he necessarily knew how it could be done. But the days dragged on, and still he did not come. Of course I did not doubt that it would win, and that Father Peter would be happy for the rest of his life, since Satan had said so; yet I knew I should be much more comfortable if he would come and tell us how to manage it. It was getting high time for Father Peter to have a saving change toward happiness, for by general report he was worn out with his imprisonment and the ignominy that was burdening him, and was like to die of his miseries unless he got relief soon.

At last the trial came on, and the people gathered from all around to witness it; among them many strangers from considerable distances. Yes, everybody was there except the accused. He was too feeble in body for the strain. But Marget was present, and keeping up her hope and her spirit the best she could. The money was present, too. It was emptied on the table, and was handled and caressed and examined by such as were privileged.

The astrologer was put in the witness-box. He had on his best hat and robe for the occasion.

QUESTION: You claim that this money is yours?

ANSWER: I do.

Q. How did you come by it?

A. I found the bag in the road when I was returning from a journey.

Q. When?"

A. More than two years ago.

Q. What did you do with it?

A. I brought it home and hid it in a secret place in my observatory, intending to find the owner if I could.

Q. You endeavored to find him?

A. I made diligent inquiry during several months, but nothing came of it.

Q. And then?"

A. I thought it not worth while to look further, and was minded to use the money in finishing the wing of the foundling-asylum connected with the priory and nunnery. So I took it out of its hiding-place and counted it to see if any of it was missing. And then—

Q. Why do you stop? Proceed.

A. I am sorry to have to say this, but just as I had finished and was restoring the bag to its place, I looked up and there stood Father Peter behind me.

Several murmured, "That looks bad," but others answered, "Ah, but he is such a liar!"

Q. That made you uneasy?

A. No; I thought nothing of it at the time, for Father Peter often came to me unannounced to ask for a little help in his need.

Marget blushed crimson at hearing her uncle falsely and impudently charged with begging, especially from one he had always denounced as a fraud, and was going to speak, but remembered herself in time and held her peace.

Q. Proceed.

A. In the end I was afraid to contribute the money to the foundling-asylum, but elected to wait yet another year and continue my inquiries. When I heard of Father Peter's find I was glad, and no suspicion entered my mind; when I came home a day or two later and discovered that my own money was gone I still did not suspect until three circumstances connected with Father Peter's good fortune struck me as being singular coincidences.

Q. Pray name them.

A. Father Peter had found his money in a path—I had found mine in a road. Father Peter's find consisted exclusively of gold ducats—mine also. Father Peter found eleven hundred and seven ducats—I exactly the same.

This closed his evidence, and certainly it made a strong impression on the house; one could see that.

Wilhelm Meidling asked him some questions, then called us boys, and we told our tale. It made the people laugh, and we were ashamed. We were feeling pretty badly, anyhow,

because Wilhelm was hopeless, and showed it. He was doing
as well as he could, poor young fellow, but nothing was in
his favor, and such sympathy as there was was now plainly
not with his client. It might be difficult for court and people
to believe the astrologer's story, considering his character,
but it was almost impossible to believe Father Peter's. We
were already feeling badly enough, but when the astrologer's
lawyer said he believed he would not ask us any questions—for our story was a little delicate and it would be
cruel for him to put any strain upon it—everybody tittered,
and it was almost more than we could bear. Then he made
a sarcastic little speech, and got so much fun out of our tale,
and it seemed so ridiculous and childish and every way impossible and foolish, that it made everybody laugh till the
tears came; and at last Marget could not keep up her courage
any longer, but broke down and cried, and I was so sorry
for her.

Now I noticed something that braced me up. It was Satan
standing alongside of Wilhelm! And there was such a contrast!—Satan looked so confident, had such a spirit in his
eyes and face, and Wilhelm looked so depressed and despondent. We two were comfortable now, and judged that he
would testify and persuade the bench and the people that
black was white and white black, or any other color he
wanted it. We glanced around to see what the strangers in
the house thought of him, for he was beautiful, you know
—stunning, in fact—but no one was noticing him; so we knew
by that that he was invisible.

The lawyer was saying his last words; and while he was
saying them Satan began to melt into Wilhelm. He melted
into him and disappeared; and then there was a change,
when his spirit began to look out of Wilhelm's eyes.

That lawyer finished quite seriously, and with dignity.
He pointed to the money, and said:

"The love of it is the root of all evil. There it lies, the ancient tempter, newly red with the shame of its latest victory

—the dishonor of a priest of God and his two poor juvenile helpers in crime. If it could but speak, let us hope that it would be constrained to confess that of all its conquests this was the basest and the most pathetic."

He sat down. Wilhelm rose and said:

"From the testimony of the accuser I gather that he found this money in a road more than two years ago. Correct me, sir, if I misunderstood you."

The astrologer said his understanding of it was correct.

"And the money so found was never out of his hands thenceforth up to a certain definite date—the last day of last year. Correct me, sir, if I am wrong."

The astrologer nodded his head. Wilhelm turned to the bench and said:

"If I prove that this money here was not that money, then it is not his?"

"Certainly not; but this is irregular. If you had such a witness it was your duty to give proper notice of it and have him here to—" He broke off and began to consult with the other judges. Meantime that other lawyer got up excited and began to protest against allowing new witnesses to be brought into the case at this late stage.

The judges decided that his contention was just and must be allowed.

"But this is not a new witness," said Wilhelm. "It has already been partly examined. I speak of the coin."

"The coin? What can the coin say?"

"It can say it is not the coin that the astrologer once possessed. It can say it was not in existence last December. By its date it can say this."

And it was so! There was the greatest excitement in the court while that lawyer and the judges were reaching for coins and examining them and exclaiming. And everybody was full of admiration of Wilhelm's brightness in happening to think of that neat idea. At last order was called and the court said:

"All of the coins but four are of the date of the present year. The court tenders its sincere sympathy to the accused, and its deep regret that he, an innocent man, through an unfortunate mistake, has suffered the undeserved humiliation of imprisonment and trial. The case is dismissed."

So the money could speak, after all, though that lawyer thought it couldn't. The court rose, and almost everybody came forward to shake hands with Marget and congratulate her, and then to shake with Wilhelm and praise him; and Satan had stepped out of Wilhelm and was standing around looking on full of interest, and people walking through him every which way, not knowing he was there. And Wilhelm could not explain why he only thought of the date on the coins at the last moment, instead of earlier; he said it just occurred to him, all of a sudden, like an inspiration, and he brought it right out without any hesitation, for, although he didn't examine the coins, he seemed, somehow, to know it was true. That was honest of him, and like him; another would have pretended he had thought of it earlier, and was keeping it back for a surprise.

He had dulled down a little now; not much, but still you could notice that he hadn't that luminous look in his eyes that he had while Satan was in him. He nearly got it back, though, for a moment when Marget came and praised him and thanked him and couldn't keep him from seeing how proud she was of him. The astrologer went off dissatisfied and cursing, and Solomon Isaacs gathered up the money and carried it away. It was Father Peter's for good and all, now.

Satan was gone. I judged that he had spirited himself away to the jail to tell the prisoner the news; and in this I was right. Marget and the rest of us hurried thither at our best speed, in a great state of rejoicing.

Well, what Satan had done was this: he had appeared before that poor prisoner, exclaiming, "The trial is over, and you stand forever disgraced as a thief—by verdict of the court!"

The shock unseated the old man's reason. When we arrived, ten minutes later, he was parading pompously up and down and delivering commands to this and that and the other constable or jailer, and calling them Grand Chamberlain, and Prince This and Prince That, and Admiral of the Fleet, Field Marshal in Command, and all such fustian, and was as happy as a bird. He thought he was Emperor!

Marget flung herself on his breast and cried, and indeed everybody was moved almost to heartbreak. He recognized Marget, but could not understand why she should cry. He patted her on the shoulder and said:

"Don't do it, dear; remember, there are witnesses, and it is not becoming in the Crown Princess. Tell me your trouble—it shall be mended; there is nothing the Emperor cannot do." Then he looked around and saw old Ursula with her apron to her eyes. He was puzzled at that, and said, "And what is the matter with you?"

Through her sobs she got out words explaining that she was distressed to see him—"so." He reflected over that a moment, then muttered, as if to himself: "A singular old thing, the Dowager Duchess—means well, but is always snuffling and never able to tell what it is about. It is because she doesn't know." His eyes fell on Wilhelm. "Prince of India," he said, "I divine that it is you that the Crown Princess is concerned about. Her tears shall be dried; I will no longer stand between you; she shall share your throne; and between you you shall inherit mine. There, little lady, have I done well? You can smile now—isn't it so?"

He petted Marget and kissed her, and was so contented with himself and with everybody that he could not do enough for us all, but began to give away kingdoms and such things right and left, and the least they any of us got was a principality. And so at last, being persuaded to go home, he marched in imposing state; and when the crowds along the way saw how it gratified him to be hurrahed at, they humored him to the top of his desire, and he responded with condescending bows and gracious smiles, and often stretched out a hand and said, "Bless you, my people!"

As pitiful a sight as ever I saw. And Marget, and old Ursula crying all the way.

On my road home I came upon Satan, and reproached him with deceiving me with that lie. He was not embarrassed, but said, quite simply and composedly:

"Ah, you mistake; it was the truth. I said he would be happy the rest of his days, and he will, for he will always think he is the Emperor, and his pride in it and his joy in it will endure to the end. He is now, and will remain, the one utterly happy person in this empire."

"But the method of it, Satan, the method! Couldn't you have done it without depriving him of his reason?"

It was difficult to irritate Satan, but that accomplished it.

"What an ass you are!" he said. "Are you so unobservant as not to have found out that sanity and happiness are an impossible combination? No sane man can be happy, for to him life is real, and he sees what a fearful thing it is. Only the mad can be happy, and not many of those. The few that imagine themselves kings or gods are happy, the rest are no happier than the sane. Of course, no man is entirely in his right mind at any time, but I have been referring to the extreme cases. I have taken from this man that trumpery thing which the race regards as a Mind; I have replaced his tin life with a silver-gilt fiction; you see the result—and you criticize! I said I would make him permanently happy, and I have done it. I have made him happy by the only means possible to his race—and you are not satisfied!" He heaved a discouraged sigh, and said, "It seems to me that this race is hard to please."

There it was, you see. He didn't seem to know any way to do a person a favor except by killing him or making a lunatic out of him. I apologized, as well as I could; but privately I did not think much of his processes—at that time.

Satan was accustomed to say that our race lived a life of continuous and uninterrupted self-deception. It duped itself from cradle to grave with shams and delusions which it mistook for realities, and this made its entire life a sham. Of the score of fine qualities which it imagined it had and was vain of, it really possessed hardly one. It regarded itself as gold, and was only brass. One day when he was in this vein he mentioned a detail—the sense of humor. I cheered up then, and took issue. I said we possessed it.

"There spoke the race!" he said; "always ready to claim what it hasn't got, and mistake its ounce of brass filings for a ton of gold-dust. You have a mongrel perception of humor, nothing more; a multitude of you possess that. This multitude see the comic side of a thousand low-grade and trivial things—broad incongruities, mainly; grotesqueries, absurdities, evokers of the horse-laugh. The ten thousand high-grade comicalities which exist in the world are sealed from their dull vision. Will a day come when the race will detect the funniness of these juvenilities and laugh at them—and by laughing at them destroy them? For your race, in its poverty, has unquestionably one really effective weapon: laughter. Power, money, persuasion, supplication, persecution—these can lift at a colossal humbug—push it a little —weaken it a little, century by century; but only laughter can blow it to rags and atoms at a blast. Against the assault of laughter nothing can stand. You are always fussing and fighting with other weapons. Do you ever use that one? No; you leave it lying rusting. As a race, do you ever use it at all? No; you lack sense and the courage."

We were traveling at the time and stopped at a little city in India and looked on while a juggler did his tricks before a group of natives. They were wonderful, but I knew Satan could beat that game, and I begged him to show off a little, and he said he would. He changed himself into a native in turban and breech-cloth, and very considerately conferred on me a temporary knowledge of the language.

The juggler exhibited a seed, covered it with earth in a small flower-pot, then put a rag over the pot; after a minute the rag began to rise; in ten minutes it had risen a foot; then the rag was removed and a little tree was exposed, with leaves upon it and ripe fruit. We ate the fruit, and it was good. But Satan said:

"Why do you cover the pot? Can't you grow the tree in the sunlight?"

"No," said the juggler; "no one can do that."

"You are only an apprentice; you don't know your trade. Give me the seed. I will show you." He took the seed and said, "What shall I raise from it?"

"It is a cherry seed; of course you will raise a cherry."

"Oh no; that is a trifle; any novice can do that. Shall I raise an orange-tree from it?"

"Oh yes!" and the juggler laughed.

"And shall I make it bear other fruits as well as ora

"If God wills!" and they all laughed.

Satan put the seed in the ground, put a handful on it, and said, "Rise!"

A tiny stem shot up and began to grow, and grew so fast that in five minutes it was a great tree, and we were sitting in the shade of it. There was a murmur of wonder, then all looked up and saw a strange and pretty sight, for the branches were heavy with fruit of many kinds and colors—oranges, grapes, bananas, peaches, cherries, apricots, and so on. Baskets were brought, and the unlading of the tree began; and the people crowded around Satan and kissed his hand, and praised him, calling him the prince of jugglers. The news went about the town, and everybody came running to see the wonder—and they remembered to bring baskets, too. But the tree was equal to the occasion; it put out new fruits as fast as any were removed; baskets were filled by the score and by the hundred, but always the supply remained undiminished. At last a foreigner in white linen and sun-helmet arrived, and exclaimed, angrily:

"Away from here! Clear out, you dogs; the tree is on my lands and is my property."

The natives put down their baskets and made humble obeisance. Satan made humble obeisance, too, with his fingers to his forehead, in the native way, and said:

"Please let them have their pleasure for an hour, sir—only that, and no longer. Afterward you may forbid them; and you will still have more fruit than you and the state together can consume in a year."

This made the foreigner very angry, and he cried out, "Who are you, you vagabond, to tell your betters what they may do and what they mayn't!" and he struck Satan with his cane and followed this error with a kick.

The fruits rotted on the branches, and the leaves withered and fell. The foreigner gazed at the bare limbs with the look of one who is surprised, and not gratified. Satan said:

"Take good care of the tree, for its health and yours are bound together. It will never bear again, but if you tend it well it will live long. Water its roots once in each hour every night—and do it yourself; it must not be done by proxy, and to do it in daylight will not answer. If you fail only once in any night, the tree will die, and you likewise. Do not go home to your own country any more—you would not reach there; make no business or pleasure engagements which require you to go outside your gate at night—you cannot afford the risk; do not rent or sell this place—it would be injudicious."

The foreigner was proud and wouldn't beg, and I thought he looked as if he would like to. While he stood gazing at Satan we vanished away and landed in Ceylon.

I was sorry for that man; sorry Satan hadn't been his customary self and killed him or made him a lunatic. It would have been a mercy. Satan overheard the thought, and said:

"I would have done it but for his wife, who has not offended me. She is coming to him presently from their native land,

Portugal. She is well, but has not long to live, and has been yearning to see him and persuade him to go back with her next year. She will die without knowing he can't leave that place."

"He won't tell her?"

"He? He will not trust that secret with any one; he will reflect that it could be revealed in sleep, in the hearing of some Portuguese guest's servant some time or other."

"Did none of those natives understand what you said to him?"

"None of them understood, but he will always be afraid that some of them did. That fear will be torture to him, for he has been a harsh master to them. In his dreams he will imagine them chopping his tree down. That will make his days uncomfortable—I have already arranged for his nights."

It grieved me, though not sharply, to see him take such a malicious satisfaction in his plans for this foreigner.

"Does he believe what you told him, Satan?"

"He thought he didn't, but our vanishing helped. The tree, where there had been no tree before—that helped. The insane and uncanny variety of fruits—the sudden withering—all these things are helps. Let him think as he may, reason as he may, one thing is certain, he will water the tree. But between this and night he will begin his changed career with a very natural precaution—for him."

"What is that?"

"He will fetch a priest to cast out the tree's devil. You are such a humorous race—and don't suspect it."

"Will he tell the priest?"

"No. He will say a juggler from Bombay created it, and that he wants the juggler's devil driven out of it, so that it will thrive and be fruitful again. The priest's incantations will fail; then the Portuguese will give up that scheme and get his watering-pot ready."

"But the priest will burn the tree. I know it; he will not allow it to remain."

"Yes, and anywhere in Europe he would burn the man, too. But in India the people are civilized, and these things will not happen. The man will drive the priest away and take care of the tree."

I reflected a little, then said, "Satan, you have given him a hard life, I think."

"Comparatively. It must not be mistaken for a holiday."

We flitted from place to place around the world as we had done before, Satan showing me a hundred wonders, most of them reflecting in some way the weakness and triviality of our race. He did this now every few days—not out of malice —I am sure of that—it only seemed to amuse and interest him, just as a naturalist might be amused and interested by a collection of ants.

11

For as much as a year Satan continued these visits, but at last he came less often, and then for a long time he did not come at all. This always made me lonely and melancholy. I felt that he was losing interest in our tiny world and might at any time abandon his visits entirely. When one day he finally came to me I was overjoyed, but only for a little while. He had come to say good-by, he told me, and for the last time. He had investigations and undertakings in other corners of the universe, he said, that would keep him busy for a longer period than I could wait for his return.

"And you are going away, and will not come back any more?"

"Yes," he said. "We have comraded long together, and it has been pleasant—pleasant for both; but I must go now, and we shall not see each other any more."

"In this life, Satan, but in another? We shall meet in another, surely?"

Then, all tranquilly and soberly, he made the strange answer, *"There is no other."*

A subtle influence blew upon my spirit from his, bringing with it a vague, dim, but blessed and hopeful feeling that the incredible words might be true—even *must* be true.

"Have you never suspected this, Theodor?"

"No. How could I? But if it can only be true—"

"It is true."

A gust of thankfulness rose in my breast, but a doubt checked it before it could issue in words, and I said, "But—but—we have seen that future life—seen it in its actuality, and so—"

"It was a vision—it had no existence."

I could hardly breathe for the great hope that was struggling in me. "A vision?—a vi—"

"*Life itself is only a vision, a dream.*"

It was electrical. By God! I had had that very thought a thousand times in my musings!

"*Nothing* exists; all is a dream. God—man—the world—the sun, the moon, the wilderness of stars—a dream, all a dream; they have no existence. *Nothing exists save empty space—and you!*"

"I!"

"And you are not you—you have no body, no blood, no bones, you are but a *thought*. I myself have no existence; I am but a dream—your dream, creature of your imagination. In a moment you will have realized this, then you will banish me from your visions and I shall dissolve into the nothingness out of which you made me. . . .

"I am perishing already—I am failing—I am passing away. In a little while you will be alone in shoreless space, to wander its limitless solitudes without friend or comrade forever—for you will remain a *thought*, the only existent thought, and by your nature inextinguishable, indestructible. But I, your poor servant, have revealed you to yourself and set you free. Dream other dreams, and better!

"Strange! that you should not have suspected years ago

—centuries, ages, eons, ago!—for you have existed, companionless, through all the eternities. Strange, indeed, that you should not have suspected that your universe and its contents were only dreams, visions, fiction! Strange, because they are so frankly and hysterically insane—like all dreams: a God who could make good children as easily as bad, yet preferred to make bad ones; who could have made every one of them happy, yet never made a single happy one; who made them prize their bitter life, yet stingily cut it short; who gave his angels eternal happiness unearned, yet required his other children to earn it; who gave his angels painless lives, yet cursed his other children with biting miseries and maladies of mind and body; who mouths justice and invented hell—mouths mercy and invented hell—mouths Golden Rules, and forgiveness multiplied by seventy times seven, and invented hell; who mouths morals to other people and has none himself; who frowns upon crimes, yet commits them all; who created man without invitation, then tries to shuffle the responsibility for man's acts upon man, instead of honorably placing it where it belongs, upon himself; and finally, with altogether divine obtuseness, invites this poor, abused slave to worship him! . . .

"You perceive, *now*, that those things are all impossible except in a dream. You perceive that they are pure and puerile insanities, the silly creations of an imagination that is not conscious of its freaks—in a word, that they are a dream, and you the maker of it. The dream-marks are all present; you should have recognized them earlier.

"It is true, that which I have revealed to you; there is no God, no universe, no human race, no earthly life, no heaven, no hell. It is all a dream—a grotesque and foolish dream. Nothing exists but you. And you are but a *thought*—a vagrant thought, a useless thought, a homeless thought, wandering forlorn among the empty eternities!"

He vanished, and left me appalled; for I knew, and realized, that all he had said was true.